# An Unexpected Guest

# AN UNEXPECTED GUEST

*A novel by*

# ANNE KORKEAKIVI

Little, Brown and Company

*New York   Boston   London*

Copyright © 2012 by Anne Korkeakivi

Little, Brown and Company
Hachette Book Group
237 Park Avenue, New York, NY 10017

Little, Brown and Company is a division of Hachette Book Group, Inc., and is celebrating its 175th anniversary in 2012. The Little, Brown name and logo are trademarks of Hachette Book Group, Inc.

The publisher is not responsible for websites (or their content) that are not owned by the publisher.

Lines from *The Inferno* courtesy of The Society of Authors as the Literary Representative of the Estate of Laurence Binyon.

ISBN 978-1-62090-909-6

Printed in the United States of America

*For L, S, and A*

"Needs must thou find another way to flee,"
He answered, seeing my eyes with weeping fill,
"If thou from this wild place wouldst get thee free;
Because this beast, at which thou criest still,
Suffereth none to go upon her path,
But hindereth and entangleth till she kill,
And hath a nature so perverse in wrath,
Her craving maw never is satiated
But after food the fiercer hunger hath."

*The Inferno,* Dante, Canto I, 91–99

# An Unexpected Guest

# ONE

Time rained down on Clare. 8:30 a.m. on the clock hanging above the breakfast alcove. Twenty-five years of pretending Ireland never existed.

She would have to step again into that air terminal. Stare into the dark waters of the River Liffey. Look over her shoulder at every instant.

Remember.

"The ambassador has just been diagnosed with viral pneumonia," Edward had whispered last evening, sliding his BlackBerry into his inner jacket pocket, as they entered a cocktail reception for the Franco-British Entente Cordial program. "And the permanent under-secretary's flight touched down at Charles de Gaulle forty-five minutes ago. He's requested the dinner in his honor tomorrow night be shifted to our place."

"How many people?"

"Twelve. With us included."

The permanent under-secretary could have easily asked Edward—who, as British minister in Paris, was deputy head of the embassy—to take over as host in the *Salon Bleu*. If the P.U.S. wanted dinner moved from the ambassador's residence to their place, he was seizing the opportunity to size Edward up in his own territory. The P.U.S. was in charge of ambassadorial appointments.

She'd touched Edward's solid wrist. "I've got it." She'd given him a thumbs-up and begun mentally planning. She'd been happy.

She hadn't yet known what country the P.U.S. had in mind.

Now she was drinking her morning coffee in the Residence's spacious white kitchen, calmly making a list for this evening. She did not glance at Edward, reading through a pile of briefs beside his tea and toast and marmalade. She continued drinking her coffee and eating her own toast quietly, as she did every morning. She did nothing that might betray her anguish.

If tonight's dinner went well, Edward would be named the new ambassador to Ireland.

"Word is," Edward had said after they'd gotten home last night, unwinding his tie from his neck, "Michael Leroy is being named to Israel."

"Michael Leroy? The ambassador in Dublin?"

"Not after August. Apparently he's wanted Tel Aviv for ages. Not enough chaos for him in Ireland currently."

She'd allowed her nightgown to fall over her head, obscuring her expression just long enough to erase it, and slipped in between their bed's cool sheets, pulling them up close to her chin. Edward didn't know with what care, during the two decades they had been married, she'd avoided stepping foot on Irish soil. He didn't realize she'd ever even been to Dublin. Edward knew when she woke she would brush her teeth both before and after breakfast. He knew that even in the flurry of preparations she would not tell Amélie, their well-meaning housekeeper, what a pain it was to communicate in Amélie's broken English. But Edward knew nothing about her really, because he knew nothing about her life before him. He knew only the part she'd chosen to show him.

Thanks to her serene efficiency all these years—not just in entertaining but also in deception—Edward had probably thought he was handing her a present.

"So," she'd said, "Dublin will soon be vacant."

Edward had kissed her forehead. "Yes, Dublin will soon be vacant." He'd turned off their bedroom's overhead light, and she'd heard his measured tread move down the hall towards the study. He'd have meetings to prepare for now that he would be replacing the ambassador throughout the following day.

*Ireland.*

"Portobello Road, number eighty-three," she told the cabdriver after she climbed into the cab at the Dublin airport, taking care to cradle her tummy in a protective fashion. When they pulled up in front of the unmarked brown building, the River Liffey seething below, she hoisted her long frame back out of the cab in an awkward motion, almost forgetting her suitcase, and hastened over the heaving paving stones to ring the entrance bell. "I need a room," she announced to the jug-eared red-faced boy who appeared at the door and stared at her without saying a word, looking her up and down until his eyes landed on her stomach. "I need a room," she repeated, insisting, a sudden desperation to get the whole thing over with as swiftly as possible rising up inside her. She heard the tires of the taxi bumping away along the cobbled road but didn't look backwards.

\*　　　\*　　　\*

Edward was ready for his own ambassadorship. He'd devoted his entire adult life to the British Foreign Office and had served as the British minister in Paris, second only to the ambassador, faithfully and effectively for the past three years. He had done the prerequisite tours in hot spots—Lebanon, Kuwait, and Cairo— earlier in his career, and had spent a tour each in London and Washington, with Irish Affairs as part of his workload. He'd married her, an American woman whose maiden name was Fennelly. All that was left standing between him and the top slot in Dublin was the dinner she was now charged with hosting.

"Everything all right, then?" Edward said, taking off his reading glasses and standing up tall from the breakfast table. "Are we on course for this evening?"

"I have it all under control."

"Of course you do."

He kissed her, and she smiled as he closed his briefcase, and smiled as he drew on his suit jacket. She smiled until she heard the front door of the Residence click shut behind him. Then she stopped smiling and placed both hands on the breakfast table.

Here were her choices. She could put on a perfect dinner and end up moving to Dublin, where, if someone didn't actually recognize her and call her to account, she at least ran the risk of going crazy. Already in the past couple months, she'd begun imagining she saw Niall's face in every crowd again.

Or she could purposefully make a mess of this evening's event and destroy the chances of her loyal, deserving husband.

Clare checked the clock again. 8:37 a.m.

Last night at the reception, after she'd learned she had twenty-four hours to put on the dinner that could make all the difference for her husband's professional future—but before she'd understood Ireland was the country at stake—she'd shaken hands and kissed cheeks exactly as much as necessary, then withdrawn to a powder room. Balancing against a marble sink, cupping her phone in one hand, she'd reeled off instructions with the precision of an airline hostess intoning safety measures. First to their cook, Mathilde. Then to Amélie—remembering to ask whether Amélie's cousin might be available to offer an extra set of hands in the kitchen. Third to Yann, an embassy waiter she particularly trusted. *"Donc, vous annulez,"* she'd told him when he'd protested he already was slotted for another assignment. The butler, Gérard, was away in the south of France—unlucky timing, but they'd had nothing planned for these nights and it was his niece's wedding. She couldn't call him back to Paris. She would cover his organizational work, and Yann would do the greeting and managing of the guests. Amélie's cousin would help serve. And Amélie would supervise the wine and tableware deliveries. Mathilde—she stayed in the kitchen.

Her dinner staff lined up, Clare had tapped out an e-mail to the embassy, requesting that the official plate embossed with the queen's emblem be sent over in the morning, not too late, and then another to Edward's secretary, requesting the guest list, with annotations about recent personal events and food preferences. She'd extracted the notepad she always carried and begun a to-do list—butcher, wine, flowers, etc.—careful to think as well of anything the butler normally would handle. Last, she'd sent an e-mail to the publication office at the Rodin Museum to say she'd likely have to delay dropping off the translation she'd just completed. This was her other job, the one she got paid for—she translated art books and catalogs.

She'd done all this in slightly over ten minutes, then returned to the reception hall in time to switch off her phone and listen to Edward give the absent ambassador's welcoming speech. She'd kissed more cheeks amongst the circulating hors d'oeuvres, greeted more acquaintances, asked about more children, wives, and husbands. She'd been the picture of calm and competence. As she'd lain in bed later that night, trying to process Edward's news about the embassy in Dublin, she had carefully tugged on this earlier sanguinity, reeling it back in until her breathing slowed, her heart stilled. She'd willed sleep to come to her.

Clare folded her breakfast napkin. If she could keep her cool last night, she could keep it this morning. She could keep it through the day, and through the dinner. She could even keep it in Dublin. She had experience controlling fear.

She replaced the top of the sugar bowl. She twisted the lid back over Edward's jar of marmalade and gathered the plates from their breakfast, placing them on a tray. Mathilde would be coming in soon to start cooking. Amélie was already primping the formal living room. She tipped the remains of Edward's pot of tea into the sink, then that of her cup of coffee.

She would not think about St. Stephen's Green in Dublin, where rain had once splattered the remains of her humanity. She wouldn't think about Dublin at all. She would put her all into helping Edward. She'd spent more than twenty years piling grain upon grain of obfuscation, and she couldn't go backwards. Either she organized tonight's dinner with the skill Edward knew she possessed or she'd have to tell him the truth about herself. She didn't plan to tell that to anyone.

# TWO

Clare scanned the guest list for possible food allergies, religious restrictions, or special diets and, finding none, set it down on a counter. A gust of spring wind stirred the chartreuse buds on the linden tree outside the kitchen window, and unfastening the hinge, she opened the window so the scent of blossoms could enter. After weeks of gray and drizzle, the sun was shining on Paris. Morning light spilled over the cobbled courtyard below. Tiny sprigs of green peeked through the crags between the stones, blades of grass too young to be cut down by the concierge's weaponry. Somehow, overnight, the wisteria had fanned out in a flash of purple against the side of the building, like the imprint of light seen after squeezing one's eyelids shut.

"You'll catch a chill like that."

Clare drew her head back in. "Good morning, Mathilde."

"Hmph." Mathilde, who was half Swiss and half Scottish, and always prepared for a sudden snow- or rainstorm, pulled a heavy wool coat off and hung it in a closet by the service entrance. "You have the menu for me?"

"Yes."

A menu had already been planned for the ambassador, but the *Salon Bleu,* where dinner was to have been held at the ambassador's residence, was a pageant of sweeping ceiling, gilt wall ornaments, blue satin upholstery, and the tinkling of crystal, with a richly colored rug the size of a small sea. The dining room in the minister's residence, while handsome with its mahogany furniture and dark-green painted walls, and large enough to seat twenty at dinner, felt intimate by comparison. In other words, what would have succeeded amidst the splendor of the *Salon Bleu* wouldn't work for the minister's more discreet residence. Moreover, Clare wanted a meal that would show off Mathilde's particular culinary talents and make subtle reference to Ireland. If she was going to help Edward, she was going to do it right.

She refined her thoughts as she spoke. "New asparagus from Alsace, wrapped in *jambon de bayonne,* to start. Your lovely Chilean sea bass crusted with almond and bathed in leek and lemon cream as the main course. Salad, and I'll get whatever we need for the cheese course when I go to buy the flowers. You decide the dessert. Whatever you think fit—your desserts are all brilliant. Just please make it seasonal."

"You can't do the Chilean sea bass. Too controversial."

"Overfishing?"

"Overfishing." Mathilde shrugged. "Vietnamese farmed basa. I can cook it up the same way as the Chilean, and it tastes almost the same. I'll dress it with potatoes in fresh pesto."

"Perfect." Clare heard the ring of the phone in the study, the sound of the housekeeper's slippers padding their way down the hall. She paused to listen for the name of the caller.

"*Oui,* wait, please." Amélie's voice carried into the room. "I will go to the Madame, James."

James? Had she heard Amélie correctly?

"*Donc,* asparagus and ham, basa in leek and lemon cream. It's no bad," Mathilde said, offering a begrudging nod, "for a spring menu." She crossed her arms over her ample chest. "All right, then, if you don't have anything else, I'd best get started. Nae the way one is supposed to do these things. A V.I.P. dinner on one day's notice."

Jamie had barely ever rung in the morning since he'd begun at boarding school last autumn. Once, when he'd forgotten to finish an essay for history: "Come on, Mom," he'd said, "just a short little e-mail, saying my computer exploded or something." Another time, when he'd been called down to the headmaster for throwing a currant bun (that hit a teacher). He normally timed his daily call for early evening, when Clare was most likely to be in but Edward not yet. At fifteen, he didn't want his father to know how unhappy he was away from home, nor how dependent he was on his mother to stick it out.

She checked her watch: 9:10 a.m.

Jamie *couldn't* have gotten into some new trouble on this day of all days.

"I'm truly sorry," she said to Mathilde, "especially after I'd given you the day off. Thank you again for coming in. You're a treasure."

Mathilde snorted and began tying on her apron.

"Madame, eet's James," Amélie said, extending the phone towards her.

"Oh!" She accepted the handset from the housekeeper with a careful smile on her face. "That's nice. Thank you, Amélie. I think I'll just take this back in the bedroom."

She walked the long hall back to her bedroom, half shut the door, and sat down on the edge of the mattress. The plastic of the receiver felt cool against her cheek, unyielding. It was tricky with Jamie. He wanted her help, and she wished she could do more for him. Things certainly were not going well at his boarding school. But nothing annoyed him more than unsolicited interference from his parents. "Jamie?"

There was a pause. *"James."*

*"James.* Is everything all right?" To herself she thought, Please, at least don't let any bones be broken. Or any school property.

"Yeah, sure, Mom. Two hundred thousand people died in Iraq this morning. But it only rained three inches in London this week."

She transferred the phone to her other hand and frowned. "Two hundred thousand? That seems like rather a lot."

"Okay, *two.* Does it really make a difference?"

"Well, to the other one hundred and ninety-eight thousand, probably. But I see what you mean. Even one is one too many. So, is that what's up? Are you having nightmares again?"

He sounded so close, she could have sworn he was calling from downstairs. "Oh, Mom," he said and groaned. "Can you stop with that? I should never have told you."

"It's okay, Jamie. I'm not going to tell anyone."

"Did you tell Dad?"

"No. But is that why you're calling?" At the other end of the apartment, the service doorbell rang. A delivery; she could hear the soft tones of Amélie's voice again. A man's voice; she couldn't distinguish whose. She checked her watch. It had to be the wine.

She'd missed how Jamie had responded.

"Mom?" he was now saying. "So? Has anyone called?"

"From?"

"From ... from anywhere."

"Oh, Jamie. We have a really big day here. Just tell me. Have you gotten into trouble at school again?"

There was silence on the other side of the line.

"Jamie?"

"Never mind."

She had a moment of panic. "I didn't mean that. What's the matter?"

"I just told you."

She sat up, alert. Jamie had called a few nights earlier, asking permission to send an e-mail in her name requesting access to the school's science lab after hours. Something about some homework he and his roommate, Robbie, were doing together. "I'll write it," she'd said, but he'd objected. "It's just a note, Mom. Just tell me the password for the family account. Otherwise, I'll have to give you all the times and stuff when we want to get in there." Afterwards the thought had kept coming back to her: since when did Jamie go out of his way to do homework?

"Well, tell me again."

Her son sputtered so hard into the phone, she had to draw her ear away. "Look, Mom," he shouted, "I'm just saying, whatever they tell you, it's not right that only one person carry all the blame! It's not right!"

She tugged on a lock of hair. "Listen, honey—"

"I gotta go, Mom. I just wanted to speak to you first. Before *they* do." His voice broke. "I wanted to tell you I'm...I have to come home."

Christ, she thought. That's it. He's going to be suspended. "Jamie—"

But he repeated, "I gotta go. Bye," and hung up.

She waited, as though some part of her younger son might still linger, ready to talk more, before she clicked off the phone. She'd been apprehensive about sending Jamie to boarding school; their older son, Peter, had been at Edward's alma mater in Scotland, Fettes, for two years and professed to love it, but Jamie called Fettes "Fat-Ass" behind Edward's back. "I know you were pleased with your years at Fettes," she'd said when Edward had first brought the idea up the winter before, "and Peter has done fine there. But Jamie isn't Peter. Edinburgh only gets seven hours of daylight in winter, and Fettes does have those red-striped blazers. And the bagpipes..."

Edward had squeezed his hands together once in front of him, as he always did when he was about to capitulate. Clare had seen the movement and had suppressed a smile. For a moment, she'd been happy to think Jamie would be spending another year at home and at the International School in Paris.

"Very well," Edward had said. "I thought he might do well to be near his older brother. But if not Fettes, he will still have to go somewhere. We'll be leaving Paris soon, and in these last years before university, a child's education must have continuity. Besides"—and he'd paused to reach for *The Guardian*—"the security risk will be smaller at a British boarding school. There will be gates, there will be grounds, there will be less of a spotlight on him than on a diplomat's son rambling the *septième arrondissement* with a schoolbag over his shoulder."

And so, she had come up with the Barrow School, because it was in London and near an airport, and a friend of Jamie's from their posting in Washington, Robbie Meriweather, had just been sent there while his father was relocated for the World Bank to Jakarta. She'd asked Robbie's father to write a letter supporting his candidacy and, when Jamie was accepted, had had the two boys placed in the same dorm room.

But being reunited with Robbie hadn't spared Jamie from homesickness, nor had being just an hour's flight away from Paris. *Home*-sick? Could she even call Paris his home? Jamie had been born while they were posted in Cairo, but that city had never been home to any of them. When her thoughts returned to those couple of years, Clare *felt* Cairo rather than remembered it: the weight of her belly, then the weight of James in her arms as she'd walked him up and down the halls of their apartment, trying to calm him. The hooded eyes of their nanny whenever she'd hand James over to her, the *siss-siss* sound the woman made between her gapped front teeth. Stepping outside, the sun beating down, bludgeoning the back of her neck and shoulders, the smell of mint and tea and excrement heavy in the still air, the assault of car horns and shouting. Back inside the haven of their apartment, more painful sounds: the ring of phones bearing Gulf War updates, the penetrating silence of whispers and furtive conversations, and, always, the wails of the baby. James had cried steadily for the first six months of his life, his little hands screwed into tiny balls, fighting a war of his own. Why didn't you go *home* to have him? the other expat wives had asked. But even then, where was home? Hers or Edward's? Though she was married to a British foreign servant, Clare was still an American.

"Not homesick, *heart*sick," Edward had corrected Clare the last time she'd brought up James's struggles at Barrow. His studied patience had weighed on her like a heavy blanket. "Heartsick for the indulgences of his munificent mother."

Jamie *should* have gone to Fettes. At least Peter would have been there to take care of him. Peter was solid, like his father. If Edward did get posted to Dublin, she'd spend more time in their London apartment and arrange for Jamie to come stay with her weekends. *She* would help him.

For a moment, Clare almost felt positive about Dublin. Then she remembered, and a wave of cold rode over her.

\*    \*    \*

She entered St. Stephen's Green earlier than agreed, hastening past the fountain with three stoic-faced Fates perched on a slab of stone in its center, tightening her navy sweater around her waist. Who'd think Dublin could be so chilly in August? In Boston, the heat had shown no sign of letting up; by now, even the roses had drooped from heat exhaustion. When she arrived at the memorial to Yeats, she sat down on a bench and pulled the sweater on. A man wandered in—not him—and she hunched over her now flat stomach.

A tiny yellow-and-green finch flitted down onto the bench beside her. He twittered, cocked his head left, then right, eyed her, flew away. She waited. Couples walked by, college kids like herself toting knapsacks, gray-haired men gripping newspapers, a mother with three small children. Even as the park began to fill with workers going home for the day, she waited. She couldn't believe the person she'd become, and yet the last thing she could do was go backwards.

Still she waited.

Clare folded her hands over the telephone. If Jamie hadn't been suspended yet, he would be in class now, and they weren't allowed to have cell phones in class—or anywhere outside their dorm rooms. If she rang him straight back, she could get him into still more trouble.

She rose from the bed and opened the door all the way. There was something happening in the front of the Residence—she could hear Amélie arguing. She had to get out there and ensure things stayed on track for the dinner.

# THREE

Amélie met her at the mouth of the Residence's hall, shadowed by a short man in a gray jumpsuit.

"*Madame,*" he said, folding his arms over his chest, "*on régle
avant que je pars.*"

"Zis man," Amélie repeated, shaking her head with the special
disgust she reserved for deliverymen who spoke even less English
than she, "he wants zis house pay him."

If the butler were here, he'd be handling this—not Amélie and
not Clare. And he would do it with his usual aplomb. But what was
the point of thinking about that? Gérard wasn't here. And it wasn't
fair to expect Amélie to manage in his place. Clare would manage.

"*Mais non, monsieur, je vous en prie...,*" Clare began, trying to
explain to the deliveryman their special circumstance. Since they
were holding the dinner in the ambassador's stead, the cost of
the wine would go on the ambassador's residence's account rather
than on theirs, although she'd still have to keep a record of it.

"*C'est pas normal,*" he interrupted.

"*Mais si, monsieur.*" Unlike the ambassador's wife, whose residence had its own huge wine cellar of Pol Roger Champagne and Bordeaux and Burgundies, Clare regularly used this purveyor for the minister's residence, where they didn't entertain in such enormous numbers and thus didn't keep such large quantities of wine always handy. The wine merchant knew her well enough to know she wasn't going to try to cheat them, even if she were able. *"C'est normal pour aujourd'hui."*

The man shrugged and made an abrupt about-face towards the front door. He did not wait for Amélie to let him out or steer him to the service entrance; he twisted the doorknob himself. *"Très bien, Madame,"* he said. *"Je sais où vous habitez."* And with this vague threat, and a dismissive flick of his wrist, he swung the door open, leaving it to thwack shut behind him.

Amélie shook her head and returned to her work in the dining room. Clare made a mental note to check that they had a full selection of single malt whiskies in stock, as well as a few bottles of Somerset Alchemy Fifteen-Year-Old Cider Brandy. If only she'd heard everything Jamie had said.

The phone was still in her hand, and she walked to the study. The last time Edward or she had tried to pin Jamie down over some school infraction, it had taken more than a week to pry any details out of him. The more they would ask, the less he would tell. She sat down behind the study's large walnut desk and rapid-dialed the Barrow switchboard. Jamie wouldn't like it, but she'd call the headmaster directly. At least she would both skip the whole part where she had to get Jamie to talk and avert any possibility of the school ringing Edward. If Jamie was being sent home, this was serious.

She heard someone pick up.

"The headmaster's line is engaged," the school's receptionist told her. "Would you like to hold?"

She tapped the broad face of the desk with a fingernail. "That's all right, thank you. I'll call back in five minutes."

She set the phone down and opened the laptop in front of her. As it booted up, she took her notepad out of her cardigan pocket and surveyed her to-do list. Drat Barrow. They should never have sent Jamie there. He hadn't been a brilliant student at the International School, but nothing like this. The computer screen blinked at her, then stabilized, and she clicked on Outlook.

Like rows of black ants, a slew of new e-mail messages appeared.

Towards the top:

> Madame Moorhouse, It is with urgency that I request to know whether you are in knowledge that the Permanent Under-Secretary has expressed great desire to meet M. de Louriac's son, Frédéric? Monsieur de Louriac le fils and his fiancée, Agathe Gouriant D'Arcy, are in Paris from Bordeaux for this one night. I wait your communication. With my sincerest respect, Mme. Gens, secrétaire de direction, M. Rémy de Louriac, The Ballaut Group.

Clare scrolled down the screen.

A few e-mails farther down, from Edward's secretary:

> Good morning, Mrs. Moorhouse. We received a call from M. de Louriac's personal secretary this morning...

More portions of fish would have to be ordered, Mathilde would have to adjust her measures.... Why hadn't Lydia called instead of sending an e-mail? Clare felt in her sweater pocket; she didn't have her phone on her. She might not have taken it out of her purse the evening before. After Edward had dropped the bomb about Dublin, she hadn't thought about checking e-mails.

She pulled the laptop towards her and began typing.

> Madame Gens, c'est avec grand plaisir que nous accueillerons ce soir Messieurs de Louriac, père et fils, et Madame de Louriac, et l'invitée de M. de Louriac fils…

She finished the note, pressed "send" on the keyboard, and added "order more ham and more basa" to the bottom of her to-do list. She also added "rethink the seating arrangement" and "request two more official place settings from the embassy." The de Louriacs had owned the same landed estate in Aquitaine since the fifteenth century. De Louriac senior had been the P.U.S.'s tennis partner during the P.U.S.'s years in Paris. They were what passed for intimates in the diplomatic world. Also, he controlled Ballaut, the titanic French aeronautics concern, which was of vital interest to the British government at this moment. Edward had explained it briefly to her yesterday on their way home from the reception. She had not probed the details. They would be fourteen total now at dinner.

9:40 a.m. Time to call Barrow again.

As she reached for the handset, sunshine slashed through the broad windows of the study, impaling her hands against the study desk, translucent in the sharp light, an older woman's hands. Were they *her* hands? A touch of freckle sprayed across the top of the right one, the skin so thin the tendons were almost visible. The knuckles rose into a puckered ridge.

Was it possible that someone had once kissed each of these knuckles, telling her how he dreamt of her hands when they were separated? She'd sat down beside him at the kitchen table and watched him drink his Coke and noticed the curl of hair rolling down the back of his neck. He'd plunked down his bottle and, without asking, slipped his palm under hers.

"You surely have beautiful hands, Clare," he said.

His eyes were so blue that they left her feeling as though she'd stared too long up into the sky. She looked away and was unable to see anything.

She was tall and fair-haired, good-looking without being striking, and plenty of boys had been happy to have her as their date for a movie, on a hike, to a house party. "Why don't you ask Clare? She's okay," she could imagine them saying about her. But she was never part of the golden circle of popular girls, and the boys in the suburbs of Hartford were as vague about their attentions as they were good at playing lacrosse. Not one of them had ever called anything about her beautiful. None of them even seemed to have opinions.

She began to unfurl her fingers, for him.

Clare drew her hands back from the phone, hid them behind her back, brushed them against the front of her cardigan. And if she hadn't followed Niall into her aunt's kitchen all those years ago? If he hadn't touched her hand and she hadn't looked into his eyes? Would she still have ended up agreeing to help? Would she now be in this predicament?

She pressed the rapid-dial button for Barrow on the phone again. She was not going to think about Niall, especially not now. This time she told the main switchboard she would hold; while she waited, she fired off an e-mail to the fishmonger, as well as one to the butcher, ordering the extra portions. She was Clare Moorhouse, wife to the British minister in Paris, cool, collected, the picture of composure. Still on hold, she sent e-mails to the pantry at the ambassador's residence, requesting the two additional place settings, and to the ambassador's secretary asking whether either of the two new guests had any dietary requirements. She modified both her guest and her to-do lists.

The switchboard put her through. "Mrs. Moorhouse. Of course," the headmaster's secretary said. Clare thought she could hear her reach for the pearls she always wore around her neck and click them together. "Mr. Hennessey just stepped away. But he will call you and your husband back straightaway. As soon as he sorts out this other...business."

"Mrs. Thomas, I have a busy day. I will be out most of the afternoon. And my husband will not be available at all. Perhaps, *we* could talk now?" Hearing the secretary's hesitation, Clare continued, careful to be as definite and no-nonsense as possible. This was what worked best with Barrow. "I just spoke with James, and he's very upset. He really has been trying to make an effort. He may make his mistakes here and there, but he means well."

The headmaster's secretary cleared her throat. Clack went the pearls; now Clare was sure she heard them. They must have thumped against the phone receiver. *"Indeed,"* Mrs. Thomas said.

"Mrs. Thomas, I can assure you we take both James and Barrow very seriously. I'm very worried." She hesitated. "The minister is, too. I've spoken with him."

The secretary was quiet for a moment. "It would be better if you talked directly with the headmaster. But I can tell you that Barrow does not intend to ask for James's removal. Some type of punitive action has to be taken, a suspension, but there will not be a request for permanent withdrawal. But really, you need to speak with Mr. Hennessey."

"Mrs. Thomas," Clare began, buying time to think of the right way to phrase a question without sounding too blunt and, thus, American or ignorant, things that might prejudice them further against Jamie. She didn't want Barrow to know she hadn't got out of Jamie in detail what had happened, that Jamie wasn't easy to handle in his home life either.

The sound of a crash echoed through the dining room into the study. Mathilde! Either the fishmonger or the butcher must have called back on the kitchen line to confirm Clare's e-mails, and Mathilde was upset that Clare hadn't gone in there right away to inform her about the additional guests. This could mean trouble for tonight's dinner. If Mathilde felt really put out, she was liable to burn the fish, or the equivalent, in retaliation. Mathilde's temper was as impressive as her cooking.

"Mrs. Thomas," she said. She could hear the pad of footsteps. That would be Amélie fleeing the pantry. "Please tell Mr. Hennessey that James's father and I will try him back this afternoon. He doesn't need to try me."

She hung up the phone and extracted her pad. *Call the headmaster at Barrow again,* she added to the bottom of her to-do list, right after *Check on the single-malt whiskey and the British brandy.* She wouldn't try to get it out of the secretary. That wouldn't help anyone.

That call about the science lab—she should have followed it up. Winter term, Jamie had been caught cheating on a science test and he'd been on academic probation ever since. Indeed, the only reason she'd agreed to let him write that e-mail in her name was that she hadn't wanted in any way to discourage him. Jamie had had trouble with the science teacher, Mr. Roach, from the start. Already in the autumn he had given Jamie a week of detention for spilling some chemical material. "He's dangerous," Mr. Roach had said. "He doesn't think through what he's doing and could cause real damage." He'd ragged on Jamie ever since—probably half the reason Jamie had cheated on that test. Jamie had never done anything like that when he was still at the International School. He knew Mr. Roach was looking for any excuse to fail him. And no one else at Barrow would be sticking up for him.

She sighed and stood up. At least he didn't seem to have hurt himself. Not this time.

"What a busy morning!" she said to Amélie, passing her en route to the kitchen, preparing herself for what she would find in there. She'd have to set Jamie's problems aside for the moment to sort out whatever had happened to upset Mathilde; the tiniest perceived slight could set Mathilde off, and her means of revenge were typically disproportionate. About two months after Clare had hired her, Mathilde had gone so far as to produce an authentic haggis in response to being asked to do lamb for a member of the Kuwaiti royal family. It turned out she hadn't liked the way Clare had left a note for her instead of speaking personally to her about the menu.

"Well, you wrote 'lamb,' *n'est-ce pas?*" Mathilde had said, thumping out the crust for a shepherd's pie when Clare had gone to speak with her the following morning about having served their royal guests animal entrails mixed with oatmeal. Flour rose like an atomic cloud around her. "You wrote 'traditional,' nae? How am I to ken what you mean if you canna take the time to speak with me directly? And," she added, "it's no that simple either, producing a good 'aggis here in Paris."

Now *that's* a contradiction in terms, if ever there was one, Clare had thought, and for a brief moment, she had considered simply hiring a new chef. But Mathilde had already made them the envy of dinner hosts all over the city, and in Paris that was no mean accomplishment. Moreover, Edward liked Mathilde's cooking. Maybe because of her curious heritage, Mathilde had an uncanny talent for creating rewarding culinary experiences out of the type of mild simple dish that best pleased Edward.

So Clare had made a study of how to work with Mathilde, learning to check in often but gently, without ever appearing to interfere. And, above all, never to underestimate Mathilde's sense of self-importance. As for the other stuff—the fits of temper, grunts, and snorts—Clare ignored it. She *needed* Mathilde. Especially on a day like this.

"What a formidable diplomat your mother would make," Edward had joked to the boys this past New Year's Eve after she'd earned a spontaneous rendition of "Auld Lang Syne" from Mathilde over a cooling pot of cabbage, "If only she showed the slightest interest in politics. Really, it's thrown away, spending her days translating museum catalogs."

"I think it was the bottle of Madeira I brought in while she was cooking," she'd said, but secretly she'd been pleased with her accomplishment.

"Oh, Mathilde," she said now, entering the kitchen. The cook was standing by the back door, her apron flung across the kitchen table—a favorite symbolic gesture. Clare picked up the apron and smoothed it as though she were petting the head of a child. "I've just had to add two more guests! Thank heavens I can count on you to manage."

"Two additional? Right good of you to let me know."

Clare held the apron out. "I put in the extra orders right away. I know you have enough on your hands without having to start calling around to the fishmonger." When Mathilde didn't move, she added, "Oh, I know you'll make me look a better hostess than I deserve. I don't know what I'd do without you."

Husbands and wives were teams in the Foreign Service, although only one got to wear a mantle, and a spouse's ability to put on a good dinner was a crucial part of the package. No one at the Foreign Office would soon forget France's President Chirac pronouncing food from Finland the only thing worse than British cooking. If humoring Mathilde's conviction that she was the most important personage in the Residence kept the kitchen working smoothly, Clare was happy to oblige.

Mathilde rubbed a thick arm. "Spring weather's murder on my rheumatism. All that air moving around. And me in here by the cooker." She marched over and closed the window. Then she came and took back the apron.

"I'll stop in the pharmacy and see if I can't find something for you," Clare promised.

In the front hall, Amélie was balanced on a step stool, polishing the crystal chandelier. The glass glistened in the sun streaming in from the study, splashing prisms of light all over Amélie's sturdy calves. She peeked down at Clare questioningly, and Clare nodded. Crisis averted.

"*Behn...,*" Amélie said.

"Mmmm...," Clare said. She felt inside the Regency console in the foyer, where she always stored her handbag, taking in the marine landscape by Turner that hung above it. An early watercolor of breaking dawn, the Turner was even more precious to her than its pedigree might warrant, for reasons she'd never been able to pinpoint; she hung it by the door wherever they lived so it would be the first or last thing she saw as she exited or entered. "I shall be going out now. While I'm gone, can you go through the liquor cabinet, please, and make sure there's Somerset Brandy and at least twenty-five choices of whiskey? If there isn't, call Jane in housekeeping at the embassy and ask that a car bring them over."

"Ze Zomerzet Brandy and twenty-five whiskey."

"Exactly. I have a few quick errands to run. Unless something unexpected comes up, I will be back within a couple hours." To make certain Amélie had understood, she repeated, slowly: "I-will-come-back-soon. Nothing-will-happen-when-I-am-out."

Amélie's English skills left much room for improvement, but Amélie was keen to improve them and Clare felt she had to support her in the effort, even at moments as critical as this. Maybe, to build her confidence, especially at moments like this.

Amélie squinted at her from above. Clare refrained from repeating herself one last time, in French. It would be so nice to feel sure she'd been understood. "And, if ze new *Madame Conseiller* does not speak French so well as you? She will cut me!" Amélie had burst out a few months ago, anticipating the end to Clare's time in Paris. They'd already been there three years, and regardless of whether or not Edward got an ambassadorship, they would be reposted somewhere new soon. That's how it was in the Foreign Service: never too long anywhere. Amélie knew the score.

"Not cut. Not *cut,* Amélie."

"I must make better my English," Amélie had announced, nodding. "Now, I speak *only* English. *C'est bien?*"

So, Clare left the English words hanging between them and hoped Amélie had understood everything. The door to the apartment thumped shut behind her; there was the twang of the elevator cage, starting its way up. She set her wicker shopping basket down on the inlaid tile of the landing and loosened the thick silk scarf she'd knotted over her sweater as she waited for its arrival. Today was a beautiful April day in Paris, filled with promise. Jamie was in trouble yet again, but she'd accomplished what she'd needed for right now. The silver would all shine. Bread dough would soon begin rising in a basket. Fresh herbs would be cut and pounded into a pesto.

She wouldn't think about where all these dinner preparations might propel her. She had to believe everything was going to be fine.

Composure was a quality like gold in the diplomatic world, and she had built a reputation for having it in spades. She wouldn't let it now fail her.

# FOUR

Clare stepped out into the gated courtyard that separated the Residence's building from the pale stone-lined walks of the neighborhood and swung her shopping basket into the crook of her arm.

"*Bonjour, Madame,*" she said to the woman polishing the front door handle.

"*Bonjour, Madame.*" The woman stepped to one side and nodded. Clare stopped to button up her cardigan and tried not to feel the woman's eyes taking in every garment she was wearing, noting that Clare hadn't had her hair done this week.

*Hairdresser—4 p.m.* She had it on her to-do list.

Running a diplomatic residence was easy, but living in it was harder. In addition to the loss of privacy was the shortage of free will—so many things that had to be said and done each day, no matter how she might feel about them. Then, the constant menace of relocation and the conservation of a pristine public image. Not to forget the security issues—always be on guard, a fellow ex-pat wife had told her during the Cairo posting, stirring a spoonful of sugar into her coffee cup. A few years after, Clare had picked up the morning paper to see the same woman's face staring back at her from beneath the fold; she was being held for an undisclosed ransom by kidnappers in Venezuela. The kidnappers had gotten the wife by mistake when she'd picked up her husband's car after a routine check at the garage.

"My God, Edward," she'd said, holding up the paper to show him.

"They weren't Foreign Service. They were oil," he had pointed out, after taking the paper and studying the article. "Much more money."

Still, Jamie had *had* to be sent away, to someplace with gates, someplace culturally welcoming. While the chances were greater that one of them would get hurt falling down stairs in a crumbling building in Paris than that one of them would be kidnapped, the peril of terrorism seemed all the greater for its intimacy and immensity. Nine eleven had changed everything, throwing the already fragile balance between estranged worlds into both disorder and relief. She overheard the hostility in both the *tabacs* and from well-dressed professionals at multinational cocktail parties. *"Americaine?"* a key cutter had asked the day before, lifting an eyebrow in a way that conveyed a thousand words of disapproval. There'd been sympathy for a while, but the war in Iraq had changed that.

The joyous wave of wisteria against the building's facade caught her eye. Yet, she had to consider herself lucky. Paris was beautiful. The creditability of Edward's work made hers feel like a treat rather than a duty. And, in the end, what was the use in worrying, particularly on days like this one, when the sun's rays were borne lightly about by a spring wind and even the plane trees outside their apartment building seemed to be dancing? The breeze caught in her hair and caressed her cheek, coaxing a younger Clare to step out from her middle-aged shell. She could almost feel a heavy braid swing against her back as it had during the days when she was a student at Radcliffe, and for a moment she allowed herself to revel in the phantom sensation. At Harvard, she'd padded her long frame with woven Aran sweaters in honor of her Irish heritage, played Ultimate Frisbee on the campus quad barefoot, and pulled overnighters with her roommate during exam periods. Never one to proclaim her views loudly, she'd nonetheless emptied her pockets for any worthy-seeming cause, offered her floor to anyone visiting the campus for a valid-seeming protest. She'd believed the world could be better. Only after she'd met Niall had she learned to be suspicious, and *that* was the real reason for her innate apprehension; she was expecting the past to raise its angry head, hoary and covered with the cobwebs of recrimination, to point its finger at her. Neither 9/11 nor Edward and the lifestyle he'd brought her was to blame. If anything, that was *why* she'd married Edward. She had hoped the profundity of his decency might shield her.

Clare touched the fragile flat bell of a purple blossom with the tip of her finger and turned to address the charwoman, who she knew would still be staring at her.

"*Très jolie,*" she said.

"*Oui, Madame.*"

She adjusted her scarf and basket and continued across the courtyard. Every morning, she managed to push Niall away, his phantasmal arms still clasped tight around her from the night's dreams. Now, buoyed by the spring breeze, she willed him to leave her entirely, until she was just another well-dressed middle-aged woman in a solid marriage with two almost-grown, healthy children. She wasn't going to allow Niall to recede quietly into the back of her thoughts today. She wanted him out completely.

She nodded to the concierge, who stood talking with a co-worker in a corner of the entrance gateway, both wielding brooms like medieval soldiers ready to sally forth in battle, and let their sudden silence glance right off her. Not gossiping about us, at least, she thought. What would there be to say? By now, they knew she was an American. Other than that, she'd made sure that she and her family would make disappointing fodder for chatter: the children were reasonably well behaved, at least in public; the father spent nights in his own bed; she came home with shopping bags from the right boutiques, neither too many nor too few. The previous inhabitant of their apartment had enjoyed his drink more than was customary even for a diplomat. Worse, his wife, though only in her forties, had been at least fifty pounds over-weight and, of marginally aristocratic country stock, had donned galoshes whenever it was wet, which in Paris was often. Even being American seemed mild next to such transgressions.

The Rue de Varenne was empty, as usual outside rush hour, but for the pairs of gendarmes stationed along it like pats of butter on bread plates the length of a formal dining table, assigned to guard the many buildings like theirs on the street that housed govern-mental offices or official residences. The French prime minister lived in the grandest building of all, at number 57; the Italian Embassy in Paris stood at numbers 47–49–51. The French minister of agriculture and French secrétariat général du gou-vernement occupied, respectively, numbers 78–80 and 69. The rest of the seventh arrondissement hummed with visitors, thanks to the Eiffel Tower and Les Invalides, but on the Rue de Varenne, her street, tourists stuck to the beginning stretch by the Rodin Museum, wandering on and off the narrow sidewalk before it in the dazed manner so particular to the idle in Paris, return-ing to reality only at the chiding of a taxi or limousine horn but rarely making it as far even as the front gates of the building that housed the British minister's residence, just a coin's throw down from the museum.

From the Residence, the street continued in a long, nearly straight line, the cobblestones of the sidewalk just slightly uneven. Solemn gray and beige stone facades flanked either side of the road in a unified front. Edward had once commented on how well Clare fit in here, and she'd known he meant this as a compliment. She was pale, smooth, beige, a sea pebble of the kind one picks up along the beach and slips into one's pocket to run one's fingers over while pondering the meaning of life—or where to eat dinner. She knew it, she had even cultivated it—as much as she had ever manufactured anything about herself, for her development had been more like an act of erosion, a sanding away of all extraneous or undesirable elements, and this was how she felt more and more, as though each year were a grand wave washing away a little more of her. But something in her had begun to balk at the sentiment. Edward's compliment had left her feeling deeply wounded, and she'd never forgotten it.

Now, however, she looked up and down the Rue de Varenne, not to judge the validity of Edward's remark, nor to see if anyone was hovering about, as had been suggested as a simple precaution in one Foreign & Commonwealth Office post report, but to soak in the sunshine and attendant feeling of optimism. She left all second thoughts behind her, forced aside anything negative. The only things on her mind were the flowers and cheese and new asparagus from Alsace she needed to buy. She'd heard from other wives that there was a daily covered market in the Marais district that attracted vendors of fresh produce from all over France, but its name, Marché des Enfants Rouges, troubled her; translating as "market of the crimson children," the name left her with visions of an enormous cage filled with children stained red, as though their little bodies had been dipped in blood. In the almost four years they'd now been living in Paris, and in the three years they'd lived here back in the '90s, she had kept her distance. She would count on finding the asparagus at Le Bon Marché department store's food hall, as well as the oatcakes and Irish cheddar she planned to serve as a subtle reminder to the P.U.S. of her heritage and confirmation of Edward's Irish interests.

But ordering the flowers came first. An excellent florist stood on the Rue Chomel, near the end of the Rue de Varenne. She started down the street, nodding as usual to the first group of gendarmes she passed. The young gendarme with apple cheeks and a knobby neck was in his shirtsleeves in the brisk spring sunshine, an act of bravado that did not surprise her. He and his partner nodded back at her; the guards always did, except for whichever duo might be stationed in front of the prime minister's residence. One or two might even touch the small blue box with a visor they wore atop their heads in guise of an actual cap. "They're flirting with you," Edward had commented one obscure Sunday morning when they had breakfasted at a café. Mathilde, perhaps in an act of vengeance, had used the last of the milk, leaving them either to face Edward's tea and her coffee black or go out for breakfast. "They stay poker-faced for me, I can assure you." For a few weeks after, she'd avoided walking down the street and stopped greeting the guards when she did, fussing with her handbag or buttons as she passed by them, until she'd woken up to the absurdity of such behavior. She was forty-five, a wife and a mother. She was past feeling shy or flirtatious.

She quickened her pace. Of course, she could have called in an order to the florist, but as with the asparagus, choosing them herself was better. That way she could be assured of their quality. The first time Edward had visited her after they were introduced over an uncomfortable luncheon with her father and one of her father's Irish-American colleagues, he'd brought a large bouquet of lilacs to the dilapidated town house she was sharing with other recent college graduates in Washington, D.C. He was living in Washington then, too, posted there for the Foreign Office and already in his thirties. Though she'd hoped he wouldn't realize it, she'd seen right away that the flowers were no good and would never be any good; to this day, she remembered how sad they'd looked on the table. It had been March and too early for lilacs, even from a hothouse, and though the carefully trimmed and sprayed sprigs might endure without wilting, their delicate blooms would never open nor exude the sweet scent that makes lilacs precious. She'd cut them at a forty-five-degree angle and placed them in a vase filled with lukewarm water, but her heart had sunk even as it had risen at the promise of Edward's gesture.

"Lilacs were amongst the very first flowers that the colonialists brought over from England," he had said, watching her set them down on the center of her dining table. "But they originated farther east, in eastern Europe and Asia. Just one of the scores of wonders spread throughout the world by international trade."

"They have lovely lilacs at George Washington's old home, Mount Vernon." She'd been there just a few weeks earlier and read a pamphlet on the garden that had explained that the Dutch brought the first lilacs over to the New World—not the English. But she wouldn't say so. Nor that the lilacs there hadn't even begun budding. "It's not far from here. Have you visited it?"

"I haven't had the pleasure. Perhaps you will take me on a tour there sometime?"

"If you'd like me to."

"I would consider it a great favor."

How foreign Edward had seemed to her then, and how instinctively this had pleased her. Not just his gentlemanly form of courtship but everything about him: his neatly groomed short hair, his array of dark-colored wool suits, his self-assured long-legged stride, his feet armored in polished black-leather shoes. He was thirty-two to her twenty-three, nine years that somehow seemed more like nineteen. His careful British accent went down like ice tea, cool and smooth. She couldn't claim to have been sexually attracted to him from the start, not as she had been with Niall at least, but the response she'd felt to him was certainly physical; she'd wanted to burrow within his discreet tailored clothes, ruddy skin, clear gray-blue eyes, substantial hips. In the disorder of her earlier youth, she'd confused conviction with strength. On meeting Edward, she'd understood it was the absence of mania that guaranteed potency. Edward was the personification of solidity.

The night he'd proposed, he'd taken her hands but skipped right past their extravagant beauty and looked straight into her startled face.

"You are ideal for this life," he'd told her.

"I don't know if I'm . . . chatty enough. I mean for the wife of a diplomat."

"The wife of a diplomat is a diplomat, too. And a chatty diplomat is a hazard. The thing is to know when to speak and when to listen." He'd given her the look of careful esteem she would come to see daily over the next twenty years. "You do yourself discredit, Clare."

Suddenly, she'd understood that her self-perceived faults—her intuitive reserve, emotive pallor, innate discretion—were virtues in his eyes. He'd been admiring her newly sheared shoulder-length hair, the cool beige she'd begun using to cloak her own long limbs and secret emotions, and her ability to appear neutral at all times, at all costs, before anyone. "If you are sure," she said, and he'd slipped the platinum engagement ring that had once belonged to some illustrious ancestor of his onto her slender finger. Its weighty diamond had caused it to slip sideways. The following week, he'd taken the ring to a jeweler's to be resized. Five months later, in a church filled with her family and a few members of his, he'd slid a diamond-encrusted wedding band next to it. There were no tears, no sighs nor moans nor shouting, in their new life together, just a great calm that fell over her like seaside dusk. Exactly what she wanted.

Every morning since, when they awoke, in whatever bed, in whatever country, Edward reached over to lay a hand on her back and wish her good morning. He'd done it again this morning. And, all day long, she'd feel the reassuring weight of his trust guiding her forward.

This was why she could not let Edward down; even more than the love she felt for him, this was what made her so determined to ensure that this evening succeeded. Of course she believed he deserved the ambassadorship and wanted him to have all he had worked so hard for. Of course she loved him and wanted him to be happy. But above all, he had offered her a share in his future, she had accepted his offer, and she had never given him any reason to believe this trust was misguided.

Boxes of red and yellow and orange and purple tulips lay strewn across the floors of Fleurs Richert. A thin young man in a smock bent over them—the shop assistant, Jean-Benoît. Seeing that he was alone in the shop, she resisted an urge to walk right back out and return later.

"Ah, Madame Moorhouse!" Jean-Benoît twisted his head around at the sound of the door. Rising slowly to his feet, he wiped his hands on the apron and pushed his glasses up the bridge of his nose. "*Quel dommage!* Madame Richert is just go out."

Jean-Benoît's insistence on speaking English with her was different from Amélie's. Her housekeeper was desperate to learn the language to keep her job. Jean-Benoît was desperate to keep French out of a foreign mouth. However, Clare had long come to understand that being condescended to in barely intelligible English, with labial contortions beyond imagining, was the price she had to pay for having a mother tongue that also was the international language of communication. All over the world, people had made English their own; it had spawned bastard children on six continents.

"Oh, well, I know *you* will find something wonderful for me," she said. "We have an unexpected guest this evening."

Jean-Benoît led her around a stand of ranunculus, their plump faces looking like the layered tulle skirts of old-fashioned coming-out gowns, in brilliant yellows, pinks, whites, and oranges. Clare had been to a ball once in England where half the girls were wearing similar items, remembrances of another, more optimistic century, when girls were eager to look like candy packages. She couldn't imagine either of her sons dating a girl like that. Peter's girlfriends always were stylish in a discreet expensive manner. They wore luxuriant corduroy pants cut just a bit lower on the hips than their mothers would wear, wool jackets in black or brown or navy and tailored close around the bosom. Jamie hadn't had a first girlfriend yet in Paris, and the all-boys

Barrow School seemed to offer little opportunity to find one now. But the girls he'd been friendly with at the International School in Paris had worn studs in their eyebrows and relegated bright colors to streaks in their hair. Particularly the ones she'd seen him eye wistfully.

"Eh, *voilà,* Madame, zees is what I want to show *you!*" Jean-Benoît pointed to three large vases filled with tall white calla lilies. Behind them, a fourth vase held yellow callas. "Zees is nice, very nice."

"No, no, Jean-Benoît," she said. "They're beautiful. But I already have an idea of what I want."

"No, you don't." Behind his glasses, Jean-Benoît didn't blink, his arms stayed pinned close to his sides.

Clare smiled. "Well, I was thinking of dog roses. Could you get any dog roses?"

"Dog ro-zes?"

*"Rosier des chiens."*

He shrugged. "Of course. Dog ro-zes. But zees is not a flower to 'ave in a nice *réception.* It is for ze outzide."

"Could you get them for me?'

He shook his head. "But ze lilies, zees is *elegant.*"

"Well, then, how about dog violets?"

"Dog violets!"

Clare nodded her head. "Dog violets."

"You 'ave zomezing about dogs, Madame Moorhouse? You are 'aving the British minister of dogs zees night?"

Clare laughed good-naturedly and thought to herself: If they don't have asparagus at Le Bon Marché, it will mean carving out some extra time to go hunting for it. She also had now promised to pass by the apothecary to find something for Mathilde's rheumatism. She could cut out delivering her translation for the

Rodin Museum today; even though she had promised the head of the museum's documentation center, Sylvie Cohen, to put the translation on a USB stick and drop it to her personally, and she did hate to go back on a promise, she had sent that e-mail last night from the reception saying she might not be able today after all. Sylvie would understand. She and Sylvie had become friends of a kind, and with the museum right down the street from her house, the publication office just behind it in the museum gardens, it had started to feel awkward for her not to pop in to drop things off or pick things up. But while translating museum catalogs was all very well, it could not compete in importance with the rites of international diplomacy, and she knew Sylvie accepted this would always be Clare's priority.

Except for the children. The boys came very first—and there was still the call back to Barrow.

And then, after lunch, and before the hairdresser's—because she had to have her hair done for this evening—there were also the place cards still to inscribe, the guest list to read over, the seating chart to arrange.

All the small details.

She would book Jamie on the Friday 3:35 p.m. flight out of Heathrow. She could do that right now while she remembered, then send a text to the embassy asking whether someone was coming in on the same flight to share a car into the city. At least that would be taken care of. Saturday morning, Jamie would sit down with her and Edward, and they would talk the whole situation at Barrow through, the three of them, face-to-face. They'd sort Jamie out before putting him back on a flight to London whenever his suspension period was over. He'd be chastened; he'd do better in the future. They would talk to the school about getting him the support he needed.

She reached into her purse for her cell phone, then pulled her hand away. She'd finish here first: what she wanted were some flowers that grew in Ireland.

"Bluebells," she said to Jean-Benoît patiently. "Primroses."

"Zis flower, I do not know." Jean-Benoît crossed his arms across his apron. His chin made a sharp little square; his eyes looked almost black behind his glasses. "Madame, why don't you just tell me what you want?"

It was just bad luck Madame Richert, the flower shop's pleasant owner, wasn't there. "Something with a spring theme, but British. Or, maybe, a little...Irish."

"Ah, Irish! We have *les Cloches d'Irlande,* not Irish, not in *origine,* but does zees matter? Your *invités* won't know about flowers. And zey are perfect with ze lilies. I put zem with ze yellow, and zis is very spring, very *élégant.* It is what you want."

"It sounds lovely, Jean-Benoît." She surveyed the rest of the shop. "All right, all right. We shall put them in the hall and the reception rooms. But, for the dinner table..."

"Ah, zere is a dinner, too. Why do you not say zis? You cannot have ze lilies for zis, zey are too tall, too...*big.* Too much *parfum.*" He shook his head at her and clucked. "But, if one has *primevères.* Zis is very British, no?"

*Primevères* were primroses. Clare nodded. "Terrific. Thank you." She leaned over a bunch of yellow freesia to drink in their heady tealike scent.

"Of course, zey will not last."

"That's all right. It's just for this evening."

Clare could hear his heels clicking as he headed back towards the shop counter. But he did make beautiful bouquets. She didn't even have to ask what else he would add to them. After he'd finished painstakingly inscribing the order, she signed it.

"For sixteen 'our?" He handed her the order duplicate.

By 4:00 p.m., the table should be set. She would be at the hairdresser, but she could put out the vases before she left, and Amélie could place them about. Clare would have time for any necessary adjustments after she returned; she would not attend the cocktail party that would be held at the embassy before dinner. She and Edward had agreed upon this.

She nodded and folded the invoice away in her sweater pocket.

"Madame, do you know what ze *primevère* signify?"

Jean-Benoît's particular passion, other than protecting the French language, was the perceived or historical meanings of flowers. Mme Richert had once confided in Clare that he was writing an entire book on the topic, a masterpiece, to be illustrated by a close friend, a very talented young artist. Clare had understood this meant his lover. Clare did not really wish to know, any more than she wanted to hear the presumed implication behind every bouquet or to read his masterpiece of a book someday. She used to like the look of a few sprigs of straw in an arrangement until Jean-Benoît had informed her it represented "a broken agreement." She had never been able to use straw in a bouquet again.

"I don't, but please tell me," she said.

"Young love. I cannot live wiz-out you." He spread his thin arms wide with a flourish before leaning forward to open the door for her.

# FIVE

**B**ack on the street, the air was still filled with the scent of spring, so light and hopeful after the thick woodsy atmosphere inside the floral shop. April in Paris, this was the celebrated time for lovers in the City of Lights, when the gray drizzle of winter broke long enough to release the fragrance of the tiny green heads of new shoots on the plane and hazelnut trees, the wisteria starting to climb its loose-limbed way up the side of old stone buildings and cast-iron gates. In truth, what a blessing this posting in Paris had been for her, surrounded by art and the languages she loved. It wouldn't be easy to leave, no matter where they were headed, even knowing an ambassadorship somewhere else less important would be a stepping stone necessary to holding the top rank back in Paris. Because, if everything went right, that could happen. Edward could end up eventually the British ambassador in Paris. He was on the right track for that.

Clare breathed deeply and took a few steps down the street.

A man planted himself in front of her, blocking her way. He pressed a folded sheet of paper into her palm.

"Madame," he said in heavily accented English, his voice low and guttural.

She suppressed the urge to cry out in surprise; her free hand flew up in front of her mouth.

He leaned in closer, his legs split at shoulder width, thrusting out his elbows. There was something practiced about the way he stood, so firm and solid. His stance announced there would be no moving him; there would be no moving around him either.

Avoiding eye contact, she took the quick measure of him: dark, with an ashy colorless type of complexion—Albanian, at a guess—and the threat of black hairs about to burst forth from just-shaved skin. A slippery-looking leather jacket, much too hot for this warm April day, much too cheap for this fashionable street, and his respiration was labored. She could smell his body heat. She made a tentative motion to the left. He shadowed her shift in balance, a complicated pas de deux where neither of them moved more than an inch but he clarified that she would not step around him.

He was shorter than she was but wider, aggressively muscular. She glanced over his shoulder. A couple were crossing the road in their direction: young, dressed in pressed jeans and expensive loafers, deep in conversation. Students from the nearby Grande Ecole, Sciences Po. Words poured from their lips, words that she could not hear. One stopped to light a cigarette. They swung to the left when they reached the sidewalk and started down the Boulevard Raspail. A moment more and they were out of sight.

"Madame," the stranger repeated. He pushed the piece of paper against her hand. She knew what might be written on it: *Do not shout.* Or: *Do not try to run.* Scaffolding swathed a building across the street. She scanned its metal web, but the workmen must have been on break, or on strike. She glanced around the empty street.

What had the U.S. done to Albania in recent weeks? Or could his nationality be something else? Iraqi, even? If it was *that,* what could anyone say?

Except...and a part of Clare flew up to view herself from afar, as though she were one of the pigeons roosting in a cote above. Or, better yet, an anger-filled terrorist hiding in a nearby car. There was nothing to indicate she was American. If anything, she could be taken for British. She had on flat Tod loafers, ecru woolen slacks, a cream-colored sweater set. The heavy silk scarf. Tall. No makeup. No hair spray.

Except...he could know *exactly* who she was. He could have been following her this whole time. She hadn't looked around when she'd stepped out of the Residence's courtyard. American wife to a high-powered British diplomat. What a twofer she represented for a terrorist—and the children, offspring of both nations. Thank God it wasn't Jamie standing on this street right now. Edward had been right about sending him away.

Clare reached her left hand up to pull on a strand of hair, then quickly dropped her hand back to her side. No reason to flash the diamond.

"Uh...," she said. "I..."

"Please, to help me?" One of his eyes was smaller than the other, heavy-lidded. He unfolded the paper and lifted it.

She stopped trying not to look and, instead, looked closer. The paper contained a photocopied map of the center of Paris, torn maybe from a phone book, in faded black and white and gray. Written in round blue script along the margin of the sheet were a couple of phone numbers and the address for what was labeled as a medical clinic.

The labored breathing, heavy jacket, resolute stance...Color rushed to her cheeks. The man was *ill.* He was speaking in

English with her not because he knew *she* could but because *he* could. He was sick and lost, and looking for a doctor. And *she* was everything bad in the world, a racist, a profiler. She didn't know what she felt in greater quantities, relief or shame.

"Let me see," she said and took the map from him.

Hardly a week after she'd married Edward, she'd received a booklet from an association of spouses in the FCO with advice on keeping safe. And that was twenty years ago, before it had become commonplace for people to turn their own bodies into bombs and acceptable to broadcast images of people jumping out of blazing skyscrapers. Maybe her reaction had been inevitable; violence was the shadowy partner of the tea-and-handshake life of the diplomatic corps. But she couldn't blame Edward or the world he'd brought her into. Her life of violence had begun before she married Edward, the day she said yes to Niall, maybe the very day she met him. Certainly the day she allowed him to wrap her abdomen with layers of hundred-dollar bills, pounds of paper taped to her tall frame, and then headed for the Boston airport.

"We'll be safe coming in," Niall had assured her. "No one looks twice at a pregnant girl in Dublin, no one looks twice at an American tourist either," and she'd clung to that word "we."

"That's why you're carrying the money into Dublin," he'd said. "No one would believe a tourist arriving up north. But we get it safely onto the island, and the lads will ferry it up to Belfast. No worries."

That "we" again. Still, as soon as they boarded the plane in Boston, bound for Dublin, the "we" seemed to disappear.

She was alone, just she and the phantom child, and the fear she felt, as the plane took off, as they sailed above puffy white clouds and plunked down on the Irish tarmac in a gust of rain, as she undid her seat belt, stretched to accommodate her extended midriff, and padded along the jetway, trying to remember everything Niall had told her about how a pregnant woman shifted her weight from hip bone to hip bone. The arrival terminal in Dublin sucked her in, and she gave herself to it, all the time half wishing she was back at Harvard studying how to say *amar,* the Spanish verb for "love," in the first-person past-perfect subjunctive. During the flight, she'd resisted the temptation to make eye contact with Niall, seated two rows ahead of her under a separate booking, even as she made her way up and down the airplane aisle to the lavatory—"You be remembering to go often," he'd instructed her. "Women with child do."—but as she and all the other passengers tottered towards the baggage carousel, she had to restrain herself from using her long legs to catch up with him. "I can feel the baby kicking," she might say, making light of this whole crazy escapade, when she realized she couldn't see him anymore, that he'd walked straight through the baggage claim and disappeared into the crowd of Irish voices. Was the rush of panic that overcame her from fear of the customs authorities or from having lost sight of him? She felt herself sway. For a moment, she thought she might faint.

"Last months, eh?" A woman put a hand out to steady her. "Difficult time to travel."

A jolly man with white hair and red cheeks offered to lift her bag. By then, she was half convinced that she *was* with child, Niall and hers. "How kind," she mumbled, repeating something she must have read in a book or seen in a movie. Nothing felt real anymore, not even herself. She added, "I'm all right. Just a little tired."

He wasn't outside the terminal either, and she slid into the backseat of a taxi, stumbling over the address Niall had made her memorize: Portobello Road 83. Dublin.

"Portobello sounds like someplace in London," she'd said when he'd first given her the address, spelling out the word in the notebook by her mattress, under a list of texts about courtly love in Italian. They were in the dark of the tiny room in Cambridge she'd signed the lease on for the upcoming school year, as the end of summer approached. Her skin still felt sore from the mysterious, fleeting trip they'd made, renting a camper, to the Eastern Shore the weekend before. She'd moved in right after their return.

"Well, this one isn't," he'd said and scrutinized her sunburned face in the dim light, as though he were looking to see whether he'd made a mistake in trusting her. "Focus, Clare."

She'd nodded, feeling heat rise in her face, laying down her pen. "Will you meet me there?"

He shook his head.

"Where, then?"

He shook his head again.

She'd never asked him for anything, never dared. She steadied her voice. "Not at all?"

"Here, in Boston. I'll get back over before the winter comes."

She kept her eyes on him.

"All right, then, Clare."

Still, she waited. This much she needed from him.

Finally, he acquiesced. "St. Stephen's Green. The Yeats Memorial. An hour after noon, the next day. I won't speak to you. But I'll give you a sign so you'll understand if it's all right for you to follow. I'll stop to light a fag."

He'd never bent in any way to accommodate her before, and his compromise sent a surge of astonishment through her. His plan wasn't what she'd hoped for, but his offer felt like so much more than she'd ever had from him before.

She picked up her pen to finish writing the address in her notebook. "Portobello Road...?"

"It won't have a sign outside. It's just a small, gray stone building. Don't write it down," he'd continued, "in case you get caught and they search you," and she'd torn the page out of her notebook and ripped it into a hundred small pieces before she even got around to writing down the number.

"Portobello Road, number eighty-three," she told the cab-driver after she'd climbed into the cab, taking care to cradle her tummy in a protective fashion, trying to keep her voice from quivering, and when they pulled up in front of the unmarked square building, she made a mental note to point out to Niall that the building was brown, not gray. Something about this mistake, this proof that even Niall was fallible, gave her courage. She rang the front door of the shabby building and announced to the big-eared boy who opened it, his face and body remaining passive as his eyes swept all over her before stopping on her belly, "I need a room." She heard the slippery sound of the taxi taking off but didn't look backwards. Her only thought was to complete her mission, to move on from this horrendous task so she and Niall could be reunited. She didn't even think about what could possibly come next for them, what it would be like when he returned to Boston as he'd said he would. She just wanted it to happen, to have Niall's focused energy beside her again, as soon as possible. St. Stephen's Green. The Yeats Memorial. "Here, take them," she said to the man who appeared in her squalid room shortly after her arrival, entering without knocking, a knife glinting from under his shirt cuff, the River Liffey rushing past below them, and she didn't bother to turn her back as she stripped off her dress, unwinding the money-filled bandages, throwing them over to him one after another, as though each handful was payment to bring Niall back. "What's this, then?" he said, his heavy eyebrows rising, as though he'd hadn't known what she'd be delivering or at least the quantity. And maybe he hadn't, maybe he'd been told even less than she about the mission, but she didn't say a further word to him, not even when he pointed to her worn backpack and said, "Empty it." She dropped her passport and wallet and the copy of *Thérèse Raquin,* which she'd brought to read on the flight over, onto the bed. "Well, that was some day's work," he said, letting out a laugh when he'd finished stuffing the bills into the pack. "You never saw me, mind." She spent the night huddled on the room's lumpy bed, waiting, flat-stomached again but full of expectation. Next day, she moved into a different hotel, as Niall had instructed her to do when they were still back in Boston, an only slightly less dismal affair she'd picked out of a *Let's Go* guide. "I can't know which one," he'd told her. "That way, if they lift me before you leave, they can't get it out of me. No one will know, not me and not the man they send down." She arrived at St. Stephen's Green well before the appointed time, a sweater pulled around her once-again svelte torso. And if someone from the plane should see her? She sat down on a bench and folded her arms over her stomach.

And she waited. Even as the park began to be crisscrossed by people leaving work for the day, she waited. She folded and unfolded her arms.

She was so tired. What time was it back in Boston now? She gathered her stiffened limbs up and wandered the park as dark began to settle in. All around her, she heard Irish voices. Could he have passed by, but in disguise? Had she missed him? But she knew how he moved, as though he were a song that she heard over and over in her head. She knew the way he held his head up, the strange scar like a sickle on his neck. She spent another sleepless night in the *Let's Go* hotel, and the next day was back amidst the half-hidden stone amphitheater surrounding Henry Moore's sculptural paean to Yeats, even as raindrops began to plop down like huge cold tears. She moved under a tree. She pulled her sweater in around her. Still, she waited.

He'd had her book a return trip for five days later, but after a third empty day, she went to the airport and asked if there was room left on the next flight to Boston. She knew now that Niall was never going to join her in Boston either. She had brought the money over to Ireland as he wanted, and she would never see him again.

"Aren't you having a nice time?" the ginger-haired lady at the ticket counter asked, looking concerned.

"My father's not well," she answered, and realized she'd learned how to lie.

She climbed onto the plane home, feeling sickeningly weightless, half numb and half terrified. If anyone in her family found out about her trip, she had been instructed to pretend she'd taken off as a lark to find her roots, normal enough for an Irish-American girl of twenty. Niall had pretended to leave days earlier, hiding out in her room, and in other rooms he didn't tell her about, so no one would connect their departures. But no one was likely to find out about her trip. She'd been instructed to lose her passport as soon as she got back, and school hadn't started back up yet. No one would notice she wasn't around for a week; she had no roommates, and though she was friendly enough with other students, she wasn't the sort of girl people instinctively kept track of. But there was still the risk someone from the flight over would make the flight back with her and remember how recently she'd seemed so very pregnant.

"You just tell them you lost the baby," Niall had advised her back in Boston before they'd set off, narrowing those eerily blue eyes at her. "You tell them you're grieving."

Clare stared down at the heavyset stranger's street map in her hand, trying to bring into focus the lines and addresses, but all she could see was herself, after her plane had touched down in Boston's Logan Airport, throwing out every last piece of evidence from the flight, even the small suitcase she'd carried and the clothing she'd worn and the book she'd brought on the plane with her and never opened. Already beginning to hate herself for having smuggled money into Ireland. At the request of a man who'd abandoned her.

"We'll see in Dublin, then," Niall said, as they stood face-to-face, eye-to-eye, their bags at their feet, their bodies separated by her now-expanded abdomen, preparing to leave separately for the airport. He didn't kiss her. He reached out and clenched her hands, then turned and walked out the door of her room in Cambridge.

"You okay, Madame?" the heavyset stranger asked, looking at her queerly. He used his hand, freed from the map now, to hold her elbow. "You okay?"

Clare flushed and nodded. "Just thinking, just thinking where...the best way for you to get where you are going. I can help you. You are on the wrong street."

She'd done what she'd done and now she was heading full speed ahead back to Dublin where maybe she'd even cross paths with the man who had taken the money from her. But there was nothing to be done about that now. Nothing but to help this man right now find his own way, as any decent human being would do.

He was Turkish, not Albanian. By the time she and the man parted ways, she felt as though she knew all about him: his former career as a wrestler, the village where he grew up, why he was in Paris, and what he thought about French food and French women.

"They are very proud," he said of the last, "and very nervous. The others, they not stop. Maybe they not understand English? This is why I make sure you stop. I think you see paper you understand and show me with hand if you not speak English. But I *know* you English."

Clare didn't correct him. "Oh?"

"You tall. And"—he hesitated—"you have very nice…" He pointed to the skin on his face and pulled on it.

Clare smiled. His own skin was thick and pocked, perhaps from repeated steroid use or some similar type of muscle-enhancement drug. He'd told her about that, too, in his broken English, how his body had been abused by the rough usage of his days as a competitive athlete. How he was sure that was why he was sick now.

"Thank you," she said.

They'd reached the intersection of the Rue de Sèvres and the start of the Rue Saint-Placide. The entrance to the food hall at Le Bon Marché was just a few steps away, but there wasn't any reason to reveal her immediate destination to him.

She stopped and pointed to the Rue Saint-Placide.

"You follow that little street two blocks until it ends. You come out on the Rue de Vaugirard. Your doctor's building should be somewhere right there." She gave him a closer look. "Do you think you can do that?"

"Yes, yes," the man said, waving a hand. "Is no problem. I good now. Back in my own country, I never am lost. You know?"

"I know," Clare agreed, nodding. Although, she *didn't* know. If anything, she usually felt less lost when she was *away* from home. In Paris or London or Cairo, she could create her person rather than try to read it off the faces of the people who'd known her all her life. That was one of the greatest unspoken perks of being married to a diplomat. She was never lost—because she made up her destination as she went along.

The man gave her a last smile and a grunt and stepped into the street, narrowly missing being knocked down by a taxi. She realized she still had his map in her hand, but she didn't want to call him back. Surely now he wouldn't need it. She stuffed it into her sweater pocket. She watched until his silhouette had disappeared down the Rue Saint-Placide and she could be sure he wouldn't turn around and see where she was now headed. Once he was gone, she thought to herself, Well, that's one thing taken care of.

She checked her watch. 10:29 a.m.

# SIX

The tall wooden doors of Le Bon Marché food hall felt stiff against her push. Inside, the store was crowded, as usual: tourists seeking mementos from France to take home, expats seeking memories from home to bring to their Paris apartments, and well-heeled Parisian housewives selecting fine cuts of meat and Jean LeBlanc walnut oil for their dinner parties. A woman brushed past, toting a camera, and a guard glided out from the shadows and raised a single finger. No words were exchanged, but the woman dropped the camera into her knapsack. The guard returned his walkie-talkie into its holster and fell back into the shadows.

Clare moved forward, giving herself up to what felt like a glorious golden machine. Pale wood, brass fittings, and countless hanging lamps pouring amber over the aisles played backdrop to the heavy jewelry and braided-chain straps of the Chanel bags of the customers. Parisians scoffed at Le Bon Marché grocery store for being un-French, with its neat mountains of flown-in foodstuffs, and greasy tubs of overcooked, overpriced ready-made curried chicken and salmon Florentine, but they couldn't stop shopping here. Over the years of moving from one city to another, she had always found grocery stores and markets to reflect each posting's inner world in a way that was so reliable as to be almost laughable. In Cairo, the souk had been a sprawling Byzantine affair, a jumble of spices, beans, teas, and fruits, not always appetizing in odor or appearance but communal, a chaotic but exacting map of local relationships and social hierarchies. In Washington, she'd frequented a Safeway where even the uncut melons had been wrapped in plastic, as remote as the smiles on the other women shoppers' faces, the only scent that of the cleaning products used to wipe the floors and the occasional underscrubbed grocery bagger. The grocery closest to their apartment in London was run by a brooding Bangladeshi family and filled with dusty tins of curry, chili, and turmeric, dried fenugreek and *dhania* leaves, jars of ghee, their labels rubbed pale, side by side with the marmalade and marmite and Walker's Shortbread that Edward liked to have around. A fast-paced Jewish bakery, popping out oven-steamed bagels, shared the same building front. The packaging on British goods seemed more charming than the food itself, and all the print was neatly spaced across the labels. In Paris, the women dressed to shop, and the way they selected ingredients was as meticulous as their appearance.

She adjusted her basket onto her left arm and lowered her eyes so they'd be less likely to fall upon the gaze of another shopper. Le Bon Marché's food hall doubled as a haven for expats hoping to encounter other aliens in the hunt for marshmallows and pumpkin pie filling. There was a pleasant feeling of camaraderie to be found in spending a few chance minutes poring over fruits and imported crackers with similarly inclined hostesses, but she didn't have time to spare today getting caught up in any extensive conversations. Adjusting her pace, she skirted the islands stacked with foreign preserves, and zeroed in on the produce stalls on the far side of the food hall. One was piled high with asparagus. She lifted a couple of stalks and examined them. Delicate lavender crept up towards their tips, a pinkish shadow on one, a splash of purple on the other. There was something animate about asparagus, the irregularity of each spear.

She brushed the thought away and began filling a paper bag, selecting only the thinnest spears, which were the most tender— and also required less peeling. With Amélie's cousin coming in to help, there'd be enough hands to manage the asparagus, but Mathilde might still get fussed about it.

The cheese counter held a fresh supply of Irish cheddar. Clare requested two small wheels, ruddy yellow cakes sheathed in red wax. When she was a kid in suburban Connecticut, she and her friends used to buy a candy that looked like that casing, ruby lips of wax that they would chew on, not for the flavor but for the delightful sensation of their teeth sinking into the pliable plastic unsticky substance.

*"Est-ce que ça sera tout, Madame?"* the white-coated vendor asked. All the servers at Le Bon Marché's market wore thin white cotton jackets, as though they were working in a pharmacy.

She shook her head and surveyed the other cheeses in the counter. She'd heard that the ambassador's wife had cheeses sent over direct from Neal's Yard Dairy in London every fortnight, but, though she and Edward entertained constantly, they hosted such lesser numbers than the embassy that ordering cheese in bulk made even less sense to her than wine. She pointed out two large wedges of Stilton and considered whether she should ask Mathilde to defrost some tayberries and fill a few small pots with chutney to decorate the cheese plates. Her free hand strayed towards the pocket holding her list. But, no, she didn't need to direct Mathilde. She'd given Mathilde the guest list, which was all that was necessary. Mathilde understood who the guests were, and she'd know to do up the cheese in a suitably British fashion that wouldn't shock the handful of French guests. That was the thing about Mathilde. Other than her personality, she was perfect.

*"Prenez ceci, Madame,"* advised the vendor, when Clare asked for two triangles of Brie de Meaux. She directed Clare to a too-firm semicircle with a chalky off-white interior. *"Celui-ci sera bien pour vous."*

Whether it was unripened or not, Edward would not touch the brie. He'd take a respectable portion of the Stilton for the sake of decorum and, perhaps, a slice of the cheddar as well. Or maybe not, as he wouldn't want to be seen as taking everything but the French cheese. She pointed to an adjacent brie, creamier in color and leaking onto the cheese counter. She herself loved the French cheeses, the smellier the better.

*"Celui-là,"* she said. *"Deux grands morceaux, emballés séparément, s'il vous plaît."*

An expression of approval flitted across the vendor's face. *"Bien sûr, Madame."*

"Good choice," a voice said from behind her in American English.

Clare turned around to find Patricia Blum, the mother of one of Jamie's former classmates, standing behind her; tiny, round, and always cheerful, with dark hair and an extraordinarily beautiful face. For reasons she herself didn't understand, Clare found Patricia alarming. Patricia's daughter, Em, had been one of the most popular girls in the class and had never had much time for Jamie.

"They're always trying to sell us the sucker slices," Patricia whispered. She flashed a brilliant smile at the vendor. "They think that's what we want."

The vendor smiled back. She handed the cheese over, wrapped and ticketed. Clare laid it in her basket and wondered whether the vendor understood English.

"How's James doing?" Patricia asked. "Em says he's gone home for school this year."

Jamie is probably going to flunk right out of that damned boarding school, and this failure would stay on his permanent record. Unless she managed to do something about it, something that wouldn't drive him crazy for its intrusiveness. And not in a million years did Em bother to tell her mother about his having left the International School. Jamie's absence would barely have registered on Em's radar. Jamie would conquer his long frame and fair surprised face someday, but he was too obscure, too erratic, to rate amongst girls like Em at present.

"Very well, thank you. Yes, he's gone to England," she said, exchanging first one and then a second cheek kiss. Patricia had probably learned about Jamie changing schools from another parent. There was a lot of talking within the expat community. Although true intimacy was rare, everyone knew everyone else's business. She'd just have to hope word wouldn't get around about the troubles he was having. At least he hadn't been kicked out— yet. Suspension wasn't expulsion.

"Ahhh, his father's school, I bet," Patricia said. "What was it? Like, Eton?"

"No," she said. "I mean, my husband didn't go to Eton."

She shifted the basket in her hand. She wanted to call Barrow by 11:40; any later than that and she might catch the headmaster just as he was heading out to eat, which was never the best time to catch anyone.

"He's at Barrow, on the outskirts of London," she added. "How's everything at the International School? James misses it. I mean, he didn't leave because we didn't like it. We just thought it was the right time."

Patricia laughed. "I understand. Well, everything's fine. They had to cancel the annual class trip to London. You know, security reasons. But I'm taking Em and a couple of her friends up there, anyway. Week after next. Maybe we'll even run into James!"

"Maybe." This was neither within any realm of likelihood nor particularly to be desired, and Clare knew that Patricia knew this. "Well—"

Over Patricia's shoulder, she glimpsed a familiar face disappear behind a row of juice bottles.

Her heart froze up inside her rib cage. His face, thinner, grayer, but *him.* The same pale skin and hollow cheeks, the same high ridge of cheekbone buttressing a stare so brilliant it entered her in a way no one ever had before or after.

*Niall.*

The first time she saw him, he was standing atop the stone wall surrounding her aunt's house in Newton, outside Boston, and she'd ever after have an exaggerated sense of his height.

The face didn't reappear. Her breath caught in her throat, and she felt her hand reach out.

I must not be alone, she thought. He won't come to me if I'm not alone.

He'd been standing atop the stone wall, chewing on a stalk of grass while he watched her cousin Kevin change the oil in his car, in the driveway. "You aren't going to get nowhere like that," she'd heard him say, and she'd known he was different. Not Irish-American like her or Boston-Irish like Kevin, but Irish-Irish.

She gripped the closest thing to her, Patricia's arm. But she couldn't have seen him. Already she was going crazy. And yet, it had looked so like him.

\*     \*     \*

"Come on, Clare. Hand me that wrench, will you," Kevin grumbled, and she understood her cousin was trying to ignore the stranger. Beads of sweat rolled off Kevin's dark blond hair and jiggled on his earlobes. One dropped onto the tar of the driveway. The heat was a net, trapping everything and everyone. The temperature must have been about ninety degrees.

She was twenty years old, and the summer seemed to drag as heavily on her limbs as the heat wave. The summer internship she'd been so happy to land at the Isabella Stewart Gardner Museum in Boston had turned out to be hours of cataloging in an office with a small window and even smaller fan, and sometimes the days felt so heavy and still, she could hardly bear it. Even the green of her aunt's suburban lawn when she returned in the evenings provided no relief.

"Which one?" Tools lay sprawled out across the drive. She spotted at least three wrenches, each slightly different.

"Fuck if I know," Kevin had said. "That one."

She picked up the one Kevin had indicated, trying to ignore the stranger as well, but his eyes bore into her. She let her hair fall over the wrench and stole a glance, not towards his face but at the rest of him: he had on threadbare corduroy pants that seemed impossibly heavy for a day this hot. The skin of his knees, visible through the worn cloth and almost at her eye level, was white as birch. He looked unlike anyone she knew, not least because of the blunt way he was examining her.

Kevin grunted and threw the wrench back at her. She had to hop to one side to avoid being hit. "Too big. Give me another."

"You aren't going to get nowhere like that," the stranger said, after she'd handed over the second wrench. His voice was soft but not gentle. He jumped down from the wall, and using one booted foot—despite the heat, he was wearing leather boots—kicked the remaining wrench towards Kevin. "You need that one, you stupid feck," he tossed over his shoulder, sauntering towards Aunt El's kitchen. The door slammed shut behind him.

Clare sat down on the wall where he had been. "Who was that?"

"Aw, fuck. *Him?* Some cousin. Some ten-times-removed fucking cousin. One of my mom's charity cases."

She tried not to cringe. Aunt Elaine had had her move in with them in Newton after seeing the dank, cramped room Clare had planned to rent for the summer in downtown Boston, not far from the museum. Aunt Elaine had a big heart for everyone.

Kevin reached out for the final wrench, the one the ten-times-removed cousin had kicked, and applied it to the gasket. Oil came rushing out. He cursed and grabbed for a bucket. "Motherfucker!"

She got up and went into the kitchen.

And there he was, seated in the kitchen alcove, one hand clasped around a glass bottle of Coke. A film of condensation had developed around its neck, and water sweated down its sides. He flicked a few drops from his fingers and lifted the bottle to his mouth.

She sat down beside him on the bench and watched his Adam's apple as he drank. He was barely older than she was, maybe twenty-one or twenty-two. He wasn't taller either. They were shoulder to shoulder at the table, and she could feel his exposed knee beside hers. The smooth heat of his skin penetrated through the stupor of the summer, through her lanky, indolent limbs. She had to move her leg.

He drained the contents of the bottle in one go, set it back on the table, and belched. Then he looked at her. She looked down at her hands. He looked at them also.

She raised her head. Their eyes met, and she saw that his were very light blue, and as cool and glittering as winter. Despite how they'd burned into her earlier, there was nothing sunny about them.

"I'm Clare."

"I know who you are." Niall reached out and lifted one of her hands. He turned it over carefully before setting it back down on the table.

"You surely have beautiful hands, Clare."

She'd unfolded her hands in front of him. One by one, her fingers; long, thin, pale. The gentle lift around her first knuckle and slender knob of the second knuckle, the soft mound of the third, and then the broad, flat, pearly nails, fingers longer than the palm, tapering only slightly, graceful without appearing fragile. First her thumb, then her index finger, then her middle finger, her ring finger, her pinkie. They stripped for him without having worn clothing.

"Thank you," she said.

The heat had gotten to her. The heat, and she'd been too hot to eat breakfast that day. It had weighed down on her, drowning her better judgment, had drowned it that whole long hot summer. She wiped her brow and realized she'd been clutching Patricia's arm.

"Heavens," she said, loosening her scarf.

There was no Niall here, just row after row of tins and cardboard boxes and rounds of cheese and bundles of asparagus. Still, she had so thought she'd seen him this time for real, and then she had grabbed Patricia Blum's arm. She didn't even like Patricia Blum. She stepped back from her.

"Hey, that's okay!" Patricia patted her. "I've been there. Hot flashes?"

"No, no, nothing like that. It's just...Oh, too much to do today." She smiled and tried to erase her foolishness. She was barely forty-five. Hot flashes? Did she seem older to Patricia? "Please pass along greetings to Em on Jamie's behalf. It was lovely to chat."

She pushed off from Patricia, like a canoe from a dock, backwards, wobbly but sliding, trying to hide her embarrassment. The false sightings had begun the first time she and Edward lived in London, continuing after they were subsequently posted to Paris. Not all the time, but in random flurries—months would go by, even a year, then for a few weeks she'd be sure she saw him almost daily. They'd subsided when she and Edward had been moved back to Washington and had remained dormant upon their ensuing return to Paris, and she'd thought finally she was done with thinking she saw Niall in a crowd when she was just seeing another pale blue-eyed man disappearing into a sea of people. Now, lately, they had returned to her. And, like today's, they'd become so real.

The problem was Ireland. Just the thought of moving there and already she was losing her grip.

She lifted her shopping basket sternly and, in the aisle devoted to imported British foods, collected all the boxes of oatcakes on the shelf. As she waited by the checkout, she tried not to peer around her, tried not to use her height to glance over the heads of the others. She busied herself instead by verifying the expiration date on the biscuits. The point was to stop struggling with regret. Niall would never seek her out. Niall couldn't seek her out. His body had been lowered in a casket into the moist earth of Derry the November after she met him. Niall was long dead and buried.

# SEVEN

She reached the courtyard of the Residence, basket of cheese and asparagus hanging over one arm, homeopathic drops for Mathilde tucked away next to the to-do list in her sweater pocket, just as the men delivering the official plate and silver crested with Her Majesty's royal emblem from the embassy pulled up. She checked her watch: 11:45 a.m. Too late to call Barrow before lunch.

She nodded and slipped past the men, into the building's downstairs foyer. Outside, the sun was still shining, the wind still light and playful, but upstairs would soon be the table settings to unpack and lay out, and she was going to make sure that was done correctly. Her determination to make this dinner right had started to feel almost religious, like an act of penance. They were in the first decade of the third millennium, nearly three thousand people had been killed on one day alone in New York City by lunatics, some forty thousand civilians had since died in Iraq, more were dying daily, maybe right at this very moment, due to a war begun by British and American politicians, a war that neither she nor Edward (although he took care, like any good British foreign diplomat, never to promote his own political leanings) supported but that had affected their personal lives to the degree that they'd felt compelled to exile their younger son, and she was fixating on silverware. She couldn't be stopped for directions by an innocent stranger on the street without scanning for escape routes — she did wonder what had happened to that man, if he'd found his doctor, and if so, if the doctor had managed to help him; he'd looked so ill — but aligning china plates was her mantra. And there was her youngest son, imploding at school, and she'd had to put off speaking with the headmaster. It sounded ridiculous. But upholding standards was part of Edward's job, and she believed in Edward. Edward furthered the cause of civility. He would not bring anger to Dublin if he got the top post there. He would bring discussion. So she would let the building's door swing shut behind her, closing out the breeze and sunshine as well as the disorder and chaos of the external world, and train her thoughts to tableware and wineglasses.

Her next set of business would be to inscribe the place cards; years of experience had taught her to wait until now to get started on them, because of the real possibility of last-minute changes to the guest list. Usually it wasn't a question of gaining new guests, as with the de Louriacs, but losing one. Numbers had then to be swiftly made up — most often with someone "below the salt," as they called a guest recruited from amongst the embassy personnel, typically one of the first counselors, referring to where protocol would put them around the table — and the seating arrangement rapidly reconfigured to adjust for the difference in clout between the person who dropped out and the person who'd been added. And all the above meant that if the place cards had already been done up, some would need to be discarded and new ones written, a needless waste of both card stock and effort. Despite what most people seemed to think and newspapers liked to print, "thrift" was a byword for diplomatic personnel and their spouses, both regarding time and materials, even as they spent hours of each year entertaining lavishly. One was just not to show it.

There was a delicate rhythm to the whole thing. Living within the diplomatic world wasn't just a matter of smiling, shaking hands, and wearing attractive clothing. That's what most outsiders didn't realize, and that it was possible to take pride in the skill it required, even when it came to something as trivial as knowing how and when to do the place cards. A few years ago there'd been a big stir in the British papers over the revelation that the embassy in Paris spent more than any other British embassy in the world. But did they have any idea how difficult it had become to keep the whole thing going? With the emergence of instant global communications, some pundits had even begun to question the modern-day relevance of diplomats. A clerk was all that was required to authorize passports and sign birth certificates, the argument went, and individual experts could be sent here and there, as needed. Clare thought these were the opinions of people who never traveled.

If anything, today's world required on-site national representatives more than ever. She had seen firsthand how difficult relations had become with the French for Edward and his colleagues since Britain had joined the U.S. in invading Iraq. The man at the *tabac* once told her to her face he believed the U.S. was asking for more 9/11s to occur; obviously, the politicians he voted into office weren't going to be the ones eager to make deals with Americans or their staunch ally, the British. Captains of industry had to be constantly reminded, too, why doing business with the

U.S. or U.K. was still in their interest. And these same dynamics were true in countless permutations around the globe, involving countless other combinations of countries. There were layers of ill will out there, and it took ceaseless effort within the diplomatic sphere to keep the machinery of détente from collapsing. Dinner after dinner, lunches and breakfasts, receptions, conferences, workshops, one-on-one meetings; Edward was always busy. Meanwhile, trouble percolated as pervasively as global power was restructured: between India and Pakistan, between Pakistan and Afghanistan, between North Korea and everywhere. There was even talk that new splinter groups of the I.R.A. might rise up against the Good Friday agreement.

The elevator was already waiting on the ground floor, and she stepped into it, swinging the door shut after her. She pressed the button for her floor. And if some radical elements began taking up arms again for the union of Northern Ireland with the rest of Ireland? Would she in some way still be implicated? She leaned against the elevator cage. At least her guilt remained her own; surely no one in Dublin could recognize her. Niall was dead, and she'd given her real name to no one at the hotel. Only the one guy had seen what she was carrying. Was there any chance in a million she could run into either him or the desk clerk anyhow? Or that if one of them saw her photo in a magazine or newspaper, wife to the new ambassador to Ireland, he would recognize her? She looked utterly different than she had then—a middle-aged woman now, well-groomed and confident, transformed by the mantle of respectability and societal stature. Besides, even if one of them did claim to recognize her, she could deny it; airlines didn't keep records that long of their passenger lists. There was nothing to disprove her claim she'd never been to Dublin.

The elevator rose so slowly, so noisily. She resisted pressing the button for their floor again; it wouldn't make the old cage rise more quickly. Instead, she adjusted her scarf and sweater. Had she remembered everything for the dinner? But of course, she had. There'd been so many distractions already this morning, and here she'd missed calling Barrow. Still, she was efficient. She could lay claim to that. She took care of things.

"Whenever I think of you, Mom," Peter had said while home from school over Christmas, "I think of you in beige cashmere, leaning over the dinner table, refolding the napkins while Amélie's in another room, not looking."

She hadn't known whether to be pleased or insulted. She did take a certain pride in the way she'd learned to marry tact and precision.

"Not folding the napkins, dumb shit," Jamie had said. "Sitting behind the big desk in the study, writing something, making a list or something."

They were in the car, on the way to a party. Edward had craned his neck around from where he sat beside the driver in the front seat. "It's not necessary to address your brother like that." Tiny drops of drizzle competed with the wipers on the windshield behind him.

"And, anyway, Jamie, who are you to say how I remember Mom?" Peter had objected, and the whole question of how Clare was to be remembered was forgotten, except by Clare, who'd since returned to it in private from time to time when she thought about her children and how far away from her they were now. Somehow she'd been unprepared for the inevitable separation that maturation had wrought between them; their healthy arrival into the world had filled her with such astonishment that she hadn't been able to bring herself to think of them as someday moving on. As expats you were on a magic carpet, you and your spouse and children, floating through the world together, unable to get off individually, not quite of the world around you. Clare sometimes felt she'd leaned on her children, when they were still living at home, as much as they had on her. She'd *needed* them, anchors in the floating world. Just as they'd needed her to provide a wharf, a common ground, a pillar.

"Your mum is like that lovely column over there, boys, don't you think? Tall, cool, white, smooth, and wonderfully classic," Edward had said during a visit to the Acropolis seven years ago. He'd said it with a straight face, but to this day she asked herself: Edward had a sly sense of humor, but had he really once compared her to a caryatid on the Erechtheum, holding up the firmaments of the British Foreign Service? The caryatids were voluptuous, and her chest barely offered cleavage enough to console dinner-party décolletage, much less support the workings of the Queen of England. So many things she was beginning to forget, or at least question her memory of. Most of all she seemed to keep forgetting her sons had left home. She sometimes caught herself up short, rushing back from a reception to check they were safely in bed, with the realization that this was something she couldn't know about them, might never know about them again on a regular basis, their beds being from now on distant. If only people could choose what to forget and remember; how curious that we often remember what we wish we could forget, and forget what we seek to remember.

The elevator stopped on the third floor with a thud that rocked Clare forward on her feet. She would have preferred to take the stairs, but walking up instead of riding the elevator might seem indecorous, more suitable to a schoolgirl than a diplomat's wife, the sort of thing only an American woman would do. Not on the same level as wearing galoshes, but still. When they moved on from the minister's residence, she didn't plan to leave any gossip behind her. She pushed on the cage, and the door clicked open with a big clank and a thud. She thought it all too noisy, but that was how elevators were in Paris. If no one else minded it, why should she?

"The men are on their way up with the plate," she told Amélie, finding the housekeeper in the dining room giving a last polish to the heavy mahogany table. It would soon be set with delicate china trimmed with the golden standard of the British Crown. A few hours later, she and their guests would all be lined up around it, the P.U.S. to her right, Edward facing her from the other end of the table, everyone in their evening finery, expectant. "Are we okay with the liquor?"

"*Oui, Madame.*" Amélie made one last concentric circle on the table with her cloth and looked up. "Ze table, she is rea-dy." She hesitated. "*Madame?*" She pointed towards the hall, in the direction of the bedrooms. She raised one hand to chin level and shook it.

Clare handed her basket over to Amélie, taking the homeopathic drops out of her pocket and stacking them on top. "Please tell Mathilde the chemist said to put three drops in a glass of juice, twice daily." She made a squeezing motion with her hand to demonstrate. "Three drops in juice. Two times a day."

The service doorbell rang. This would be the men with the plate.

"I open the door," Amélie said.

"Thank you."

She turned towards the bedrooms.

A few rays of electric light squeezed out from under the door to Jamie's room. Clare knocked and pushed the door open. Sprawled the length of the bed was her oversized fifteen-year-old, reading, she noted, a Philip Roth novel. Jamie pushed the book under an arm as she entered.

She took one fast step forward, then stopped herself. Instead, she said, "Jamie! How did you get here so quickly?"

"That's nice, Mom. I mean, hi and everything."

She sat down on the edge of his bed and tried to kiss him. He shrugged off her embrace but, as she straightened away from him, continued to hold on to her, grabbing one of her arms. With her free hand, she ruffled his hair. There was a faint scar still visible along his hairline from the time he'd woken from a nap in the London town house where they'd lived after the Cairo posting, heard her voice downstairs, and tried to join her while clutching on to a stuffed bunny. They'd had a nanny back then named Nia, a young woman from Wales, who was supposed to be watching him. Edward had dismissed her as soon as they'd returned from the hospital, maybe the only time he'd ever taken on a staff decision. "The point is that she wasn't doing her job. It's not an act of vengeance," he'd said. She'd nodded, relieved. She hadn't wanted to see the woman again herself, not even long enough to fire her.

Jamie released her arm and shook his hair back over his forehead.

"I was already in Paris when I called," he said. "I was at the airport."

Her young son, alone in an airport. Had he taken a bus in? A taxi? She folded her hands over each other. "How did you leave school grounds without first getting my permission?"

"I just left."

Clare heard the front door to the Residence open and shut. That could mean only one thing. Edward. What could he be doing home for lunch on a day this busy? She gently closed the door to the room. She had better warn Edward first about Jamie's latest troubles; he had a lot of other things on his plate today. "You can't just leave school, Jamie."

"I didn't. I sent them an e-mail in your name first."

"Jamie!" She lowered her voice. "*Jamie.* You can't do that."

There was no further sound from the foyer. Edward had gone either into the study or through the dining room into the kitchen.

"Yes, I could. You gave me permission."

"No, not for that. To visit the science lab after hours."

Jamie shrugged.

Clare frowned. "You may not leave the school grounds without my knowing, and you may not go sending e-mails in my name either, without my express permission. The science lab thing was just that one time. And you certainly may not go around hopping on planes." She heard more sounds from down the hall and lowered her voice again. "Jamie, I've talked to the school. They're really angry."

Jamie rolled his eyes.

"Tell me." When Jamie didn't respond, she added, "The science lab? Did you do it?"

"They didn't let me hand it in. A-holes."

"No? Although you did do it? And though you did go to the lab after hours?"

The hint of a grin flitted across his face. "Yeah, well. I did *that*."

She sighed. "Do you think this is funny? 'Cause I don't think this is funny."

The smile disappeared. "I was just trying..." His voice trailed off.

She stood up. He did the homework, but they wouldn't accept it. She could think of one sole explanation. She could only hope there was another. "What exactly happened?"

"I thought you just said you talked to Barrow."

"I did. But they didn't tell me the details. I'm giving you a chance to tell your side first."

He shrugged. "A prefect saw. The fascist. He didn't have to go and tell on us."

"Oh, Jamie."

He looked towards her suddenly, his face searching hers. "Mom," he said. But nothing followed. Finally he said, "Whatever."

She surveyed him, a heap of adolescence. He didn't need to spell it out. He had been caught cheating again. "How many days?"

"A week."

A week. Jamie was lucky the school wasn't kicking him out altogether; still, a week was a major suspension. He'd get F's on every test or assignment he missed and not be allowed to make them up. The offense would go down on his permanent school record. She sighed again.

"Okay, well. Stay here for now. If we're going to have a week, there's no point getting your father involved when he's so busy. You and he can talk once we've gotten through tonight's dinner." Jamie would understand she meant he wasn't to let on to his father he was there, not before tomorrow. He could be naughty, but he would never interfere with his father's work. "But you know you're in trouble. Have you had any lunch?"

"I'm not hungry."

She turned to go, when Jamie bolted up and snagged on to the hem of her sweater. "But you don't understand, Mommy! It's just mean what they did. They wouldn't even listen!"

Clare smoothed her sweater and took his hands firmly into hers. Where had things gone wrong with this wonderful son of hers? She wished it would all go away: the dinner, Ireland. Here was

Jamie. She didn't want to go tussle with Mathilde and fill out names on place markers. She wanted to hug her son and rock him and make every mistake he'd ever made—and they were piling up so fast now—vanish.

"James, I don't know what is going on in your head." She held up her fingers and started counting. "Forging my signature? Flying from London to Paris without telling me first? It's all just crazy. You know this. How did you even get started on this? What were you thinking? Your father and I made it very clear: better you flunk honorably than get into this sort of trouble again."

Jamie drew back. He examined her as though there was something viscous between them. When he answered, his tone was soft and almost dreamy. "You didn't really speak to anyone at Barrow, did you?"

"Of course, I did. What are you saying? I spoke with Mrs. Thomas. But they're giving you another chance. You are being suspended, not expelled. So I'd say they were being fairly generous. They could kick you out, you know, altogether." She hesitated. She hated to go there—Edward would say it was none of their business. He'd say everyone had to take responsibility for his or her own actions. "Robbie didn't also get into trouble?"

Jamie's face fell shut. "Robbie wasn't part of it. It was just me and Rian."

"Who's Ryan?"

He stuck his lip out. "You're busy." He flopped back on his bed and folded his hands on his chest.

She knew that sullen face, the hands closed up like an oyster. Whoever Ryan was, and why Ryan was involved rather than Robbie, his lab partner—Jamie wasn't now going to explain, not until he was ready. Jamie was like the shower they had in that first home in London. Sometimes the water would suddenly turn cold, sometimes hot, sometimes the pressure would disappear altogether. You had to be ready to jump in and out accordingly. She shook her head. "I want you to stay in your room until I tell you that you may come out. I'm going to see Mathilde about fixing you something. Did you see her?"

Jamie shook his head. "I said I'm not hungry," he repeated. "I bought two Camembert sandwiches at the airport. I ate them on the bus."

Her heart swelled up against her rib cage. He knew how to take the airport bus by himself; he bought himself stale sandwiches wrapped in paper. He would have been sitting there, in the same city as she, without her even knowing it, chewing on his baguette, his heart a mix of joy at being back home and dread over being in trouble at school. Maybe dread also at having to face his parents—at having to face her. Jamie. However bad what he'd done was, he'd done it just out of desperation. He didn't want to disappoint them. "Okay."

"Don't go bugging Mathilde," he said and raised an eyebrow. "If you know what's good for you."

"That's enough." She would not laugh. "You just sit tight."

She shut his door behind her and made her way back down the hall. The door to the study was closed. She could hear the clip of Edward's voice behind it but muffled by the heavy wood of the door such that she couldn't make out what he was saying. This was not the first time she'd faced this same scene, a closed door, the sound of her husband's voice on the phone behind it in midday. She shook the thought from her mind. If something terrible had happened somewhere, she probably would have heard it from Patricia Blum. Bad news spread faster than a virus amongst the expat community in Paris.

"Did you speak with the minister?" she asked Amélie as she passed through the dining room into the kitchen. She couldn't go in there while he was on the phone, talking.

"Excuse me, Madame. The *ministre* goes to ze study and closes ze door. *Clac!* I do no speak with him."

The harder she worked at it, the worse poor Amélie's English seemed to be becoming. Clare tugged on her hair. If something had happened, surely Edward would have looked for her before closing himself into the study. At the very least, he would have asked her whereabouts from Amélie.

She noticed a bit of dust on the back of a chair but resisted the urge to flick it. Amélie might take it as a reproach. "Well, let's go see about the plates," she said.

The men had brought the crates all in by now and opened them.

"*Votre signature, Madame, s'il vous plaît,*" one of the men said, handing her a clipboard.

She signed her name at the bottom, added the date, and handed it back to him. She took one last look around the dining room while Amélie showed them out. Their dining room might not be the *Salon Bleu* of the ambassador's residence, but rich with polished wood and sparkling crystal it did look attractive. With Amélie no longer watching, she removed that one tiny piece of dust. Then she followed the deliverymen's path through to the kitchen. As she passed the pantry, she could see the wines in their wooden boxes. She hoped Amélie had thought to check the contents against the order sheet, but she refrained from asking. Amélie didn't usually make mistakes, other than grammatical ones. Amélie, for example, would intuit she shouldn't mention Jamie's return to Edward. Clare couldn't count on Mathilde for the same sort of discretion. But maybe Mathilde hadn't seen that Jamie had come in.

The cook was standing beside the kitchen table, a huge bowl pushed up against her abdomen, a whisk the length of a donkey's tail in her hand. Clare could smell freshly sliced onion, mint, and basil; Mathilde must have already prepared the sauce for the potatoes. For one sweet second, she was swept back outside, into the spring, into the light.

"Well, Mrs. Moorhouse, the minister is home *à midi* and a bit early at that, *n'est-ce-pas?*" Mathilde commented, without stopping her flaying of the pale yellow yolks in the bowl. "And now I suppose you'll be needing a lunch for him, and me trying to make a miracle out of these here eggs. They're a right waste of good money, they are, these eggs. He's no good, *ce marchand.*"

The image of Jamie, alone in the airport, buying sandwiches, came to her. As much as the idea disturbed her, she couldn't help but think he'd done well to get them. She wouldn't want to ask Mathilde to prepare a lunch for him now, and Mathilde probably wouldn't accept anyone else mucking about in the kitchen. Mathilde was in a creative fury. "That's all right, Mathilde, I'll find something for Mr. Moorhouse."

"Oh, and be leaving the minister with a cold sandwich at lunch? Anyhow, I can't have anyone fussing about in my kitchen right now."

Clare smiled; Mathilde was as consistent as a toothache. Knowing her so well gave Clare a curious sense of satisfaction.

Then she remembered the closed door to the study.

"Did the minister come to speak with you when he came in? I mean, he didn't come to say anything about having to cancel?"

"Cancel!" Mathilde dropped the whisk. "*Ça va pas ça!* First you announce we'll be putting on a V.I.P. dinner on one day's notice, and a night off for me, too, then you add to it just hours before *without telling me,* then you want to take everyone away! Were you planning to tell me that *after* I finished preparing dinner? And me already with the dessert half done and the bread rising?"

"No, no, no," Clare reassured her, inwardly scolding herself. If something serious had happened, something that might demand cancelation, like another bombing in London, Edward would have called her before he even got home. And he wouldn't have been the one to tell Mathilde about it. Dealing with staff was her job.

Where was her phone? She reached into her sweater pocket— but her BlackBerry was still in her purse. She hadn't used it while she was out, although she almost had, to call the embassy to find a ride back from the airport tomorrow for Jamie. Wasn't she glad now that she hadn't! How embarrassing if word had gotten round that James was already in Paris when she'd called: the minister's wife didn't even know in which country her younger son was. Still, it was odd she hadn't *received* any calls. Had she neglected to switch it back on after Edward's welcoming speech at last night's reception? Maybe Jamie *had* tried to call her on her cell phone to ask permission to leave, to fly to Paris. Unable to reach her, he wouldn't have tried the home phone, because he'd have had to call when his dad was still home in order to catch that morning flight. It didn't make anything okay, but it did explain things a little.

"I found some nice cheese at Bon Marché," she said, and prayed for Mathilde to pick her whisk back up without further remonstration. "Some very nice Irish cheddar."

"Well, Irish is better than English," Mathilde said, eyeing Clare. A Scottish nationalist when she wasn't being a Swiss loyalist, Mathilde enjoyed taking whatever swipe she could at England. Not that she had any reservations about working for the British Crown. Clare wouldn't be surprised to discover she had heard about the post in Dublin opening up and was worrying it, in her mind, just as she was the eggs. Mathilde seemed to know everything, especially anything that might pertain to her own work status. After all, this evening had its meaning for Mathilde as well. Unlike Edward's secretary, for example, who was within the British Foreign & Commonwealth Office system, if Edward and Clare left for Dublin, Mathilde might well be out of a job, as would Amélie. They'd been independent hires by Clare, and the next minister couldn't be counted on to hire either of them.

Clare was careful to keep her face as neutral as possible, until the whisk resumed its rounds. "You won't get any argument here, Mrs. Moorhouse," Mathilde said. "But, the minister might find Irish cheese strange, no? A bit of an unusual choice? Instead of English? By the bye, I checked the wine boxes myself this morning. All the wine's there. The right wine."

There were moments when Clare worshipped Mathilde's uncanny ability to read her mind, but most of the time it frightened her. She picked up an eggshell, examined its thin bluish edge. Mathilde was right about the eggs, too; the shell looked unpromising. She would have to speak with the grocer tomorrow. Thank heavens Mathilde was able to scare anything into rising.

"I like a little Irish cheddar every once in a while. My family was Irish, remember."

Mathilde stopped beating her yolks long enough to pour in a large measure of sugar. "Well, isn't that right, nae? You were a young Irish lass when your English husband plucked you from the tree. County Clare, I reckon?"

Clare laughed. "I'm from Connecticut, Mathilde."

"Aw, go on. I know how 'tis stateside. They had all those I.R.A.

supporters coming out from there, didn't they now? More Irish than the Irish themselves. They're the ones half kept the movement funded."

Clare backed slowly from the table. "I better see whether Amélie has everything sorted out." She stretched a hand behind her for the door, missed it, reached again.

"Just one wee matter," Mathilde said.

Clare stopped short, her hand falling. Mathilde pointed an elbow towards the shopping basket that Clare had left on the floor by the kitchen's central island.

"You're forgetting your *reçu*. You're going to need that for your ledger."

Clare took care not to breathe out too deeply. She retrieved the receipt from the basket, folded it once and then again, folded it as though she might be able to fold everything that worried her away into that little corner of paper.

One of the things Niall used to say to her—and she'd never known if he was ridiculing Americans or grateful to them—was that without their American brethren and all their pretty green dollars, the IRA would have had to pimp its leprechauns to raise money.

He'd said a lot of things, Niall had. Her first mistake had been to listen to them.

"You come make up my bed for me, why don't you?"

She hadn't seen him since that first time, when she'd watched him drink soda in the heat of that summer afternoon, feeling as though she'd been inside that glass, and when he'd consumed all of it, as though she'd also been swallowed. He'd disappeared from her aunt's place shortly after, and her aunt had been frantic with worry, knitting her brow and fingers as she contemplated whether she'd have to call someone in Ireland, until Uncle Pat had laid down his newspaper and grinned.

"Oh, El," Uncle Pat had said, "Niall's a young man, his first time in America. He's found some friendly American girl. He'll be back when the beer runs out. Or the loving."

Aunt Elaine's eyebrows had lowered into a frown and her hands had moved away from the phone. She'd set down her old address book, with half the pages falling out.

Clare's stomach had threatened to crawl into her mouth.

And then, there he was, sitting at the breakfast table three mornings later, pointing at Clare's hands while she buttered her bread. As though he'd never been gone.

"I'd like to see your fingers smoothing back my sheets, wouldn't I." But, softly, so no one heard but she, and she had to keep herself from knocking over her orange juice glass. "Spreading. Those beautiful hands, spreading."

Later, when she began to understand where he really went during those sudden absences, because the first one was followed by more, she was relieved. She was happy. Anything but other girls.

In the dining room, Amélie had already begun unwrapping the plate, and there was Edward filling up the doorway. "I thought I heard a commotion in the dining room," he said.

"It was the men bringing in the plate. I was...in one of the bedrooms. And then I had to speak with Mathilde."

"Everything in the kitchen coming along all right?"

"You don't dare go in."

Edward laughed, a good sign.

She smiled back. "We had to add de Louriac *fils* and de Louriac *belle-fille,* and then I neglected to tell her straight off. Amélie, did I tell you we need to add two places?"

"Yes, Madame. All is here."

Clare looked at the table and realized how foolish her question was; the settings were there, the two extra ones included. Amélie had already put them out. She laughed and shook her head. "But you knew that, too," she told Edward. "You forwarded the message from de Louriac's secretary."

"We all have a lot on our minds," Edward said. *"Amélie, tout est très bien. Comme toujours. Merci."*

Amélie gave a little curtsy, as she would do for Edward, and blushed. Edward slipped a hand around Clare's elbow. "Come. Tell me where we are with everything."

Clare gave in to the pull of his hand, so warm and steady through the fabric of her sweater. This was when he was going to shut the door and tell her what had happened. There was some reason he'd come home at lunchtime on such a busy day, some reason for the shut door to the study. She walked with him into the study, sat down in the armchair across from the desk, and pulled out her little notebook just in case something would need to be added to her to-do list. Sitting there, waiting for him to say whatever he was about to say and knowing that Jamie was secretly down the hall, she felt as though she could almost hear Jamie's breath pushing in and out of his shallow chest, as she'd done when he was a baby, leaning over his crib as he took his afternoon nap. She just had to keep her fingers crossed Jamie would stay put. One of the first lessons one learned in a life of diplomacy was that timing was everything. And now was not the time to break the news of Jamie's latest disaster to Edward. If Edward found out what Jamie had done—and really she wasn't sure what was the worst part of it, the cheating or the forging her signature and flying home without permission—he'd consider it his duty to speak with Jamie immediately. Not only did Edward not have time for that today, but Jamie might become defensive, in which case they would not be able to count on him to keep a low profile through the evening. The more she thought about it, the more sure she was that the best thing would be not even to tell Edward for the moment that Jamie was home, much less that he'd been suspended. She could reveal all tomorrow.

Edward closed the door and came around to sit behind the desk. His face looked calm; his expression pleasant and neutral. But she saw the set of his eyes and knew something serious was coming. He folded his hands over one another. "Two more de Louriacs, then?"

"The son and fiancée. They're in Paris."

"How lucky."

"They'll probably be better dinner companions than the parents."

Edward laughed. "Oh, well, he's an all right sort. Where will you seat Madame?"

"You want the fiancée, do you? I'm pretty sure she won't be in a miniskirt."

Edward laughed again, this time cracking his wide knuckles. They both knew he wasn't interested in other women. "Just as long as the mother-in-law isn't. What are we having?"

"We'll start with baby asparagus and *jambon de bayonne*. And there will be some nice fish, with new potatoes in a spring-herb pesto, but I asked Mathilde to go very light on the garlic." Edward wasn't any bigger on garlic than he was on spices. "I think it's going to be brilliant. Mathilde's whipping something amazing up for dessert."

"Literally, I suppose."

"Oh, yes. She's got her favorite instrument of torture going around as we speak. Well, second favorite, after the cleaver. She's making her chocolates, of course. And fresh rolls. And, for the cheese course, I found some really nice cheddar. I bought oatcakes to go with it."

Edward nodded. "Sounds super." She stared at him through the following silence, waiting. This had all been filler. Now, he would tell her what was going on. He tapped his desk a few times. "There's been an incident."

Clare nodded.

"An assassination." He spoke softly now, with the gentleness he always brought to bad news. "Not one of ours. A French parliamentarian, at Versailles this morning."

"Do I know him?"

Edward shook his head. "I've never met him myself." He ran a hand over his brow, rubbing as though he hoped to smooth it out. "Phff," he said.

She stood up and touched his knuckles gently, leaving her fingers on his until he stopped rubbing. He caught her hand with his, and pressed the cool skin of her fingers against his forehead.

"Do they know...?" she said. She withdrew her hand and laid it on his shoulder.

"An idea. There have been numerous threats since the French State passed the law officially declaring the Armenian business genocide. Now there's some talk of making it against the law in France to deny it. A Turkish nationalist group."

"Oh." She remembered hearing about the controversy when they first arrived back in Paris; how furious the Turks were that the French, with whom they'd painstakingly cultivated diplomatic relations for centuries, had officially decided to call the death of more than a million Armenians under the Ottoman Empire during and just after World War One by the term "genocide." The Turks themselves never accepted that this had been a situation of deliberate extinction of the Armenian people, insisting the deaths were a by-product of the war. She recalled a heated discussion at one dinner party, just shortly before Christmas; the British still refrained from using the word, which stance some people had supported and others had considered morally reprehensible.

She sighed. "Dinner tonight?"

He shook his head. "No need to cancel dinner."

All right, she thought. The guests would be upset, especially the French ones; everyone would be uneasy. Before he returned to the embassy, she and Edward would have to come up with a master plan on how to handle the situation. The correct mood had to be created—sober, respectful—but unbowed.

But they would go on. That was the essential. One had to keep going.

# EIGHT

Clare picked up her and Edward's dirty lunch plates from the small table in the study and carried them towards the kitchen. She and Edward had spent some time discussing whether to ask Reverend Newsome to lead a prayer for the slain politician when they sat down for dinner. Having decided yes, they had agreed not to allow the assassination to dominate discussion throughout the evening—one of the duties of the Foreign Service was to maintain balance. Then Clare had gone into the kitchen to fetch the lunch Mathilde, before leaving for her break, had quickly fashioned. She must have found her way back into Mathilde's good graces, because there was a plate of chicken in cream sauce waiting for her also. She and Edward had eaten mostly in silence as Edward went through a briefing he'd brought from the office for a workshop he was attending in the ambassador's place that afternoon. He'd shuffled the papers into his briefcase and announced he was heading back out.

"There's a chancery post in Manama coming up," he'd said as

he'd shut the clasp on his bag. "The P.U.S. asked me in passing—I was reading from a French document—this morning whether I still had my Arabic."

"Bahrain?"

"Bahrain."

"What did you say?"

"That I figured it was pretty rusty."

She'd smiled. "I hope you didn't make any bad jokes about oiling it. How much longer do we have in Paris?"

"We've been here more than three years," he'd said, adding, "there's also something in Bishkek."

She wrinkled her brow.

"Kyrgyzstan," he said. "Between Tajikistan and Kazakhstan. Electricity is a bit of a problem, but there are some lovely yurt stays. The mountain views are probably spectacular."

She'd kissed him. "Dinner will go well. I promise."

She'd stuck with her decision not to tell him about Barrow. If Jamie chose to unveil his presence during tonight's dinner, Edward would be caught out, surprised by his own son. But the assassination had left her all the more loath to introduce Jamie's latest indiscretion into his day. That was another thing about diplomatic life; the concerns of the wider world put one's personal issues—especially the humbler ones, such as whether Peter made the First or the Second Senior rowing team at Fettes, or the dry cleaner had left a mark on one of Edward's best jackets—in perspective. Even the shock of having your fifteen-year-old son suspended from school and left to wander around the airports of Europe slid down a notch when it came up for comparison against irrevocable tragedies such as an assassination—or, after thirty years of service, being relegated to someplace in central Asia without much electricity.

Clare pushed through the doorway into the kitchen with her shoulder, her hands encumbered by their plates. Jamie wouldn't appear suddenly during dinner. She would speak with him now, try to get some more details and, at the same time, make him promise to keep a low profile until tomorrow. They would be the only ones in the apartment for a little while, with Edward gone and Mathilde and Amélie out for their midday breaks. Moments of domestic privacy had become rare since moving into the Residence; you had to seize them.

She set the plates down and surveyed the kitchen. Everything looked in order. She peeked into the fridge; a colander of deep-red strawberries sat on the middle shelf. She stole a handful with the hope that Mathilde wasn't planning to use them to garnish this evening's dessert or, if she was, wouldn't notice. The first bite burnt into her tongue, a warm sweetness with an acidic edge. Jamie loved strawberries; she'd tote the rest of her handful to him. As a little boy he'd make himself sick eating too many at one sitting. "Moderation," Edward would tell him, and Jamie would turn his back and pop another in his mouth. "Mommy...," he'd moan within the hour, "my tummy doesn't feel good."

James would never show temperance. "Where does he get it from?" Edward would ask when James flew into a fury over being told to pick up his sneakers from the study floor or rolled off his chair in laughter during the rare state dinner he'd been invited to attend. "Certainly not you or me!"

Clare emptied her handful of strawberries back into the colander and closed the fridge. Mollycoddling. That's what Edward called her behavior towards the children on the rare occasion that they disagreed over parental decisions.

She wiped her hands with a paper towel and headed down the

hall towards his room. There was no longer light streaming out from under his door.

She knocked softly.

No one answered.

Had he fallen asleep waiting for her to return? He would have gotten up at dawn to catch the flight for Paris.

She turned the knob and pushed the door open.

On Jamie's empty bed lay a note, written on a page torn from the Roth novel. Jamie had folded the page in two, with "Mom" scrawled across the outer flap. On the inside was written "Gone out. Don't want to make any more trouble. I'll steer clear of Dad until tomorrow. Jamie."

Clare sat down on the bed. The warmth left behind by her adolescent son's lanky body pressed into her thighs, and she ignored the urge to lean into it. She'd told Jamie he was to stay put; why did he have to burrow himself into even further trouble? She didn't want to have to fight with him. She didn't want to have to punish him. But these things he kept doing—the forging names, the sneaking around, the coming and going without permission—these couldn't be excused, in the way even cheating might be, as a foolish act of desperation. They were just plain bad. Dangerous, even. Had she given him some reason to think he was to get out of the house for the evening? Or could she have sounded too unsympathetic to the way Barrow had handled his latest mess-up? What had he said? Something about a Ryan? Had she met a Ryan last time she visited? She looked around the room as though it might hold a clue, but Jamie hadn't been at Barrow long enough to have brought home a yearbook. Jamie's duffel bag lay on the floor. She made a move to pick it up, then stopped. She wouldn't look through it.

Instead, she got up and went back down the hall to the foyer console. She extracted her purse from the console and fished out her BlackBerry. It *was* turned off. She pressed the on button and waited for the sucking sound of its return to power.

The screen saver flashed up. Seven voice messages, three text messages. She scrolled through them, searching. Jamie's name wasn't amongst them.

She drummed her fingers on the console. Jamie *hadn't* called before leaving for the airport. He'd forged a message to the headmaster in her name, then flown back home without her permission. Without even trying to get it. Now he had, again, deliberately ignored her instructions and left the apartment. "You know, I was barely twenty-four when I started with the Foreign Office," Edward had said this morning, out of the blue. For a moment, she'd been startled from her surreptitious brooding over the thought of moving to Ireland. Edward was so rarely random.

"That's quite a while," she'd said.

"Yes, it is." He'd looked into his teacup as though seeing all the numerous cups he'd drunk since he'd first started out in the diplomatic service. "But I don't regret it. Not for an instant. I feel good about what I do for a living. What I could still do."

She laid her hand out flat and took a deep breath. Here was what she was going to do right now about Jamie. Nothing. She wasn't even going to worry. *Mollycoddling.* She'd babied Jamie too much already, and this was what had come of it.

She slipped her phone into her pocket. She was going to take care of the place cards. Before Mathilde and Amélie returned and required her supervision. Then, with her staff back on track for the afternoon, she was going to leave to get her hair done. Edward deserved what little she could do for him. He deserved an ambassadorship. And he deserved Ireland. For three decades, he had sat through endless meetings and downed endless cups of tea or coffee, and sipped almost as many glasses of wine. He'd nodded at appalling individuals and lent an ear to abysmal reinventions of history while his waistline expanded and his chin dropped and his eyelids grew heavier. And then he'd tried to remold those atrocities into something better—a better world, containing a better Britain. And he'd done it all with such patience, and such aplomb. Just two weeks ago, after listening to a long diatribe from the German husband of a Polish diplomat blaming British colonial policy for the mess in the Middle East, Edward had responded, "Undoubtedly, some may question the efficacy or even wisdom of the Balfour Declaration. But rare are the events in history that have not engendered mixed responses. Rare—although *not nonexistent.*" He hadn't even had to use the words "World War Two," the one historical event almost everyone in the Western world could agree upon. The man had reddened and changed the subject to the upcoming World Cup being held in Germany. Edward was fair; if anything, he was calibrated. He knew when to agree and when to put his foot down. And how to disagree.

Thanks to him she'd learn how to disagree also, with her own past—and not just to be ashamed of the missteps she'd taken. At Edward's side, she'd folded and packed away every part of her past she despaired of, like worn-out handkerchiefs in colors she no longer liked and embroidered with mottos she no longer believed in. He hadn't asked her; he never even knew of these prisms in her personal history. Meanwhile, he'd given up things also, putting away pursuits he believed wouldn't suit her. Oh, the folly of *that!* Edward had started out at the Foreign Office in a different direction, choosing Arabic for his hard language training and putting his name forth for Lebanon during the Israeli occupation. He'd lived in Kuwait, too, before he was posted in Washington, D.C., and met her. In another incarnation, he might have been happy to have a chance at Bahrain. But after they'd married, after they'd begun having the children, after Jamie's ignominious start in Cairo, he'd stopped bringing home books on the Palestine conflict, and stopped checking to see what new postings might be coming up in the Arab world. Instead, building on the part of his portfolio in the States that included Irish Affairs, he'd stacked his bedside table with tomes by Gerry Adams and columns by Gary McMichael. He'd perfected his French and stoked his knowledge of the U.K.'s involvement in the European Union. He became a recognized expert in European defense issues. At the same time, he'd never tried to capitalize on her Irish heritage, and she had easily been able to convince herself it was Europe in general he was after, not Ireland in particular. After one or two carefully fashioned displays of indifference on her part early in their marriage, he'd dropped all talk of even visiting the country.

"How about Ireland?" he'd asked the summer after they married while they were discussing where to go for their upcoming holiday. "Shall we do the ancestral tour?"

"I was thinking something more exotic," she'd responded, flipping the page in her book. "To be honest, I've heard so much about Ireland all my life that I feel as though I've already been there many times over. There are so many other places in the world to see."

And despite the inanity of her excuses—too much rain, she'd said with a shrug the second and final time he'd proposed they tour the country—he'd left it at that. He hadn't even urged her to join him when he'd had to hop across the Irish Channel during his two postings in London. Instead, just as he'd respected all her other personal inclinations, he'd gone along with celebrating her Irish heritage in the vague noncommittal way she'd developed—making jokes about the gift of gab when she was called out for keeping quiet, attending the works of new Irish playwrights each season, donning a spot of green when St. Patrick's rolled around—accepting her indifference without discussion. If others, less circumspect, might express dismay, saying, "But no coastal stretch can compare to the Cliffs of Moher," or "But you haven't seen anything until you've seen the lakes of Killarney," he'd leave her to answer. "Edward already travels so much," she would say, "and during our holidays, we either go home to visit family in the U.S. or England. What little time we have left, we really need to get some sunshine. But we'll get there!" And he would smile and nod as she'd start asking about someone's new book or house or grandchild, deflecting any further questions.

"Ireland at last," their friends and family would say if Edward was awarded the post in Dublin, and she would have to act as though it was nothing short of a miracle.

"Ireland at last!" she would echo.

She closed her purse back up to be returned to the foyer console, noting the USB stick containing the Rodin Museum catalog's translation still inside. Oh, to escape into one of her translations, beautiful and belonging to a world of heroes and gods and unambiguously punished sinners.

She sat down behind the big desk in the study, taking over the same space Edward had just a short while ago occupied to inform her about the assassination. The main thing was that Jamie always *meant* well. That was the big difference between her youthful acts of delirium and his. If he'd cheated, it had been to please her and Edward. If he'd forged her name, skipped onto a plane, slipped out of the house now, it was because somewhere in the fog of his adolescent mind he thought these things would make matters easier. Mental note: she had to be sure the headmaster didn't figure out Jamie had forged her signature giving him permission to leave. Then he might expel him.

Pulling her cell phone out of her pocket, she pressed the rapid-dial for Jamie's number.

The ring went directly into voice mail.

*Damn,* she thought. *Of course.*

"Jamie," she said on his voice mail, "this is your mother. I need you to call me immediately."

She knew Jamie wasn't going to call her back until he damn well felt like it. He probably was making a point of not even checking his messages. Jamie might mean well in a global sense, and he could be sweet as a charm, but keeping his own counsel just didn't bother him the way it might other kids. Family members commented on how, like Clare, he looked more like his one Swedish great-grandparent than any of his British or Irish ancestors. Clare thought he had something else of Mormor's, as they'd called her grandmother, the thing that had allowed her to conceal her true age until her death. But his inner life was unruly, and it was the combination of this trait with his opacity that caused such havoc. She never seemed to know until after the fact the problems he was having, something exacerbated by his adamancy she not get involved in his life without his express invitation.

There was nothing to do but just get on with things. She assembled pen and card stock, but the still of the room left her feeling pinioned. She got up, walked to the room's tall windows, and flung them open. Spring came wafting in, lifting the ends of her hair as though her shoulder-length locks were a curtain, stirring the scarf she wore draped around her shoulders. Taking the scarf off now, she laid it over the back of the desk chair. She shed her cardigan as well. She thought she could smell magnolias or maybe hazelnut blossoms. An urge to put her arms around someone surprised her. Why wasn't Jamie here, where she could talk with him? She went to the small television on a corner shelf and flipped on the power so as to fill the room with the sound of people. She settled herself behind the desk and began engraving.

Black loops and curls emerged from her fountain pen, and she gave in to the luxury of adding a little swagger: a twist at the end of an "e" and slight flourish at the end of a "t." Everyone said she had excellent handwriting for an American, and despite herself, despite all weighing on her mind, seeing how beautifully the lines were coming out gave her a twinge of pleasure. For some time when she was young, she'd harbored the dream of becoming an artist. Through high school, she'd even kept a secret journal of drawings, which she hid under a loose plank in the floor of her bedroom, fearing her family would tease her if they saw it. The long broad back of the history teacher who always called her Karen rather than Clare, the Frye boots of a group of giggling girls she feared, the weeping willow outside the home of a boy she secretly liked, all went in there, carefully dated and captioned. Her last year spent living at home, she'd moved on to unauthorized nudes, disrobing the brittle school principal and bossy captain of the cheerleading squad with her pencil in the quiet of her room late at night. But the figure drawing class she'd signed up for first semester at Harvard, using live models, had been a disaster. She couldn't get used to having ready and willing animate bodies before her, and the teacher had suggested she might feel more comfortable taking a still-life class the following semester. By the end of freshman year, she'd committed to a Romance languages major. Instead of painting nudes, she'd read of the forever-clothed Laura and frustrated Emma Bovary. She'd followed Don Quixote on his pointless quests and endured one hundred years of solitude with the Buendías.

A wise decision, as it turned out. Tonight, she would greet her French guests in their own language and chat with Bautista LeTouquet, wife of the director general at the Quai d'Orsay, in her native Italian. Edward would be proud of her, the home office would be impressed, and their guests would all feel more comfortable, even while English remained the lingua franca. People appreciated having a metaphoric hand extended towards them through the use of their own language; it made them feel respected. Americans and Brits, so used to hearing others speak in English, took this for granted. How that poor man, the sick Turkish wrestler, had struggled to make himself understood in English this morning!

Edward had always insisted that the children not let their linguistic luck breed complacency, and she'd wholeheartedly agreed. Peter was in his sixth year of German and fourth of Russian. Jamie was supposed to be studying Spanish. They weren't taking classes in French now that they were being schooled in Great Britain, as there'd have been nothing available for them at their levels, but they were both already quite fluent in the language. Native English speakers but born in different countries from one another, citizens of two, schooled in no less than three: where did her sons fit in? Edward would ask, Where does *anyone* fit in? but nonchalance was easy for Edward, because he did fit in somewhere: he was English from his stately toes to his thinning fair hair. His parents were English, and his grandparents and centuries of generations before them, all living and dying on the same stretch of dirt and rock between the English Channel, St. George's Channel, and the North Sea, except for one great-great-grandfather who'd spent many years as a colonel in India and a great-uncle who had somehow ended up being buried in Sumatra. And even those peripatetic ancestors hardly counted because they'd brought their Englishness along with them to their colonial postings. "The English manage to import their Englishness," Niall once said, "to every corner of the globe, like it was a digestive biscuit." And true to form, the great-uncle had died, of a sudden coronary, in a Sumatran rose garden sipping tea from a cup made of Spode china. She knew this for a fact. She and Edward had inherited the tea set the cup had come from, and the box that had held it had been covered with stamps bearing the abbreviation "Nedl. Ind.," from when Indonesia was still part of the Dutch East Indies. The set was one cup short.

"Fucks," Niall had also said, of the English. "Fucking imperialistic bastards. They'll get their orange arses off our island, won't they."

The first time she and Niall had spoken about Ireland, not predicting their future, not understanding anything yet, she'd responded as though she were participating in the Harvard debate club.

"Of course, the Catholics should be treated better. But the Protestants, the ones that have been there for some generations now," she'd said, "aren't they Northern Irish now, too? Aren't they even in the majority? Shouldn't they also have some say about what country they live in?"

They were lying on her bed at Aunt Elaine's house. Everyone else had gone to the Cape for the weekend. Niall had refused—only later would she understand why he avoided the beach, even when the summer heat was beating down on them—and she'd made up some work she'd had to do for her summer internship at the museum so she could appear to have a good reason to stay behind also. This would be her first chance to be alone in the house with him. They weren't lovers yet, not Saturday morning when the rest of the family's cars backed down the driveway, but an hour later, when she stepped out of the shower, she'd found him sitting on the sink, unwashed, dressed only in jeans, waiting for her. She hadn't been astonished.

"You—" she'd said.

He'd reached for a towel. "Come here." He'd begun to dry her, starting with her long hair, which hung almost down to her waist, then moved on to her neck and shoulders, her back, her legs and feet. He'd ended with her hands. He'd dried each finger separately.

And, later, Sunday afternoon, still lying on her bed in the heat, for they seemed to have hardly left it in the past thirty-six hours, he'd asked what she knew about Ireland. She'd been stupid enough to try to impress him with her meager knowledge of the Troubles, and with her schoolgirl understanding of magnanimity.

"Shouldn't they also have some say what country they live in?" she concluded, and he pulled his warm, sinewy body out from under her.

"You don't know anything," he whispered, stepping into his jeans. And then was gone.

Maybe she hadn't known anything. Or maybe, as an American emerging from such a different perception of assimilation, she hadn't been able to conceive of what life could be like for a poor, young Catholic boy growing up in Northern Ireland. The latter was what Niall had eventually decided when he'd apparently forgiven her and decided she was teachable. And taken her under his tutelage he had, telling her how the system had been rigged when he was a kid so the Catholics in Derry didn't even have as many votes per head as Protestants, and often no vote at all, how someone like him couldn't hardly get a job, never mind dream of going to uni, as he called college—injustices she'd heard about growing up but that took on sudden dimension when spoken with Niall's rummaging cadences.

"My da back in Derry," he'd told her. "He saw his neighbor's son, just a lad, shot down on the streets of Bogside on Bloody Sunday. You know about Bloody Sunday?"

She'd nodded.

"Lying there bleeding in the street, and Eamon just a boy, barely seventeen. My da and some men got a car and tried to get him to hospital. The Brits stopped them on the way, arrested the lot of them. Called them terrorist yobbos, and Eamon there bleeding to death in the back of the car. And you know what, Clare? They gave all those British bastards medals.

"There is no solution left but Ireland for the Irish."

And she'd believed him; she'd been ready to believe anything he said.

But, if he was right. If he, Edward, even the Turkish wrestler this morning—who'd told her so proudly of his village where his family had lived for centuries, who'd spoken with such distaste of the French, and, indeed, for Europe in general, excepting her and her dermal texture—were correct in their unfaltering visions of their home countries as unique consistent entities, where did that leave her children? Could the boys belong to both Britain and the U.S.? Where did that leave the hundreds of children forced to lay down new roots in neighboring or even distant nations thanks to wars in Vietnam or Somalia or, now, Iraq? Or by the end of colonization? Was the term "global identity" nothing more than a marketing tool? Were these children condemned to belong nowhere, ever?

"Back in my own home, I never lost," the wrestler had told her.

Clare put down her pen. She tugged on a strand of hair, shivered in the spring breeze. She drew her sweater from the back of her chair and pulled it over her shoulders. Across from her, the TV was droning. She watched the screen without seeing for a moment, the feeling of spring pushing at her shoulders, the state of her thoughts pushing back against it. The release that the fresh air had brought her just a few moments earlier had mutated into something more melancholy, a bittersweet sense of futility.

Then, she saw the face on the screen.

"My God," she said.

She rose from behind the desk and moved towards the television.

His face occupied a blue-background box in the corner. Clare squinted, stepped closer, then back from the screen, trying to shift the lines of the man's image. Could she be seeing someone else? A relative? A stranger who happened to look so very similar?

But no matter where she positioned herself, nothing changed: the pocked skin, the heavy build, the half-closed smaller left eye.

She reached for the remote and raised the volume. A tanned but grim-faced newscaster was talking, his brown eyes level.

The suspect has been identified, the newscaster announced, as a signatory member of a reactionary nationalist group that has already been implicated in a number of assassinations in its own country. This particular foot soldier has never been convicted of any crime beyond a petty offense as a youth, unrelated, for which he spent three months in prison. He is believed, however, by the authorities to have been circulating in France for some time now and has been photo-identified by an eyewitness of this morning's murder. The police were actively searching for him.

Clare clasped the collar of her sweater. In the photo they were showing, he was even wearing a cheap leather jacket.

A French parliamentarian, shot this morning at Versailles,

Edward had said, then added, lowering his voice, dead upon arrival. She'd felt something like relief, washed with shame for her callousness: no one they knew; nothing to do with their children; unrelated to London, or either of their home countries. They would still use all that asparagus, rolled up in paper towel in the kitchen. Edward would still get his chance to prove himself to the permanent under-secretary. She would remain in the predicament she'd by then accepted as her lot.

"How awful," she'd said, even as she pushed the murder a safe distance away from her own existence.

The newscaster was now riffling through a pile of papers. A communiqué, he explained in clipped French, lifting a sheet so stiff that the paper crackled, has been received by the French government from this same pro-Nationalist guerilla organization, condemning discussion of a law criminalizing the denial of Armenian genocide in Turkey in the early twentieth century and taking responsibility for the events of this morning, at 10:30 a.m. in Versailles, outside the French capital.

Clare twisted a lock of hair around her finger. His face had been shiny with perspiration. A problem with his kidneys, he'd said. He didn't like to see European doctors, but he was here visiting a cousin. "I have go see doctor. Two weeks I no . . . I piss blood." So much intimate information. "My wife, very good cooker. She makes a yogurt, mmm." He'd smacked his lips. "Very very good. Very good for body, too. You live long life. You like eat lamb?" He'd spat out a laugh like a snort. "French lady, they want look more like stick we make kebab than kebab. No meat. You come my home," he said, flinging his arms wide open, and she'd looked around them to make sure no one was nearby on the sidewalk, listening. "My wife feed you."

"I have three son, one girl. You have child?" he'd asked.

"Oh, yes, children are very important," she'd answered. "Do your children like yogurt?"

A terrorist.

Thank God she hadn't said anything about the children. Thank God she hadn't given her name either, or told him her nationality. She'd left him nothing to trace her by; all he had on her was where she shopped for flowers. *Used* to shop for flowers—she wouldn't patronize the Rue Chomel flower shop anymore. Or if she did, she would call in her orders. And Le Bon Marché? She'd waited until he'd disappeared from sight before heading into the food hall. If he was about to execute a murder, he wouldn't have bothered to double back to see where she was going. Would he have?

She had to be rational. This man hated the French, not the British or Americans. He was no threat to her or her family. He'd had other things on his mind; maybe the address he'd shown her hadn't even been for a doctor. Maybe he'd just told her that. Maybe that's where he'd gone to pick up his weapon.

The police. Could she remember the address where he was going?

She closed her eyes, tried to visualize the map he'd handed her. Rue de Vaugirard . . . but that street was long. She couldn't begin to remember the number.

She lowered the sound on the television and replaced the remote on top of it. She returned to the window, shut it, sat back down behind the desk, and picked up the landline.

No. She set the handset back down. She wouldn't call Edward right now. Edward didn't need to be interrupted by this. She stared at the phone. She wouldn't call the police either. She wouldn't call *anyone*. What would she have to say? A man looking like the man the police were seeking had asked her for directions to an address that she couldn't remember, before any crime had been committed. Calling about this would be like bragging she'd been in the Twin Towers the day before they were atomized. It would be self-aggrandizing. Petty. She hadn't seen the man commit any crime, he hadn't been anything but pleasant to her, and they already had a witness to the murder, someone who'd given his description to the police and had even picked out his photo.

This was a weird anecdote she would share with Edward over a weekend, over a private dinner. As for the police, she had nothing to offer them.

She heard the soft thud of a door. She cradled the phone back up into her hand and tiptoed towards the doorway, keeping to one side, out of view, and listened. A few moments later, the pad of slipper-shod feet in the dining room.

Amélie returning from lunch. Clare shook her head at her own absurdity. If anyone had reason to be worried, the eyewitness should be. Returning to the desk, she set the phone firmly back down again. She picked up her pen. Three place cards were still waiting to be finished. It was a crazy coincidence, the type that happened only in novels, but that was all. She didn't need to get involved. She *wasn't* involved.

Amélie knocked on the half-open door before stepping into the study. "I fineesh the dining room, Madame?"

She smiled and nodded, setting down the fountain pen, as though she'd been in the middle of writing. "Yes, Amélie, please. You can get out the vases also. We will need four large ones for side tables and two small ones for the dinner table. The flowers will arrive at four." She checked her watch again, out of habit. "The flowers will be delivered in about two hours."

"Yes, Madame." Amélie dipped her chin. "All is good?"

"Yes, everything is good."

"Yes, Madame." Amélie shut the door behind her, making a soft clicking sound.

In movies, jail cells clanked. They didn't click.

Clare looked again at the TV screen; the regular programming was back on.

There was nothing on the screen, no sign of there having been a news flash, or of political turmoil. On 9/11 four years ago, and last summer on 7/7, the coverage had been inescapable—the hunted, haunted faces of people wandering Wall Street or emerging from the London Underground by Russell Square. But, here, on the screen, she was looking at three men and one woman, all dressed in either gray or black, as they sat around a table discussing something, a book one of them had recently published, as though nothing beyond the norm had happened to anyone.

Of course, it was just one individual, not a mass slaughter. Still, it had been a parliamentarian. Maybe she'd imagined the whole thing, or at least, maybe, in the same way as she kept thinking she saw Niall, dead these two decades, she hadn't really brushed shoulders this morning with a political assassin. Maybe their contact was equally illusory. Maybe she was cracking up already, even without having moved to Dublin.

The map.

She reached into her sweater pocket and pulled out the piece of paper the Turk had thrust at her. There were the dim street names, faded from being photocopied. There, at top, was the address of the health clinic. There was the phone number.

A part of her wanted to throw it out right then and there, and in doing so wash her hands of the whole encounter. The dinner, Jamie. Dublin. She couldn't cope with a murder. But something stopped her, a sense of justice bigger than herself. She folded the paper back up, doubling the sheet once and then twice and then a third time, and returned it to her pocket.

She got up and shut off the TV, came back to sit down behind the desk.

Enough.

She looked at her watch. 2:25 p.m. Five more hours.

She took out her to-do list and checked off everything she'd accomplished. She read the newly shortened list through and replaced it in the pocket that did not have the map in it. She extracted a sheet of paper from the desk drawer, drew a large rectangle and, on top, wrote, "Seating for Dinner." At one end, she wrote Edward's name. At the other, she wrote her own.

She set her pen back down. She picked up the phone and dialed. Three rings, and he answered.

"Edward?"

"Hold on, just one moment, I just need to—" There was the sound of shuffling papers, the scratching of a pen. "Yes, what is it?"

"Edward…" She tapped the paper on the desk before her. He sounded so preoccupied. This day meant everything to him. This appointment.

She looked around the room. She smoothed her pants legs. "I meant to ask. The green-and-white silk?"

"For dinner?"

"You know, with the wraparound waist. The background is green, the white is flowers."

"Not green. Just wear your emerald."

The emerald, of course. She would have to clean it. "That beige suit, then?"

"Clare, darling. I'm awfully busy. Did Mathilde make a fuss about the strawberries?"

How did he know she'd dipped into the strawberries? "I don't think she's back yet."

"Cover for me, will you? We don't need the wrath of Mathilde tonight. Shouldn't she be back from lunch by now?"

"You stole from her strawberries?" Clare tugged on a loose strand of hair. She touched her pocket. "Edward, you know what you were telling me? You know that man?"

"A strawberry man?"

"At Versailles."

There was a silence, then a sigh. "Oh, yes. Versailles."

"They think they know who did it."

"Yes, I heard. Wait, hold on a sec—"

She could hear the sound of his secretary's clipped tones in the background. "Edward," she said into the receiver, "are you still there?"

"Yes."

"The man. At Versailles."

"Yes. Bruno Molyneux. No, no, that's all right," he finished by saying, but not to her. She again heard the distant voice of his secretary.

She stared at her hands. A wisp of blond hair was caught under a nail. She disengaged the strand and let it flutter from her fingers into the wastepaper basket. Once she told someone about her encounter, that strange episode would become reality. Until then, their meeting was a truth only to her and her Turk. If one of them denied they had ever crossed paths, it might as well have never happened.

"Never mind," she said. "It's nothing. I'll wear the beige. And the emerald."

She replaced the phone and took out her list. The emerald was her most tangible link to Ireland. The ring everyone wanted;

the ring she wore as seldom as possible because it meant too many things to her. Her wealthy Irish grandfather had used it to woo Mormor—a platinum claddagh with a spectacular 5.5-carat emerald and two enclosing diamonds.

"Why did she leave the emerald to Clare?" her sister-in-law, Amy, had asked at the luncheon after the reading of Mormor's will. "She could just as well have given it to Rachel."

Clare had been upstairs changing Peter's diaper in the guest room bathroom, directly above the kitchen. She'd heard the whole conversation through the grating. Rachel was the firstborn of the next generation, Clare's brother Luke and Amy's daughter, then five years old.

Her other brother, Aidan, who wasn't married back then and still wasn't married now but was always very mindful of the politics of family order, had said, "Probably she figured there'd be more granddaughters to follow. She didn't want to seed any future jealousies amongst them."

"Or to the estate. She could have left it to the estate. That would have been the normal thing to do. The estate sells it and divides the proceeds equally amongst the heirs," Luke had said.

Silence had wafted up the vent. A metal door had gone clunk—the oven.

"Because," her mother had said, "Clare's got those hands."

"What about her hands?" her sister-in-law had squeaked.

"Haven't you ever noticed them?"

Clare had thrown a towel down over the duct so she couldn't hear the rest of the conversation. No one other than Niall had ever mentioned her hands. She didn't know why if her mother had noticed them, she'd never said anything about them. Mormor neither. She'd looked down at them, water spilling over them, and wanted to clothe them. It had taken her a long time after that to get over her feeling of nakedness about them.

Clare stared at her hands, now slightly veined, the skin just beginning to thin on them—these hands that had gotten her into so much trouble. Then she picked up her pen and across the bottom of her pad, wrote, "Clean emerald."

She shoved the pad away. She would make a few necessary phone calls, complete this week's expense report, then head out to the hairdresser's. Was Mathilde back from lunch? Did she dare go check up on her? Only Mathilde could manage still to inspire fear after all else Clare was facing. If only Mathilde had become a nursemaid instead of a chef. She would have sorted Jamie out in a way Clare never was able.

Yet again Clare pulled the BlackBerry from her pocket. Nothing. Even as he became in many ways more dependent upon her, Jamie was spiraling further out of control. He would falsify a message from her and jump on a plane without any adult's knowledge, much less permission. He would come and go when he wanted, and explain himself only when he was good and ready. What did she know about what had really happened? She'd told Barrow she'd call them rather than the opposite; she had to try now to put this conversation off until she'd managed to rein Jamie in enough to find out why he'd done what he'd done.

And she wasn't going to talk at all, to anyone, about this latest strange encounter, with the Turkish stranger. She'd file it away amongst the other experiences in her life she didn't intend to reveal to anyone.

# NINE

C lare closed the door to the study softly behind her as she stepped into the hall, and paused to listen. There was no sound coming from the kitchen. Either Mathilde wasn't back yet or she was back but wasn't unhappy.

She headed down the hall towards the bedrooms. She'd check just once, on the off chance Jamie had snuck back into the Residence while she was in the study with the door closed, as quietly as he'd snuck out while she was having lunch with his father.

She stopped at Peter's door first. Maybe it would be a better place for hiding. Or maybe Jamie'd looked for inspiration in the way his careful older brother differed from him, so apparent even in the state of his bedroom. When Peter had left for Fettes, he'd folded every article of clothing he wasn't taking with him, sorted them by season, and placed them in separate drawers in his room. He'd cleared his desk of all paraphernalia, tossing into the garbage anything less than vital, and organizing whatever was left into boxes that he labeled and lined up along the top shelf of his room's armoire. Looking around, the week after she had returned from delivering him to Scotland—not to snoop, but to check whether he'd left anything important behind—Clare had been struck by how similar the interiors of his desk drawers now appeared to those in finer hotels. A few neatly piled notepads, a handful of sharpened pencils and capped pens, the leather-backed Bible he'd received from his American grandparents for his first Communion, a box of throat lozenges, and a flashlight. Only a teenager like Peter would leave a room like that. "I am in control," the room said. "I don't require—or wish—anyone else's help to keep my life in order."

Peter's room looked as clean and organized—and empty—as ever.

She shut the door again.

When Jamie had banged out of his room for the last time before heading off for boarding school last fall, he'd left dirty pajamas in a tangle on top of his bed and an explosion of books shooting out from under it, along with a few unmatched socks, a half-drunk bottle of water, and a bent ruler. Opening the door to peek in upon returning from dropping him off in London, Clare had almost been able to believe Jamie had gone just for the night, for a sleepover at a friend's, and would be back in the morning. In some way, the casual mess he'd left behind had made Clare feel better.

"Do you think it made Jamie feel better, too, a way of pretending he wasn't actually leaving?" she'd said to Edward over their third or fourth solitary dinner together. Of course, she and Edward didn't usually dine as a duo; most nights brought some sort of engagement, or else Edward might be traveling.

"Oh, it's James, that's all," Edward had said. "Not the most orderly boy, is he?"

Clare had cut her veal cutlet, releasing a trickle of blood towards her potatoes. Pink had swirled into white, laced the taupe edges of mushroom sauce. "He's not used to having no one around to care for him."

"All the more reason for him to start learning," Edward had said, reaching for his water glass. He was compelled to consume so much alcohol during work-related lunches and cocktail parties and dinners that he stuck to water when it was just the two of them. "And he will. I wouldn't worry. Not about Jamie's house-keeping, I mean."

"I won't. I'll let his roommate do that," she'd said, and they'd both laughed. "Can you imagine?"

She'd never mentioned Jamie's empty room to Edward again. Increasingly, she and Edward avoided the topic of Jamie alto-gether, other than the inescapable, such as any report that had been sent home from Barrow. Edward had suggested early on that it wasn't helpful to Jamie to be able to return home from Bar-row whenever and as often as he wanted—it wouldn't aid him in adapting to becoming more independent. Having made clear his thoughts on the subject once, he was not one to harp. She persisted in allowing Jamie to return as often as he wished any-how, and Edward greeted him on each visit with affection and no outward hint of disapprobation. She knew Edward called Jamie from the office once a week to chat, too, and she supposed Ed-ward had figured out that Jamie called her nearly every evening. But she and Edward never discussed the contents of their separate phone calls with each other, any more than they returned to the subject of Jamie's lack of self-sufficiency, except when she had something very specific to relate. And even then, sometimes she didn't. Instead, they talked about Peter's college search or where they should take their annual summer holiday as a family.

She pushed open the door to Jamie's room. There was his duffel still on the floor, inked up with phone numbers and names. On top of his desk lay a jumble of flyers. She tapped the papers into a neat pile without reading what they announced and put them back on the desk. Here's how she'd handle it. She'd phone Edward around 6:00 p.m., before he headed for cocktails at the embassy, to explain there'd been some new trouble in school, and she wanted Jamie to come home for the weekend. She'd claim she was the one who'd made the decision. She wouldn't specify when Jamie was scheduled to arrive, and Edward wouldn't ask— he had other things to think about. Then, if Jamie did come back during dinner, Edward wouldn't be startled to see him, although he might feel frustrated. Edward didn't fall apart; Edward compartmentalized. In the morning, he would ask, "So, what is going on with Jamie now?" They would go in together to wake Jamie and speak with him briefly but somberly before Edward headed in to his office. When Edward heard that Jamie had been caught cheating again, he would tell him he was sorry Jamie felt he had to keep doing this, but he had no choice but to take his punishment. They would not ask about nor listen to any claims regarding anyone else's involvement; Edward would insist whatever anyone else had done was irrelevant. And they would not discuss Jamie's unauthorized flight. This last could remain between her and Jamie, something for her to deal with separately and in confidence.

"I do clean linen, Madame?"

Amélie stood behind her, viewing the duffel bag. It lay there in the center of the room like an enormous telegram, heralding the arrival of its owner. In one hand, Amélie held a duster. In the other, the phone. She held it out.

Was it Jamie?

"Madame Gibson," Amélie said.

Clare took the phone, cupping her hand over the mouthpiece. "Draw the curtains and open a window. But no need to change the sheets. They're clean, aren't they?"

*"Oui, Madame."* They left unspoken the fact that enough time hadn't elapsed since Jamie's last visit for the sheets to have grown musty. Clare would miss Amélie when they went to Dublin, for the opposite reason she would miss Mathilde. Mathilde kept the household on its toes, and life interesting. Amélie was safe. She was kind also. Never grow too close to the staff was one of the first rules of diplomat living but when they were the people who knew her family's secrets, when they were the people she saw day in and day out, the people she sometimes saw more often than her husband, substitutes for the spinster aunt or longtime neighbor or friend from grade school or widowed grandma, becoming attached to them was difficult to avoid.

In Dublin, there would be a whole new set of staff members to get to know, then have to say good-bye to. If they went to Dublin. There was tonight's dinner still to get through. Plus Edward knew of other rumored candidates for British ambassador to Ireland.

"But none," he had pointed out this morning, as they dressed, "is married to a girl named Fennelly. If nothing else, that should prove my commitment to continued good relations between the Crown and Ireland. You are my trump card, Clare. As always."

"You mean continued domination," she, at that moment crouched down giving a last-minute buff to one of his shoes, had said.

"I mean continued subjugation," he'd answered, reaching over her for the violet tie she'd given him for his last birthday, which they both knew he hated, and looping it around his neck. She'd stood up to knot it for him. Then she'd turned her back, and he'd closed the clasp on her necklace, his warm fingers brushing her neck. That might have been the real moment she'd committed herself to getting him Dublin.

"Hello, Sally," Clare said into the phone.

Sally Gibson's son, Emil, had played soccer with Peter at the International School during their first posting in Paris. She and Sally had ended up manning many a soft-drink stand together and chaperoning numerous bus trips. Ever since their return to France, Sally had been after Clare to help with every committee she herself got involved with. Her latest was the Paris chapter of Democrats Abroad.

"I'm sorry, Sally, I really can't join," she said. Sally was a very nice person, and much too smart to be nothing more than a soccer mom in Paris, but she had the habit of acting like a dog with a bone when she got her mind set on something—maybe because she was too smart a woman to be simply a soccer mom in Paris. She and Clare had had this same exchange enough times already; Clare might have to tell Amélie to say she was out next time Sally called. "Never mind my own personal inclinations, which I've already told you are zero when it comes to politics, for me to join wouldn't be right. The Foreign Office is devoutly apolitical, and expects its personnel, and their families, to be that way in public also."

She checked her watch. 2:55 p.m. She'd lost too much time on all this other stuff already.

"Everyone is political, Clare. Especially in these days. You can't avoid it."

"Well, I am not."

"You're holding out on me. I know where your loyalties lie. And, Clare, this is important. We're heading towards disaster. The sanity and safety of our entire globe could depend on this."

Clare sighed. "Listen, Sally, I just can't. I'm sorry. But are you running something for the school *kermesse* this year? Maybe there's something I could do for that, even though both the boys are gone now. Maybe Mathilde can send over a couple cakes." That sounded bad. She added, "I mean, maybe we could still contribute something."

After she hung up, she headed down the hall towards the kitchen. She hoped Sally wouldn't go talking behind her back, saying she was starting to act snobbish. People forgot—or maybe never knew in the first place—that none of the pomp and circumstance that surrounded a diplomatic family's daily life actually belonged to them. The splendor belonged to the Crown; she and Edward were just staff (and she unpaid staff, at that). If anything, she and Edward belonged to the Residence more than it belonged to them. Not only would they pack up their things when Edward's job in Paris was finished and move on as though from a hotel, she didn't have much say about life within the Residence now.

*"Attention!"* Mathilde hissed before Clare managed to clear the kitchen doorway. She pointed a finger towards the oven then raised it to her lips.

"Is there a baby sleeping?" Clare said and immediately regretted her flippancy. She lifted the cloth covering the asparagus to check that the stalks hadn't begun to yellow. They lay there like a mass of entwined lovers, lovely shades of white and purple. "They're nice, aren't they?"

"Hah, hah, *très amusant,* Mrs. Moorhouse, but *un bon gâteau* is as delicate as a baby." Mathilde swiped the platter of asparagus from under Clare's eyes and whisked it over to the sink. She ran water from the tap until she was satisfied at its chill, collected a few drops on her naked fingertips, and shook them over the stalks as though she were a priest anointing them. "Tastes better, though."

"How do you know that, Mathilde?"

Mathilde laughed, not with her usual loud bark—so as not to disturb the cakes—but in a sort of silent version of it, hacking at the air. "A little backjaw from the minister's wife, nae? A little cheeky? You feeling yourself, Mrs. Moorhouse?"

Despite her determination not to think about him anymore, the image of the wrestler's shiny forehead rose in her mind. Clare looped a strand of hair behind an ear and crossed her arms across her chest. "*Can* an employer be cheeky to an employee, Mathilde?"

Mathilde wiped her damp fingers on the apron covering her broad chest and straightened the kerchief she wore over her graying hair. Then, gathering herself up as high as her diminutive height would allow her, especially when confronted with Clare at well over half a foot taller, she answered, "Anyone can be ill mannered. Even *Monsieur le Président* to a street cleaner."

She looked fierce, and Clare remembered what Edward had said: *We don't need the wrath of Mathilde tonight.* Besides, Mathilde was right. Everyone deserved respect. Even if that hadn't been what Clare had been asking, and Mathilde knew it.

"You're right." She left the asparagus and peered into the fridge. The strawberries had been impounded. She shut the door. "Although, somehow I can't imagine a French president chatting up a garbage collector."

Mathilde snorted. "Neither can I. The French wouldn't have it. So, I'll be putting an orange Bundt into the oven tomorrow, *n'est-ce pas?*"

Orange Bundt cake was Jamie's favorite. This was Mathilde's way of making peace, at the same time as keeping the upper hand; tendering both a spontaneous offer to please Jamie and evidence of her awareness of his mid-school-week arrival. She probably also thought Jamie had eaten the strawberries. Well, good. Let her. She would forgive Jamie for it more easily than if the thief were she or Edward.

"That would be lovely, Mathilde."

Two large tubs of plain yogurt stood on the counter, like country cisterns, white and thick.

"My wife, very good cooker," the Turk had said, "She make very good yogurt, very good for body."

If they were in America, this wouldn't be true for him once they brought him in, no matter whether his wife was allowed to send him yogurt. If caught and convicted, the Turk could be sentenced to death. Hard to imagine of the man she'd walked down the street with just a couple of hours earlier, listening to him praise his wife's cooking. Clare felt a pain in her chest, the wind knocked out of her. But no, capital punishment didn't exist in Europe, neither in France nor Turkey. Only Americans, amongst the Western nations, clung to killing their killers.

That's nuts, she thought. I'm feeling sorry for this man? He's a terrorist.

He'd stepped out in front of her, holding a piece of paper in his hand, pressing it on her. But, back then, he'd been just some poor lost guy, sweating in a cheap leather jacket. How could that same man be an assassin?

There must be a mistake, she thought. *Her* mistake. There was an eyewitness.

"If you will be tearing your hair out, Mrs. Moorhouse, I'd ask you don't do it around my cooking," Mathilde said, pulling a tray of fish out of a fridge, where it had been marinating.

Clare dropped the wisp of hair she'd yanked from her skull,

without realizing it, into the garbage. She noticed the clock on the oven door, which used the international standard notation: 15.25. Her appointment at the hairdresser was at 4:00 p.m. "What's the yogurt for?"

"The dessert," Mathilde said. She plopped the fish down on the counter, suddenly heedless of the cakes in the oven. "Along with the strawberries."

Time to leave, Clare thought.

"What's left of them, anyway," Mathilde called after her.

Before going out, Clare slipped back into the study and turned on the television. But it was before the hour: no headline news. She flipped to CNN. Sports coverage. She flipped to BBC. A world business report.

She had arranged for a car to take her to the hairdresser's; unless there was a demonstration clogging the streets, she had time to do a quick check on Google. She sat down at the desk and tapped the space button to close the screensaver. While she waited, she burrowed her hands in her sweater pockets, the triple-ply cashmere warm and soft against her fingers. She felt the cold crepe of thin paper and pulled a sheet out, not her to-do list, nor the Turk's map, but the forgotten flower shop receipt. She'd failed to enter the sum into the day's expense sheet.

She reached for the drawer containing the Residence's expense ledger, but before opening it, she tapped a few words into Google. Then, as the site loaded, she trained her eyes over the receipt. Jean-Benoît wrote with a strange angular tilt, and his notation was as meticulous as his lettering. Instead of scrawling out the ultimate price, after calculating the fifteen percent embassy reduction, he'd begun at the beginning, marking down the precise number and regular cost of each element of each bouquet— *lys jaunes/48 tiges/6,50 euros/312,00 euros*—followed by the price adjustment. Even the exact time of purchase was specified: *10.12.*

Clare glanced up at the computer screen, fixed now into a crossword of calibrated print and graphics.

His face was still there, his same droopy eyelid, his cheap jacket. She couldn't have been mistaken. Her wrestler was wanted for shooting a French parliamentarian in front of Versailles at 10.30 this morning.

*But that was not possible.*

She checked Jean-Benoît's receipt. There it was at the bottom. Time of purchase: 10.12.

He'd crossed the street and almost been hit by a car. She'd waited to see he reached the other side safely and then waited to be sure he wouldn't turn back. She'd seen his wide, dark form lumber down the Rue Saint-Placide, until he'd become just another urban spot amongst many. And then she'd glanced at her own watch.

*10:29 a.m.*

Her watch had read 10:29 a.m., and she'd calculated in her mind how much time she had left to finish her shopping and also stop at the pharmacy to pick up some homeopathic medicine for Mathilde before they arrived with the plate back at the apartment.

Clare looked at her watch now. The gold around its face twinkled up at her in the light reflected off the computer. 3:41 p.m. She checked the clock in the far right bottom of the computer. Also 3:41 p.m.

She picked up the desk phone and dialed. A sensible male voice: *quinze heures, quarante-et-un minutes, trente secondes.* She waited. *Quinze heures, quarante-et-un minutes, quarante secondes.*

She looked back at her watch. Even the second hand was accurate.

There was no way her Turk could have gotten to Versailles in one minute. Not even if he'd sprouted wings and flown. Versailles lay fifteen miles southwest of Paris.

Clare touched her spidery fingers to her forehead. She was careful not to groan or sigh, or make any sound the staff might hear.

She reached for the phone, but her hand stopped before dialing a number. She sat there for a minute, feeling the press of time, both past and present, on her. Then she laid the phone back down on its cradle. She still wasn't going to call anyone—not the police, not Edward. Not until she'd thought this over. Never do anything impetuously. Never do anything without thinking through all the repercussions. She'd made that mistake once. She would not repeat it.

Her situation was complicated.

If she was wrong—although how she could be, she didn't see at present—and provided this man with an alibi, she could be abetting an assassin. A man would have been murdered, his murderer would come away scot-free, and she'd be responsible.

If she was right about the timing but some other detail was wrong—maybe the wrong time had been reported to the news stations, either by mistake or on purpose for some tactical reason—the police wouldn't take her support of his innocence seriously. She *wouldn't* become responsible for freeing a murderer—but she might come under scrutiny herself. What's this woman doing, not Turkish, not involved in this case, the Irish-American wife of a British diplomat, getting involved in this case? Defending a presumed political assassin? At best, this would be uncomfortable for Edward, particularly at such a sensitive professional moment. At the worst...

Not to be considered.

Either way, she'd have to search out the correct police station and go in to make a statement. That would mean, at the very least, abandoning her hair appointment, but God knows what else also, because how long might it take? French bureaucracy wasn't exactly known for its efficiency, and this was the murder of a high-ranking French official. She could be down there for hours. She and Edward might even have to cancel the dinner.

Impossible.

If she was right, however, and her Turk was innocent...

She could single-handedly keep the police from following the wrong lead, and get them on track to searching for the real killer. She could be pivotal in catching the murderer. And she could be pivotal in sparing her Turk unnecessary harassment.

Unless...

Maybe they'd still hunt him down, even with her statement. There was an eyewitness. He was believed to have belonged to that organization. Why would they instantly believe her word about it?

So, it would become her word against that of the other witness.

Again, the police might have to start delving into her own history.

That was not going to happen.

She would wait. Meanwhile, tonight's dinner would go on.

She pulled her sweater sleeve over her watch and, selecting a fine-tipped blue ballpoint pen, copied down the pertinent information from Jean-Benoît's receipt in the ledger, immediately under the entry she had already made for the cheese and asparagus.

After she'd transcribed the amounts, she reviewed her work carefully. She did this, as she always did, because—just as she hadn't immediately put together the time problem between when she'd last seen the wrestler and the reported time of the murder—numbers were the one weakness she couldn't seem to shake. "Clare can't remember our phone number," one of her brothers had ratted her out to their mother when she was still in grade school, and she'd had to write the number on her thigh in ink before they'd sat down to that night's dinner, slipping her skirt up high under the table to read it so as to prove him wrong. Even as she'd excelled in all her other courses, math class had always been a struggle. As she'd gotten older, she'd learned ways for coping with the problem without ever managing to overcome it. She'd devised elaborate tricks for memorizing her own cell phone number, and all the others she called regularly she had relegated to rapid-dial. "Don't fuss too much over it. Everyone has to have some little foible and at least yours isn't biting your nails or drink or betting on the horses," Edward had said a couple years back when she'd stumbled upon an article about mathematical dyslexia. But she disliked having any perceivable weakness, and she continued to triple-verify any number she touched, including those on the Residence's expense ledger.

She found one mistake. She searched in the desk drawer for white-out, blotted over the incorrect digit, waited a moment for the white-out to dry, and wrote in the correct figure. When she was sure the page was dry, she closed the book and replaced the ledger in her drawer.

His face was still staring at her from the computer. She might occasionally make mistakes with numbers, but she had not made a mistake about the time she'd met him.

She checked her watch yet again. The car she'd ordered to take her to the hairdresser's would be waiting downstairs. There would be other cars blocked behind hers in the single-lane street, honking. Maybe one of the guards or a gendarme would approach the driver to complain. She looked at the phone but did not touch it again. She capped the pen she'd been using and placed it back in the desk's pencil holder. She clicked off the Internet, the wrestler's face popping out of sight at her touch. She rose. She withdrew her scarf from the back of the chair and wrapped it around her shoulders. Tonight's dinner was fast approaching, and a distracted wife with unkempt hair was not the ideal spouse for a future ambassador to Ireland.

# TEN

Clare could see her hairdresser, Marco, inside the salon, adjusting a square of foil in the hair of a seated customer. The woman looked like a project Peter had done for science class while he was still in elementary school, a doll robot with rolls of tinfoil encircling its head. Like the woman, the robot had borne a brightly painted smile.

Behind her, Clare felt the weight of her driver's gaze. She was grateful embassy drivers considered themselves quasibodyguards, but his present concern made her feel as though she were a bug squashed between two glass slides under a microscope. There he was, waiting behind her, and there Marco was, waiting before her. She stopped in the middle of the sidewalk and waved to the driver that he should leave. But she couldn't bring herself to go into the hairdresser's salon.

She pulled her cell phone out of her bag and, in her mind, rehearsed what she might say.

"I'm really sorry to bother you again, darling, but I have a quick legal question. If you were wanted by the police for a crime, here in France, but someone came forward who could provide an alibi for you, would the police stop hunting for you? Before you'd been caught and questioned? Would it change the investigation? And could that person offer the alibi, say, over the phone?"

She didn't unlock her phone. Edward would think she was nuts interrupting him, today of all days, to ask something like that. What explanation could she possibly come up with that he wouldn't see through? Especially when she got to the next part.

"And how about if there was a second witness, who claimed to have seen you commit the crime? Would they check into the backgrounds of both witnesses? Would it become a question of seeing which was more credible?"

A trail of smoke, the remnant of a passerby's cigarette, curled up into her face. The cigarette had been hand-rolled, of the sort she had smelled on her Turk's jacket. When they were walking down the boulevard side by side, she'd contemplated how foolish he was to smoke, considering his medical problems. Good grief! She'd been worrying about his nicotine habits. They'd both had much bigger worries ahead of them. If she went to the police, at the very least there would be statements, and officials, and documents, and the press, and lots and lots of talk. Back when she first met Edward, she'd felt fear at the very sight of a policeman. She'd crossed streets not to pass in front of them; she'd turned her face so there was no chance they would see and recognize it from a description or drawing. In twenty years, she'd managed never even to be stopped for a traffic violation. She could smile at the gendarmes on her street, without a hint of hesitation, and wait for them to nod their hats back at her. She'd cleared her slate. She'd washed away the traces of her iniquity.

Clare flicked the smoke out of her face with as subtle a twist of her hand as possible and glanced at the salon window. Marco was very specifically now avoiding looking in her direction. She was late for her appointment, and still she was on the street, standing there dumbly, cell phone in hand, acting like a confused puppy. She tucked the phone back into her purse, and tried to tamp down her thoughts in the same neat fashion.

If the police managed to apprehend her Turk—which was in itself unlikely—she *would* step forward, if she had to. But she probably would never have to because the doctor he'd gone to see would be able to identify him just as well as she could. In fact, the doctor had probably *already* come forward to identify him. Or would this evening, once he turned on the evening news and saw the picture. Or would tomorrow morning, after he'd seen the morning paper. If no doctor ever came forward, that could only mean there *was* no doctor. That, in turn, would mean the Turk had lied to her—proof he was mixed up in this whole thing after all. How, she didn't know, because the time conflict was undeniable. Either way, there was no need for her to get involved with the whole mess, and certainly not today.

She reached into her sweater pocket, withdrew the Turk's map, in its many folds, and zipped it carefully shut within her purse alongside her phone. Dinner was just over three hours away.

She opened the door to the salon and entered what felt like a different world, adjusting her step to fit the beat of a female singer's smoky alto. Carefully coiffed heads turned and nodded in her direction, a chorus of *bonjour*s over the hum of blow-dryers and the tinkle of water running. Marco was waiting, with a shiny black smock in his hands. While an assistant hung Clare's sweater, then placed her scarf and earrings on a black velvet tray and stowed them behind the salon counter, her hairdresser slipped one sleeve of the smock over one of her arms and, then, the other. The smock flapped and slid over her, as light as a casing of feathers. On an ordinary day, she would have smiled at the sensation, so reminiscent of Dorothy when she entered the Emerald City. But she felt a sudden chill, and shivered.

"Are you cold, Clare?" Marco asked her in French, emphasizing her first name, as though he realized he was virtually the only service-providing person in Paris who didn't "Madame Moorhouse" her. He probably *did* realize. He traveled regularly to London, where the salon had a sister business, and undoubtedly spoke fine English, but they always conversed in French, to the point of pronouncing immutably English-language words in a Gallic manner: *le blow-drying, le hamburger.* Marco was very chic, and very discreet.

"I'm fine," she responded, also in French.

She allowed him to lead her to a chrome-colored seat before a large gilt mirror. "As usual?" he asked, pushing a few strands back from her forehead.

Her face stared back at her, his face hovering just above hers and, beyond their two faces, the street. She felt as though she were looking at gradations of animation: her face pale, her hair pale, her expression as calm as usual, betraying none of the turmoil she'd been feeling; his face also serious and pale but his hair a brilliant reddish-black, and his eyes enflamed and searching; the world outside awash with the buoyant passage of pedestrians, the colors of spring.

Tall plane trees, vibrant with shimmering chartreuse leaves, lined the traffic island in the middle of the avenue.

She clutched the edge of her chair. The profile of a man's body. The way he moved, just as she remembered. Lean and economic. Unpredictable. His body had never enveloped hers; instead, it had carried hers along. They'd been the same height standing face-to-face, the same length lying side by side. She turned her head to look directly through the windowpane. But there was no one on the traffic island, not even a body on which to pin a mistaken identity. She stared again at her own image in the mirror. She saw her face, her eyes, her hair. She closed her eyes, reopened them. She was still looking at her own pallid image. Everything as it should be, and yet, she'd had two sightings of Niall now, in one day, both of them so convincing. This shouldn't still be happening to her. In the first years, decades even, she'd catch her breath and swallow her heart, sure she was catching a glimpse of him, and then the man she was looking at might turn his head and she'd see someone much older, or someone much younger, or maybe even a woman. Increasingly, however, the vision would move from her sight without her getting to view a face clearly, and she'd find herself left with the feeling that what she'd seen really had been him, even when there was no chance it could be.

She didn't want to think about what his face would look like now, deep in the ground, inside its casket. A dry skull, maybe some dark strands of hair. All that was left when all the bark and clamor had ended. Death knew no glamour.

"As usual," she said.

She clasped her two hands in front of her, pressing the smock down against her thighs. If she kept seeing someone who was dead, and feeling almost one hundred percent certain about it, maybe she had also dreamt up her encounter with the Turkish wrestler. Maybe she was actually hallucinating. She'd read of stranger things happening to people. A chemical imbalance. Or guilt rising up from the past to pervert her brain, like Macbeth thinking he saw Banquo, or Lady Macbeth seeing bloodstains on her clean fingers. What was insanity, anyhow? Perfectly rational people imagined enemies in their neighbors; maybe cool and collected women could start imagining encounters with murderers. Or, at the very least, dream up their resemblance to someone with whom they'd had an unsettling recent encounter. After all, bad skin and a cheap leather jacket—that could describe a good portion of the world's population. Could she have conjured this whole connection up, just as she seemed to be conjuring up the figure of Niall on every street corner? Was the man she saw on television even the same person as the wrestler?

"Perfect," Marco said. "Shall we wash your hair, then?"

She was glad she hadn't bothered Edward. Really glad she hadn't gone down to a police station. She lifted her hands and watched the bottom of the smock slither towards her calves, as she stood. Marco's assistant led her to a washbasin, and she allowed her head to be tilted back, her neck to be slotted into cool porcelain. Water began to pour over her skull, filling her ears with warm, soft liquid.

There were many dark-complected heavyset men with skin ruined by steroid consumption. Why shouldn't there even be more than one with a droopy eyelid? How carefully had she really looked at him? She'd avoided his eyes at first and then they'd walked down the street side by side. It's not as though they'd sat at a table across from each other. Just imagine if she'd gone in to defend the guy, they brought him for questioning anyhow, and it wasn't even the same person. Not only would she have jeopardized tonight's dinner for nothing, people would laugh at her. And then they might start saying she was crazy. Or had lied on purpose because she sympathized with the assassin's cause. This was how it was nowadays—disagreeing with the authoritative majority was tantamount to being subversive, especially when related in any way to terrorism. When Jamie had bought a T-shirt condemning the war in Iraq, Edward had asked him not to wear it. "Not to school, at least," Edward had said. "I know you do not

mean it this way, and I completely agree with your right to disagree. But there are some people out there who will say it means
you are supporting Al Qaeda."

Of course Jamie had worn the shirt anyway. From the youngest
age, Jamie had bucked against anything he perceived as unjust.
In kindergarten already, he'd come home with a bite on his arm
for defending his snack against a bully. When President Bush had
threatened to invade Iraq, he'd insisted on joining the throngs
of protestors in the streets of Paris. He'd even begun interro-
gating a dinner guest from the American embassy one evening,
until Edward had intervened. *That* had been embarrassing. But
Jamie was young. Younger people were more quickly forgiven
their opinions and the actions they took based upon them—until
they came back to haunt them. The police had said the man in
the photo belonged to an extremist organization, but they hadn't
said when. Maybe he was just a poor devil who had gotten himself caught up in more than he intended when still a kid—signed
a petition written by an old school friend, attended a meeting or
two run by a neighbor, and ended up with his name on a mailing
list for the wrong organization, all back when he was an ardent
innocent college student. Or a young man trying out his first job.
Maybe he was just an ordinary fellow who'd made one very big
mistake that would now follow him around forever, at the urging
of a friend, or family member, or a lover. If he was apprehended
and his case went to trial, this one mistake from his past would
be his undoing.

But, still. Even if he hadn't been involved in the assassination,
he couldn't be considered entirely guiltless, could he? He did
once make that choice, regardless of his age at the time. And if
he had been involved in the assassination, even remotely? The
thought left her dizzy. And she'd been standing on the street cor-

ner with him, chatting about yogurt and the eating habits of French women! He might have had the blood on his hands of civilian children and women, the invisible wing tips of their souls brushing his broad shoulders.

There would be huge political pressure to solve this case, and quickly, to keep fear from growing amongst the populace. People were ready to believe anything about anyone once the word "terrorism" was mentioned. Terrorism was too frightening, too inhuman. The utter breakdown of civilization.

Clare started up, causing water to cascade down her neck and into her collar.

"*Ça va, Madame?*"

"*Oui, oui, excusez-moi.*"

She lowered her head back down, leaving her neck lifted slightly so the assistant could wipe off the back of it.

Other than Niall, whose wake had been attended by family and friends, whose body had been checked by a coroner—so why *did* she continue to believe she saw him?—no one should have known about her trip to Dublin, or any of the rest of it. *You never saw me,* the man in the hotel had warned her—and she'd understood that idea to be mutual. Just as promised by Niall, the desk clerk hadn't requested her passport. She'd paid in cash. No one who knew her had ever seen her alone with Niall, including her family. No one knew they'd become more than polite if somewhat distant housemates for two months of one summer. Even when she'd driven him up and down the Eastern corridor, she'd always stayed in the car, stayed on the beach, stayed in the motel room, stayed away from being seen with him. She could count the number of people who would have seen them alone together— a luncheonette waitress, a motel cleaning lady, a tollbooth collector. People who wouldn't remember her or Niall more than two decades later. She and Niall had been two amongst the thousands of holiday-making lovers they'd poured coffee to, straightened the sheets of, accepted dimes from. Even if they said they could remember her, they couldn't be considered credible witnesses. Twenty-plus years later? But *she* knew.

The pressure on her skull stopped. The assistant had removed her fingers from Clare's head. Clare opened her eyes and looked up.

"*Madame?*"

"*Oui?*"

"*J'ai dit: la temperature de l'eau? Ça va?*"

"*Excusez-moi. Oui, c'est parfait.*"

The water returned, bubbling along the perimeter of her hairline, the frontier of her high forehead. Instinctively, she re-shut her eyes. The hands returned. They slid down to the base of her neck and made their way back up again, kneading, pressing, stroking. Droplets dribbled over her temples, wet lapped her cheekbones. All this mess, all relating back to that moment more than two decades ago when she'd stepped out of the shower, water trickling down her back and over her breasts, and found him standing there. And if she'd cried out or grabbed a towel or turned away? If she had blushed, even? She'd said, "You—" And then she'd said nothing. She'd stood there, naked in front of him, water pooling down around her toes. She, the girl who disappeared into the private dressing room to change at the pool, who pulled her sweats and T-shirts on in a toilet stall by the gym lockers. A false breeze, maybe just the movement of his arms, had stirred the wet on her body, lifting away the oppressive heat of that summer, of her own body. He'd raised the towel in his hands and begun to dry her hair, while droplets streamed down her back.

Again and again, in her mind, over the decades, she'd revisited that moment. That delicious lifting of the heat. The delicious lifting of suspense, uncertainty, *attente.* The joy it had given her then. The horrible thrill it still gave her to remember despite herself.

"You're different from other girls in America." The evening air was viscous around them on her aunt's back porch in the Boston suburb; Clare felt it hugging her bare arms and legs like a wet bandage. Two weeks had passed since their weekend alone to-gether, and, for the first time since, she and Niall were the only ones in the house. It wasn't planned. Niall hadn't shown any deference towards her since that weekend—not a word, not a glance. He hadn't whispered a suggestion they meet someplace away from the house, nor hesitated when their paths had crossed under the eyes of her aunt and uncle. She understood he was pre-tending nothing had happened between them to save her from unnecessary trouble, because becoming a couple would cause a lot of talk amongst the family. From what she'd figured out, he was a cousin through her uncle, and it was Aunt Elaine who was her fa-ther's sister. They weren't blood related, therefore—but whether or not they were would hardly have mattered. She was a Radcliffe girl. Niall was a high-school dropout from a worn-down street in Derry. Worse, he was a "cause," she'd learned, for her aunt and uncle. *He's been getting himself into a mess over there,* Uncle Pat had said a few nights after Niall had arrived. *He'll be ending up under lock and key, just like his father before him,* before turning to flip a steak on the barbecue. *God knows how he even got the fare to come over. But you know how El can never turn them down.* He'd been talking to a friend, who'd nodded without asking for further explanation. She'd overheard, and understood the essential. Niall was never going to be a suitable match for her.

But even as she'd admired his discretion, another part of Clare had begun to worry he'd forgotten about lying in the heat after wrapping her in a towel, after putting his arms around her. He was young and handsome. He was confident. God only knew how many women he'd slept with. Was sleeping with currently, while visiting Boston.

Or was he showing no recognition of their intimacy because it was something he regretted? Could he be angry because of what she'd said about the English in Northern Ireland? Or had she been disappointing without her clothes on?

In front of the others, he acted as though he'd love to have her if only he could. He made an open joke of it. "Why doesn't Clare have herself a man?" he'd remarked over a family breakfast several mornings after he'd rubbed her naked body down with a towel and spread her wet hair across her pillow beneath him. She was on her way to work, her blond braid spun up in a bun, a clean cotton dress buttoned up her long spine. He'd been missing the last few days—or maybe just a couple days, but every day without any acknowledgment from him since the weekend that they'd spent together seemed like a month—and she hadn't expected to find him amongst the others in her aunt's kitchen.

But there he'd been, leaning against one of the counters as though he'd been leaning against it all along, knocking back a mug of thick black coffee. Wearing his same worn-out old corduroys, which she now knew he wore without anything under them, and a sleeveless undershirt. She'd had to look away. He'd kept looking at her.

"Some Harvard bastard wearing a sports coat and driving a Mercedes," he'd said. "Don't they know how to ask a girl out there?"

"That's no way to talk," Uncle Pat had scolded him, coughing into his fist, a glint of smile appearing over his closed knuckles, checking over his shoulder that Aunt Elaine wasn't within listening distance.

Clare had poured her own cup of coffee and slipped onto a chair by the kitchen table, across from her cousin Kevin. "Pass me the milk and sugar?"

"Why? You like her yourself?" Kevin had pushed the sugar bowl and a carton of milk in her direction. He'd grinned at her and shoveled a spoonful of cornflakes into his mouth, leaving tiny flakes of cereal on his upper lip. She and Kevin had grown up side by side, just five months separating their birth dates. Until they were fifteen, she'd been taller than he. She could remember the first Thanksgiving they'd spent together when he'd shown signs of whiskers. It hadn't been that long ago. "Kind of sea level up top, isn't she?"

"Don't you think it's time you got your own place, Kevin?" Uncle Pat had said, whacking her cousin on the head. Her uncle had peered into the cereal box, crumpled it up, and thrown it in the garbage. "Help yourself to toast, Clare. Looks like your aunt made a loaf's worth this morning."

Clare had dutifully begun chewing on a piece of toast, dry, without jelly.

"Personally, I don't fancy the heifers," Niall had replied, eyeing her up and down as though she were *some* sort of livestock. "But Clare's too rich for my blood, cousin. I could never have myself a woman like that."

Kevin had pushed his empty bowl away. "You never know, Niall." He'd pronounced the name like it was a long Egyptian river. "Those Harvard girls have been known to go slumming. And all American girls are suckers for a foreign accent."

Clare had finished her toast, the last bits gripping her windpipe, and stood up. "Have a great day, everyone."

"And a lovely day to you, too, Clare," Niall had said, as though they'd just run into each other at the drugstore. As though she were a girl he'd been trying to pick up in a coffee shop. As though she could have been any nice-looking girl, anywhere.

But now they were alone together again, and he slithered in next to her where she was sitting on the porch soaking in the evening smells of grass and old-fashioned roses and rhododendron, a cool glass of ice tea at her feet, a copy of Pablo Neruda's recently published *Para nacer he nacido* idle on one knee, and slid a hand onto her warm thigh. He removed the book from its perch, placing it on the ground next to her drink, and picked up her hand. He turned it over and over again. He separated one finger out and ran it down his cheek and neck, over his chest.

"You're different from other girls in America," he said.

"I am?" Was she supposed to run her finger down over his body now? No longer manipulated by him, her finger seemed powerless to move on its own. She left it where he'd left it, on his collarbone, pressing against his white skin.

"You don't squeal. They're like baby pigs in the slaughterhouse, some of the girls here, the way they will be squealing all the time."

The image of a girl, screaming with pleasure beneath the weight of Niall's dense white body appeared before her eyes. But he was talking about how so many of the girls she knew, especially before she arrived at Radcliffe, responded to any new information. High-pitched. Loudly. She didn't like it either. She'd never been able to bring herself to follow suit.

"Did you grow up on a farm, Niall?"

"Why are you asking?"

"You seem to think a lot about livestock. Heifers. Piglets."

He laughed. "Come on. We'll have something for the thirst."

"There's beer in the fridge." She poked her feet into espadrilles. He was already over the stone wall and waiting by her little Ford Fiesta.

"No, not that."

She drove in the dusk until they saw a cavernous liquor store, cars tethered around the front of it like nurslings around the teats of a sow. But *she* wasn't like a squealing piglet any more than she was like a cow. She was *different.* She felt his compliment settle over her shoulders, around her nape, like a silken mantle that elevated her from all the others. He *liked* her impassivity. He liked her reserve and quiet. He liked all the things that were supposed to be stumbling blocks for her.

"Maybe you shouldn't let her spend all that time alone up in her room, drawing," Granny Fennelly had remarked to her parents when she was still in high school. "Get her to sign up for the school musical or something." And her father and mother had guffawed at the very thought of Clare performing in public. But Niall wasn't laughing at her.

"This will be the one," Niall said, tipping his head towards the package store before she could pass it. "Have you any money on you?"

Neither the thin cotton tank top nor the Indian wrap skirt she'd been wearing had pockets. She hadn't thought to fetch her wallet before climbing into the car. That meant she wouldn't have ID to buy the liquor either. She was legal, but only just; no one would sell alcohol to her without first checking. Niall would have to go in. No one would think to card him.

She shuffled through the hair clips and sunglasses on the dashboard, coming up with a few coins. "I—"

"Keep the engine runnin'."

There was a song on the radio she recognized from hearing it on the quad, and she tried to sing along as she waited, for distraction. But she didn't know the words, other than "Celll-e-brate," and she couldn't sing well anyway and was scared he'd hear her. Another song followed on its heels, which she also recognized but didn't know the words to either, other than something about "the border of Mexico." All memories of another world, the one on campus.

Before the song could end, he had slipped back into the car. She shifted into gear and pulled out of the parking lot. He waited a few blocks before removing the half-pint of Jameson from his shirt front. He took a plug and put the top back on without offering her a sip. Instead, he settled into his seat and studied her profile.

"If you don't have your wallet on you, you don't have your driving permit on you, now, do you?" She shook her head, and he clicked his tongue. "Isn't that illegal in the States, driving without your permit on your person?"

They drove another block in silence.

He screwed up his mouth, made a little popping sound. "That's how people get caught, Clare. They don't pay attention to the wee things. They get tripped up on something ejeet."

"If I'd known what you wanted, I could have told you. Uncle Pat has Irish whiskey back at the house." Her words came out so soft that she herself could barely hear them.

He heard her, though. He clicked his tongue again. "Can't stroke my own uncle."

He studied her a moment longer, then nodded, as though he'd made up his mind about something. She felt his hand take hold of her thigh. Heat spread through her leg, into her groin, through her abdomen, and she had to focus her energies on not pressing down on the accelerator pedal. Or letting it go altogether.

"But you're all right," he said. "Why don't we go to the left up there? To the forest."

His hand gripped her thigh. The liquor store had been a test. And she had passed it. He'd taken a risk for her because he'd wanted to know whether he could trust her. Heat rushed through her arms down to her fingers, up her neck into her cheeks, burning away the swelter of the evening. She put on her turn signal and rotated the steering wheel.

"Lovely quiet here," he said.

He snapped off the car radio, even before she cut the engine. The evening was silent in the state park, so silent she imagined she could hear the trees breathing. She dropped her eyes down on his bare forearms. For the first time, she noticed that his pale skin was freckled.

*"Voilà,"* the assistant said, as though she'd just finished explaining something to a child. *"J'ai fait un bon conditioning aussi."* She wrapped a towel around Clare's shoulders and, with a solicitous gesture, gestured towards Marco's hairdressing station.

Clare followed the assistant, one hand clasping the two ends of the fresh towel, the other her purse. There was noise, the sounds of pop music and hair dryers and people chatting. She slipped into a chair and set her purse down by her feet. She looked into the mirror.

"Come on."

The car doors made a click as they opened. They walked single file, he in front, until they reached a gentle clearing, off the forest road but within sight of the car. He settled down amongst the grass and pine needles and drank from the bottle. She sank down beside him. He offered her the bottle, and she shook her head. He put an arm around her and pulled her onto her back. They lay there, under the pines and oaks and maples and dying elms, their uppermost branches scattered with yellow leaves that gleamed in the moonlight, in silence except for the sound made by the bottle when he tipped it backwards.

"You like it here," he said, more an acknowledgment than a question.

"Yes."

"You're always sittin' in the garden, or puttin' flowers on the table."

He placed a hand on her hip, and she felt as though they were carbon copies, side by side, their breath rising and falling together.

"You ever have the feeling there's something you fancy saying, but no with words?"

That was exactly how she felt, had felt, almost every day of her life.

In that pale light, she fell asleep. She woke at dawn, startled by a shaft of sunlight breaking through the tree boughs. He was already awake, staring up at the tip of morning. He got up and kicked the empty bottle of Jameson into the brush with the toe of his boot. Before following him back down the path, she stooped to retrieve it.

She only meant to keep him from littering, but it took her a long time to part with the bottle. After they got back to the house, he disappearing into his bedroom to sleep through the rest of the morning, she went into her bathroom and rinsed it out. Once everyone else in the house had gotten up, she filled the bottle with wildflowers and set it on her little bedside table. The bottle stayed there through the rest of her stay at her aunt and uncle's. It followed her to her new room in Cambridge. Until the day she returned from Dublin.

*　　　*　　　*

*"Café? Un jus d'orange?"* The assistant laid a new dry towel around her shoulders and pinned it together with a large silver hair clip.

*"Oui, merci. Un café."*

Marco appeared, armed with a comb in his right hand and an enormous blow dryer in the other. He was a terse man, a quality Clare appreciated in a hairdresser. With Marco, she didn't feel required to make conversation over the roar of a hair dryer. That alone was enough to make her a loyal customer.

They exchanged a few civilities, always in French, as he ran through her hair with the comb.

*"Les enfants vont bien?"* he asked.

*"Oui, très bien. Il fait beau aujourd'hui, n'est-ce pas?"*

He nodded. *"Il va faire chaud en juin."*

When her hair was smooth, parted, and combed forward towards her brow, the conversation stopped. He dropped the comb into a net and enveloped her head in a cloud of hair spray. From an array of hair utensils, he selected a long and thin round brush and switched on the blow-dryer, applying all his attention now to the task of making her hair flip back from her face.

The assistant returned with her coffee, and Marco waited, blow-dryer in hand, like a gun cocked and ready to go, while she took a sip. She laid the cup back down on its saucer. Black coffee, cola, and beer. That summer, she'd watched Niall gulp down gallons of all three. But, though she kept the empty bottle from that night by her bedside, she never again saw him drink Irish whiskey. The next time she could remember seeing anyone drinking Jameson whiskey was the first time she met Edward, three years after Niall's disappearance, three years since another man had managed to arrest her attention.

*     *     *

The man from the British Consulate—"Hello, my name is Edward Moorhouse," extending a hand in her direction when she'd walked into the restaurant—waited for her to pick up her ginger ale. His fingers were smooth and full on his glass of whiskey, and one bore a heavy gold ring embossed with a crest. Niall would have spat at such a ring, but she'd promised herself not to think about what Niall would think ever.

"Ireland," the man said to her father, "gives us so much that is lovely. Even the names." He took a sip, placed the glass back down on the pale damask tablecloth, and smiled at her. "May I ask whether you have a second name, Clare?"

"Clare Siobhan," she said blandly. It was on the tip of her tongue to add: "But I'm American, not Irish." But she didn't.

"Clare Siobhan," he'd repeated after her, thoughtfully.

"Clare Siobhan Fennelly," her father said, with a bit of a lilt and smiling at her. She smiled back at him. She was home visiting for a long weekend, and he'd asked her to join them for lunch straightaway when he'd picked her up at the Hartford train station the evening before: "Kennedy and I are going to the Coach House tomorrow with some British guy, Edward Moorhouse, up from Washington, like you. It's bound to be a bit dull but the food's good." She'd agreed, mostly because she didn't know how not to without displeasing her father. At least if the guy was British, no one would be trying to fix her up with him—she was growing weary of her parents' not especially subtle efforts to find her a husband, or at least a boyfriend. "Are you sure?" her mother had asked when she'd called to say she had Thursday and Friday free and would come up to Connecticut. "Isn't there anyone down in Washington you'd like to spend your days off with?"

How could she explain that, no, there was no one she wanted to spend her days and especially her nights with, how the idea of being with another man had come to seem ridiculous to her after Niall? They knew nothing of her and Niall.

"This man Moorhouse wants to talk to us about investing in Northern Ireland," her father had continued as they'd driven along the familiar streets home from the station. Barry Kennedy and her dad were on the board of a company with considerable interests in both London and Edinburgh. "That's what he does, goes around the States trying to get U.S. companies to invest, despite the MacBride Principles. You know the MacBride Principles?" Clare had shaken her head, although she had heard talk of them, so her father had explained how a movement towards legislation was growing, newly backed by the Nobel Peace Prize winner Sean MacBride, to discourage U.S. companies from investing in Northern Ireland on the basis that employment policies there were prejudiced against Catholics. She'd listened with half an ear, never wanting to hear a word again about the Troubles and having understood the essential: she was definitely safe from any awkward attempts at matchmaking. No way would her dad be hoping to fix her up with this guy. Not if this Mr. Moorhouse was trying to convince them to invest in British interests in Northern Ireland.

Still, when she'd seen the visitor from the British embassy waiting for them in the Coach House restaurant in his well-buffed black shoes, she couldn't help but feel bad for him; he looked so decent. A nice-looking man in a smooth, well-kept way, tall, solidly built, and fair, with calm, thoughtful eyes. A part of her wanted to warn him. She knew full well how her father and Kennedy were going to respond to any overtures regarding investment in Northern Ireland. Clare's father was as strong a believer in Ireland for the Irish as the next Irish-American, even if he professed to oppose the current Provisional I.R.A.'s more radical methods. She wouldn't want to ask where Kennedy stood on the subject.

"Jamesons all around! Straight up." Kennedy ordered three Irish whiskeys for the men without asking anyone's opinion. Kennedy's maternal grandfather, James O'Malley, fresh in Boston from County Cork at the turn of the century, had been a well-known pugilist. Clare had often heard her parents remark on how closely Kennedy had inherited his temperament. "How about you, Clare? What will you have? A nice Guinness?"

Edward Moorhouse waited while she ordered a glass of soda. Then he said to the waiter, "I'll have my whiskey on the rocks, thank you."

She bowed her head, waiting for Kennedy to spew forth reproach at this despoilment of good whiskey, but the Brit continued right along, in that even, elegant voice of his, giving no one the chance to get a word in: "I read a fascinating article about the Connecticut River on my way up here. It said that there were three kinds of trout living in the river, and that Atlantic salmon is currently being reintroduced. I've had the pleasure of seeing a bit of America over the past few months of being posted here, and it's rewarding to read so often about such efforts to reclaim your land back from post–Industrial Age pollution. You have an extraordinarily beautiful country."

Clare watched her father and Kennedy rendered wordless, unsure whether they were being complimented for having a handsome country or insulted for having allowed it to become polluted. In the confusion, the sacrilege of spoiling good whiskey with ice was forgotten.

My, she thought, this Edward Moorhouse is good. And she'd

taken him for a pushover. Normally she would walk a mile out of her way to avoid being party to conflict, but something in her awakened. She sat up straighter.

More thorough introductions followed. Her father took care of hers, pointing out that Edward and Clare both lived in Washington. She waited for Edward to inquire which neighborhood, but "Washington, D.C., is a beautiful city, Miss Fennelly" was all he said.

"We go by first names here," Kennedy cut in, "here" meaning in America rather than in formal, stuffy, elitist Great Britain, though almost everyone referred to Kennedy himself by his last name and he almost always referred to himself in the same way. On the telephone: "Kennedy here."

"Clare's just begun work as a language specialist," her father said.

"Museum guide," Kennedy interjected.

"And translator," her father said. "She doesn't want to do anything governmental, though. Art. She likes art."

Edward looked back and forth between her dad and Kennedy. When they were finished discussing her as though she wasn't there, he turned to her. "May I ask which languages?"

"French, Spanish, and Italian. She does all of them. And English, of course," her father said.

"And English?" Edward repeated, still smiling at her.

Somehow, she understood he wasn't making fun of her humble accomplishments, nor of her father's exaggerated pride in them, but, rather, he was complimenting her. She waited for him to add some remark about how unusual it was for Americans to speak so many foreign languages. He didn't.

She smiled back despite herself and found herself speaking up for a change. "Especially English."

"So, how long you been down in Washington?" Kennedy asked Edward, propelling the discussion towards Edward's work for the British Diplomatic Service. He let Edward speak for a while before interrupting.

"Don't you feel like an asshole going around asking people to pony up for the British in Ireland?" Kennedy plopped down his glass, splashing whiskey up onto his fingers. Clare hoped against hope he wouldn't lick them. Something about this Englishman made her want not just to sit up but to make the world around her sit straight, too. The way that he managed to create a sense of calm and civility around himself was almost hypnotic. She wanted him to respect them. She wanted him to notice her.

"No." Edward looked as tranquil as the potted fern hanging from the ceiling above them. "Because I'm not. I'm asking people to pony up for the British in *Great Britain.*"

The table fell silent.

Faced with their visitor's unruffled reasoning, and his nerve presenting it before such an obviously hostile audience, even Kennedy seemed unable to muster up an immediate counterattack. He rubbed his fingers on his napkin. "Yeah, well, not everyone would agree with that," he said finally, but too late. His retort fell over their lunch in a thousand fluttery pieces, like wisps of ash floating out from a fireplace.

Clare's dad glared into his glass. She returned to wishing she hadn't agreed to join them. "They do great steaks there," her father had said the previous evening, his face intermittently illuminated by the fluorescent street lamps they were passing. "And it'll give us a little extra time together." She knew better now. She'd been invited as a buffer, to keep Kennedy decent and her father polite. Her father hated controversy as much as she did, almost as much as he was loyal to the idea of a united Ireland, and he was old school—he thought it unseemly to argue in front of women or children. He'd never lose his temper with a guest in front of her. Especially not in front of her. Since childhood, her family had prodded her for her reserve, for her coolness, but they knew when it could be useful.

But this Brit didn't require a human shield. "I'll wager the Irish don't need anyone's help," Edward continued, passing right over Kennedy's comment and looking at her father. "Astonishing people, the Irish. The culture, what a gift. The Irish War was a setback for them, in terms of economic development. No doubt about it, they've had a lot of setbacks to contend with. It's interesting to ponder what might have happened to them had they had a different history. But mark my words, they're going to claim their place in the global economy within the next two decades. The rest of Europe is going to be on their knees to them."

Of course, he was only talking about the five-sixths of the island that comprised the Republic of Ireland. Well schooled by Niall in the wiles of the British, Clare understood this. But the hazy reference worked to soothe her father and Kennedy. To their ears, Edward was as good as admitting the British had mucked up Ireland's history. She certainly wasn't going to clarify the Brit's meaning.

"Bastard's job he's got, but he still was an awfully nice guy," she heard her father telling her mother that evening. "Suppose it's not his fault. Suppose they have to take whatever's assigned them."

"You say he lives in Washington?" her mother had asked.

To her, the following morning: "So, Clare, what did you think of your father's visitor?"

The growl of the blow-dryer stopped, tumbling Clare back into the present. Marco laid the dryer down on the counter and prodded her hairline experimentally. A strand fell loose, tickling her nose and forehead. He frowned, tucked the hair back towards her blond crown and released a fine mist of hair spray.

"With summer on its way, shall we up the highlights next time you come in?" he asked.

In a sense, Edward had stopped aiming for making a name in the Middle East and begun working on getting the ambassadorship in Dublin from that very moment they met. By the end of this summer, more than two decades later, he might finally have it. The children would come home to Paris for the last time this June; the following summer, "home" would mean Dublin or wherever they were next posted. Or "home" would, finally, once and for all, mean nothing for them, as they'd be too old and too far away, particularly if Edward landed someplace to which the boys had no connection and had never lived.

"I'm not ready to think about summer yet," she told Marco. "It's so pleasant, springtime in Paris. I just want to think about today and tomorrow."

"Of course," Marco agreed, giving a last twist to her hair.

She could see the embassy's car pull up outside, a dark shape like the shadow of a sand shark beneath a dock. Her driver was back, waiting. Marco held up a hand mirror so she could see the back of her hair, and she nodded her approval and thanked him. At the reception desk of the salon, she tapped in the code for her bank card and reinserted her earrings. In her purse still was the USB stick containing her translation. Looking at it, she thought, I need to step out of this day for a moment.

She dropped her wallet back into the bag and fished the stick out, slipping it into her pocket. She checked her watch. 5:02 p.m. She was back on schedule. She would steal a few moments to visit the publication office at the Rodin Museum.

# ELEVEN

The driver whipped them around the Place de la Concorde. From the backseat, she watched a throng of cars in all shapes and sizes join them into the centrifugal force exuded by the traffic circle, pulling them in too close to one another, then flinging them out along the Rue Royale or the Champs Elysées or, in their own case, the Voie Georges Pompidou. This was where Louis XVI and, shortly after, Marie Antoinette lost their heads, when the Place trembled not from the weight of small speeding cars but the ill-shod feet of angry republicans. Clare rubbed her neck. The guillotine wasn't supposed to be painful. But still.

They were out now, over the Seine, on the Pont Alexandre III, heading for Place des Invalides. The sudden sense of space here was uncanny, the monumentality of Paris at its most extreme. Cupids frolicking in the buff, horses with gilt wings thrust into the Parisian firmament. A *bateau mouche* appeared from under the bridge, making its way down the Seine like softened butter being spread on bread, tiny ripples following its wake.

*"Je descends devant la Musée Rodin, s'il vous plaît,"* she told the

driver. The entrance to the Rodin Museum was literally steps from the Residence. She shouldn't lose more than fifteen minutes by stopping there to drop off the translation. As soon as she'd left the hairdresser's, she'd called Amélie; everything was going according to schedule at the Residence.

The car zoomed towards the face of the Invalides and zigzagged, left, then right, then left again, onto the Rue de Varenne. The driver pulled up in front of the museum. *"Merci,"* she told him, looking around this time before stepping out into the open to see who might be on the street. Just a steady trickle of office workers coming out at the end of their workdays and a few tourists wearing fleece jackets. She shut the car door behind her.

The French Ministry of Culture had recently redone the museum entrance. She missed the shabby old entry as it used to be: a crumbling stone cubbyhole that spilled out directly into the gardens, manned by a makeshift wooden ticket booth. The magical instant of stepping through an unprepossessing break in the old stone wall surrounding the property to find oneself amidst eighteenth-century splendor. The monolithic new entrance, incorporated into a nineteenth-century chapel, looked modern in a faux-Egyptian way, a smooth, slick style that had become only recently popular amongst museums. It made her feel old. The museum entrances she'd floated through as a student trying out her nascent French, Italian, and Spanish skills on the European continent had been completely different.

The ticket seller who always wore a dark-colored turtleneck, no matter the weather, was stationed at the first cash register. He raised an eyebrow at her.

*"Bonjour—"* she began.

*"C'est dix-sept heures seize,"* he said and pointed to the clock on his cash register. *"Dernière entrée à dix-sept heures quinze."*

5:16 p.m. Last entrance was at quarter past five.

"Thank you," she responded in French. "But I am not here for the museum today. I am here for *le service culturel.*"

By now, back at the Residence, the flowers had been delivered, which Amélie would have put around in their vases. No more deliveries expected. No more surprises. Just her clothes to change, and the dinner preparations to be finished. Mathilde was giving the dinner roll dough its second pounding. Amélie's cousin had arrived, and she and Amélie were peeling potatoes to soak in cold, salted water.

She waited as the ticket seller called the museum's publication office.

*"Personne ne répond."* He set his phone back down and pointed again to the cash register's clock.

Everyone in the office had left for home already. At least— closing up the files on their desks, the files on their computers, smoothing their skirts, sealing the envelopes of their day's correspondence—they weren't answering phone calls. Delivering the translation would have to wait after all. Not a big deal, as Sylvie wasn't expecting it until after the weekend now. Certainly not worth arguing over with the ticket seller.

She couldn't bring herself to move away, however. The light shining into the entryway from the gardens was mesmerizing. All that rain, finally stopped, had brought flowers, and the air was full of their perfume. How glorious the museum gardens must have been all day under the bright sky, with the light breeze of spring rippling through them. With all that had happened since, she'd almost forgotten the morning sunlight slanting into the apartment, the fragrance of blossoms wafting in through the Residence's open windows, the thrill of a rain-free day in springtime. The wild wisteria brightening the Residence's courtyard.

The gardens stayed open later than the museum. Just five minutes—the time she would have spent delivering the translation. Just one quick turn, to see whether the wild cherry trees were in bloom yet. With all the rain and drizzle Paris had had, weeks had passed since the last time she'd so much as walked through the gardens.

A desire as deep as breath came over her. She had to go in.

*"C'est pas grave,"* she told the ticket seller. *"Merci et bonne journée."*

Instead of turning back out the entrance, she searched inside her wallet for her membership pass and flashed it at the guard by the door.

The pale monumental facade of the Hôtel Biron, the chief museum building, stood directly ahead, a maze of symmetrical rose gardens and clipped box trees fanning out in front of it. She passed before them without giving the building a second thought and headed for the main part of the garden, on the sunny southern side. She barely paused before the Gates of Hell, flanking the property's eastern wall, all those agonized bodies in various aspects of contortion, the heat of their deep bronze reflecting back at her. There was Eve, her plump arms hugging her curvy torso, her head bowed. The catalog Clare had most recently worked on suggested that the model for the statue had been in the early stages of pregnancy and had found Rodin's studio too chilly. And, yes, even in the spring sun, she looked uncomfortable.

Clare continued around the building into the garden's large southern end. Deep chartreuse leaf buds were already coursing across the trunks and branches of the linden trees. Jaunty yellow daffodils waved their strange snouts in the afternoon breeze amidst the bright blue bells of grape hyacinths. Along the garden's central alley, people stood or strolled chatting, talking on cell phones, ogling the bronze sculptures strewn here and there amongst the growth. An elderly trio nodded to her.

She stopped by the Grove of Orpheus. It seemed barren, still bereft of the lavish greenery of summer, the box trees cut low and round, the lilacs not yet in bloom. Only the bare stems and a few random sprouts of medicinal plants poked through the grove's rockery. The muscular torso of Orpheus, stretching his lyre up towards the sky, looked all the more doomed for the lack of leaves and flowers as buoys. Written by his feet: *Toi qui entre ici abandonne toute espérance*—"All hope abandon ye who enter here"— lifted from the entrance to Hell in Dante. Doubt had destroyed Orpheus and condemned his wife to return forever to the underworld, but also greed. He had wanted too much, too badly. He'd tried to insist that the pleasures of love last forever.

She continued south along the garden's central alley until she reached the path that led east to the section known as the Woods, which would take her on a loop back towards the museum entrance. Here, chestnut trees replaced the linden, perhaps the same ones whose fragrance had filled the Rue de Varenne as she'd walked along it to buy flowers and had wafted into the Residence's study when she'd opened its windows this morning. She breathed in deeply.

There, between the trees, was the huge bent torso of Andrieu d'Andres, the one of the six burghers of Calais doomed to be known through history, thanks to Rodin, not for his act of extreme bravery but for the distress he felt over his act of self-sacrifice. She moved towards the statue, as she always did when she reached this part of the garden. The college professor from whom she'd first heard the story of the Calais burghers had been a square-headed Italian who had somehow ended up teaching French history. His face had always been faintly red, and he'd worn a moustache that bobbed when he spoke. She could see it now, responding to seminar discussion with a little bounce, as she and the other Harvard and Radcliffe undergrads tried to make sense of self-sacrifice in another era. During the Hundred Years' War, in the mid-fourteenth century, King Edward III of England had laid siege to the northern French town of Calais. After eleven months, with the town's food and water supplies depleted, six of the town's most illustrious citizens agreed to offer themselves up as ransom to the king in return for his freeing their city and its people. The six burghers presented themselves on the appointed morning, divested of their rich robes, before the city gates, and the king proceeded to call his executioner. He was swayed at only the last minute by his pregnant wife, Philippa; she decided that the burghers' slaughter would be a bad portent for her unborn baby.

Most of the other students in her seminar had found the men's surprise release a letdown. Over the same semester, the class had been through the Norman Conquest and the slaughter of the Cathars. They'd come to expect tales of immolation and beheading. One girl went so far as to suggest that the Burghers' escape lessened the bravery of their action.

Clare had laughed along with the seminar group's increasingly boorish discussion, although secretly she'd found the burghers' unexpected survival all the more proof of their patriotism; to her, the arbitrariness of their deliverance served to underscore its unlikelihood. When she'd begun translating museum and art exhibition catalogs and seen Rodin's famous depiction of the burghers' arrival at the city gates, she'd realized just how foolish she and her classmates must have looked to their professor, the boys in their hardy rugby shirts and the girls in their neat Fair Isle sweaters, sitting around an oak-paneled study hall discussing sacrifice. Since moving into the minister's residence, she'd returned to their tortured hypercorporeal figures in the gardens of the Rodin Museum over and over. A full rendition of the sculpture—as Rodin, under commission for the city of Calais, had designed it to be displayed, all six burghers clustered together, of equal height, of equal stature—stood farther on in the Rodin Museum gardens, closer to the entrance. Individual casts of each burgher were strewn amidst the lindens and chestnuts and peonies. The most exalted, Eustache de Saint-Pierre, the burgher who had agreed first to surrender his life for the good of his city, stood square in the middle, looking grave but determined, a beacon for French pride. But the figure that magnetized her was that of poor Andrieu. Rodin had buried Andrieu's bronze face in enormous tinny hands, bent his dark gleaming neck with mortal sorrow; he had chosen Andrieu to represent a different side of self-sacrifice. One she thought might be more realistic. Sorrow. The quiet half-hidden bench beside him was her favorite place in the garden to sit and think.

The young grass felt soft under her loafers. The afternoon sun danced on Andrieu's dipped head and flirted with his agonized metallic fingers. She reached out to touch them.

He was there. On the bench, sheltered by a giant holly, its leaves dark and razor-sharp.

Her hand fell on the statue's hand. Her wedding ring made a ping against the bronze, into the stillness. This time he was no mirage, no fleeting vision. He was as real as the iron bench beneath him.

"You...," she said, just as she'd said so many years ago. Her voice trailed off.

The fading sun, as hot-cold on her neck as the way he was looking at her.

"How about ye?" he said.

The ticking of her watch, the ticking of the day as it passed, of the years that had passed.

*"Niall."*

He slid a few inches to his right, leaving a space for her on the bench.

She sat down.

He did not move to take her hand. She did not offer it. But she felt as though he'd slipped his whole body around her, not just an arm over her shoulder or a cheek next to her cheek. It was summer again, and she felt the heat of him.

"Poor bastard," he said. "Known forever as the one who choked at dying for his people."

How strangely familiar his voice was, still low and almost rumbling, still that distinct rhythm that rolled along, then lifted at the end of a sentence. "There was a lot of controversy over that figure," she finally said. "A real uproar. The city of Calais thought like you. They thought it wasn't respectful."

"You're not of the same mind."

She shook her head. "Andrieu wasn't a coward: he offered his life up willingly, no one forced him. He simply was human. He wept over the impending loss of it."

Niall leaned back into the bench and breathed the air. He surveyed her profile. "You've become a talker, Clare."

"No," she said. She viewed him from the sides of her eyes. "Eloquent."

Niall laughed. *"Touché."*

"You've become French-speaking."

He laughed again. "You always were a clever one. Quiet but clever. That's what first took me about you. That and..."

They both looked at her hands. They were so thin, so fine, and the rings Edward had given her sparkled. She clasped her fingers together on her lap, covering the diamonds. "Where have you been, Niall? You're supposed to be dead."

Niall closed his eyes. She could see the exhaustion in the skin around them. He looked the same but different, no longer old for his age but timeless, his body still lean, but the black of his now-cropped short hair flecked with gray. He was wearing a dark blue cotton sweater, boots, and faded blue jeans. Clare felt an unsolicited stirring in her own body. When he reopened his lids, his eyes were just the same as they'd always been: penetrating.

"You could say I *am* dead. You as good as killed me. But, Mother of God have mercy on me, I'm not here to ask you why you did what you did. I'm not here to give out to you. I just want my life back."

A sparrow flew to their feet, pecked around, and left. She searched his face for an explanation. Probably she would not have the life she had today, would never even have married Edward, if she hadn't first known Niall. She would have become a secondary school language teacher at a good private academy or maybe worked for an international bank, sending her kids to do their First Communion, wearing a claddagh ring as a tribute to her heritage. She would have married a fellow Harvard grad or maybe one of the boys from her hometown in Connecticut. They would have gone to reunions together and remembered mutual classmates over beers and sweet cocktails with other alumni couples. Without Niall, she'd have done nothing, known nothing. He'd forced her to resurrect herself from the ashes of his betrayal. But what had she done to him? She'd meant nothing to him. He'd used her, and then he'd left her.

She looked at the hands, in her lap, that had first drawn him to her, the skin on them translucent. She'd looked at them this morning and seen the spidery veins of an aging woman. She'd looked at her face in the mirror and seen the years she'd spent without him.

"I don't understand," she said.

A ringing, a ridiculous sound: a clip from Mozart's *Eine Kleine Nachtmusik.* They both stared at her purse. She withdrew her BlackBerry and saw the name of the caller posted on the screen. *Edward.*

She squeezed the cell phone between her palms, as though the apparatus were a small wriggly rodent, unruly, foreign and un-manageable, until it stopped ringing. She turned the ringer off, lodged it back inside her purse, and closed the zipper.

"The money," he said. "I'm talking about the money."

She gathered her purse up and slid to the far end of the bench, turning sideways so that she could face him head-on. The sky was brighter, the afternoon later. She could hear all the birds. She could hear the breeze in the lindens.

"Are you planning to blackmail me? Is that why you've come back?"

The eyelids over his still-sharp blue eyes snapped open and shut like a spring-jointed door over a summer's day. He started to speak, then turned his face away, lifting a forearm by his face.

She heard the footsteps too and glanced over her shoulder: Two middle-aged women were strolling up the walkway from the Woods, arm in arm. They were happy. They were laughing. Clare looked back again at Niall. She watched the light in his eyes flicker over them, then relax. Crossing his arms over his chest, he turned his attention back to her.

"Blackmail you? After what I done for you? And how could I blackmail you, even if I were wanting? Think, Clare. We're in this together."

"I'm not in anything," she said.

He shrugged. "*Were* in this. As you like."

Another twosome approached, a mother pushing her baby in a stroller, talking on her phone. The museum was closing, the park was emptying.

Niall didn't flinch this time, but he waited until the woman and her child had passed before speaking again.

"Look, you don' have to worry about anyone ever knowing about you. I never told anyone, never will. If I had done, you'd be in the ground now yourself for what you did, wouldn't you? That's why I faked my own death, isn' it? I never even told anyone you were my woman."

Heat rushed over Clare, coloring her neck and prickling the roots of her hair. They'd lain together in damp sheets, their limbs heavy from the summer heat, and beside him her body had turned from that of a gangly girl's into a woman's. His pale skin, the tautness of his energy. The hollows they'd carved out of sand as they'd traveled up the coastline. His knee right now, right next to her. *Niall.* She'd looked up the meaning of his name in Widener Library: "passionate, from old Irish."

But he was *I.R.A.* Niall had never uttered the word, but he hadn't needed to. She had been a love-besotted stooge, ready to do whatever he asked, and asked he had, and then just as swiftly discarded her. Niall, explaining they were just helping regular people. Niall, taping those bills to her torso, still warm from his own hands. Niall, walking away from her in the airport, not even looking back.

"Who was it really for?" she said. She braced herself for the words she'd never heard, and had waited for, so many years. "That money?"

Niall took a cigarette out, tapped it. But he didn't light it.

"I understand it weren't your country. That's what they told me when they gave me the ticket to come over: The Americans, they like to think themselves more Irish than the Irish, but there you are, driving to the good jobs, dropping the kids off at the good schools. No one saying, Fuck off, you Fenian bastard, burning you out your own home, hammering you just for walking down the street. No bombs exploding before your eyes either. Easiest job they could have done me, collecting the funds from the Americans."

He put the cigarette back in the pack and looked at her with that fixed way she so remembered. "But you, Clare. You were different."

The bastard. She drew her leg away from his. "You said it was just to help ordinary people."

"It was."

"And the camper? The trip we made to Maryland?"

Niall sighed. "Come on, Clare. It was a war. And we were fighting the only way we could. What were we supposed to defend ourselves with? Sticks and stones? I wish it could have been different, but I done what I done and I don't regret a second. It was for the freedom of the Irish people—it was *worth* fighting for."

"Worth innocent bloodshed? People died, Niall. *Ordinary* people."

"*We* died."

"Not just you."

Niall shrugged. "You don't really understand how it was. We didn't even have a bath in our home when I was a lad. A lad like me: either you were one of them or you died fighting. But I didn't come here to debate you. Think what you like. I'm done. I just want the money."

"What money?"

"I know you didn't keep it so you could spend it yourself. You hid it somewhere, didn't you?"

"Honestly, Niall. I don't know what you are talking about."

"The money. That money."

"*That* money?"

"*That* money."

"Niall, I don't have that money. You know that. I gave it to the man in Dublin just like you told me to do."

Here he had to come back and sit next to her in the gardens, wearing that blue sweater and with those same piercing pale eyes, his rolling voice like swells on the sea, talking about the Troubles, talking about his peoples' struggles, sucking her back more than two decades into a life she'd so carefully set behind her, and she'd gone and said it. If he was wearing a wire? Maybe he had come clean with the British government and made a plea bargain with them by handing her over. Would Edward be able to hire someone who could get her out of this? Would he *want* to?

Niall frowned. "You gave it to the man?"

He looked, if possible, more confused than she was. He wasn't wearing a wire, and Interpol wasn't waiting in a van on the street.

She tipped her head yes.

"Are you taking the piss out of me, Clare?"

A breeze brushed through the holly, causing ragged shadows to flash across his face.

She wanted to ask him the same thing. Instead she said, "No. I did what you asked. And then I waited for you. You never came." She'd come out with it; there was no turning back. "Why didn't you?"

"To St. Stephen's Green? After?"

"I waited."

"When you didn't show up with the money, I thought maybe

you'd done a runner. But how could you've done, you with a life like you had? So my next thought was, maybe she's gone to the Brits."

There must be some explanation, some code. But whatever it was, she couldn't break it. "But, I *did* show up with the money. I'm telling you, I gave it to him just like you told me."

He held her wrist fast. His skin was dry and heated, just as she remembered it. "I'm not playing games here. I've been hiding for my whole man's life now. My cousin said it was me in that casket, he the only one who knew it was really Sean O'Faolain, what was drowned and my cousin fished him out. Sean O'Faolain lying under a gravestone with my name on it, and everyone thinking he's the one disappeared and not me. The poor bastard, he looked so bad no one could tell the difference. I've been a dead man in the county records for twenty years since.

"Do you understand, Clare? I don't exist either in life or in death. You erased me."

Niall was still Niall, resolute, enigmatic, a battered but unfaltering church along the windswept shore, but now she was the one holding the door open, and from inside she heard the echo of weeping. She wanted to slam it shut. She wanted him to stay as she remembered, the stone she couldn't overturn, the fire she couldn't douse. She wanted him to stay the Niall he was in her memory. She wanted him to stay only in her memory.

She shook her wrist free from him. Still she couldn't bring herself to stand up.

"But I don' think you went to the Brits with it," he continued, trying to hold her not by force anymore but by watching her face closely. "They'd have got my name out of you whether you'd wanted to give it or not, the bastards. I would have heard about it, even as a dead man. So, what, then? What did you do with it?"

His eyes were trained on hers, completely serious. He wasn't talking in code. He meant exactly what he was asking.

"I gave it to him," she said softly. "I swear. I did just what you said." She saw it all. The airport. The taxi ride. The miserable house that had been the wrong color. The number beside the bell. "Eighty-three Portobello Road. Just like you said. He followed me right up. He came almost immediately. I gave it all to him. And then I waited."

And now she waited again. Niall said nothing. Shadows emerged from his sharp eyes, lassoed her, dissipated into the late spring afternoon. He breathed in and out slowly. He stretched his arms out across the back of the bench, and leaned his head back against it.

"Eighty-three Portobello Road? You gave it to a man there?"

"Yes. I did."

"Clare," he said. "The address I gave you was *thirty-eight* Portobello Road. You would have gave the money to a pimp. *Eighty-three* Portobello was a whorehouse. Everyone come down to Dublin knew it."

# TWELVE

A door through time dropped open beneath her, and she was falling weightless, into the past. Twenty-five years of fear and guilt, accompanying each step she put forward in life, evaporated. The ecstasy, the lightness of burden she felt, were indescribable. Replaced with something else, a strange new blend of joy and release mixed with guilt and compunction. This was the miracle she couldn't have hoped would happen. The miracle she didn't deserve. She had never helped kill anyone. She'd just helped a pimp get richer than he'd ever dreamt possible. A part of her wanted to laugh and laugh and laugh. She wanted to stretch out on her back in the budding grass and laugh until she cried, sending her howls of laughter up to the gathering evening above her. Laugh at her newfound freedom; laugh at the ridiculousness of how she'd earned it.

But seeing the expression on Niall's face, she couldn't laugh. He had trusted her, and she'd ruined him.

"I—"

Niall got up. He walked around back of the statue of Andrieu,

and for a few moments, she wondered whether he might just continue walking.

"Niall—"

She heard him sigh. He came back around and sat down again
beside her. She searched his face for anger, tears, anything, but
his expression was impassable. "I combed the streets of Dublin.
And I started thinking: could she have scared? But I saw you
on the plane coming from Boston, I saw you still had the big
stomach. I knew you must have brought it. So, I walked around,
asking myself: what could she have done with it? I even went
down to Dublin ferry, thinking you might have taken the boat to
England. I asked myself: how far could have she gone, this American girl? How far would she go in betraying me?"

He stopped, as though expecting not her but history to answer
the question. It had. Her imperfectness had betrayed him, completely.

"If you'd have gone to the Brits," he continued, "if they knew
about me and found me, they'd've put me away at least ten years,
maybe twenty. I couldn't tell my own either. Ne'er mind me.
Someone would have found you and killed you. So I walked the
streets of Dublin, walked them up and down, all the time asking
myself which would be worse: the Brits or my own. It was like a
song in my head, drumming over and over. I went out to the airport the day you were to go home and watched as every passenger
boarded, waited until the plane was but a tiny speck in the sky,
disappearin' over the water.

"Can you imagine," he said, "what that bastard would be
thinking, you unloading all those dollars on him? Must have been
one happy fuck."

"Niall—" she started again.

He shook his head and stared at Andrieu's feet. In a life of nothing but bad news, this still was a wild blow. She couldn't think of one single thing to say. They sat in silence until he looked up at her. He shrugged and released a short laugh. "Ha."

"I was not so smart as you thought," she said.

He shook his head again. "Fuck. I got what I asked for, didn't I? The whole thing was daft. The whole plan. I was just a lad, you know. It weren't as though I was the most experienced Volunteer. Throwing rocks about all I'd done before they sent me over. That's *why* they sent me."

"I'd thought you were older than anyone I'd ever known."

"So I was pretending. But I wasn't, or I would have known better than to mix up a woman and a mission. And my own woman at that. Feck, you got me goin', did'n' you?"

Her chest ached. From regret, from relief, she wasn't sure why. She crossed her arms again over it. "Look, Niall. The thing is. You—we—didn't kill anybody. I mean weren't involved in anyone's dying. That's what this means. Think about it."

He shrugged and hung his head. "Yeah, maybe. Except for myself. You just don' understand. I was a soldier. Killing's not a sin when you're a soldier."

"Maybe not—but not everyone who died in your war was also a soldier."

"Eh—" Niall started to speak, then stopped as the elderly trio whose path she'd crossed earlier in the main path of the garden came walking past. He lowered his head again, lifting one hand to screen it.

She turned from their vision also, feeling for a moment what Niall had doubtless felt every waking moment for the last quarter century.

"I have seen you, haven't I?" she said once the walkers had passed out of view.

"You're always surrounded by people. Even all the police on your street know you, so. And I didn't know if you were with them now. So, for a long time, I just watched you. Sometimes with the papers, the Internet, sometimes for myself."

She *had* seen him, not in Cairo, never when she was living in America. Visa issues would have made that impossible. But in England maybe, definitely in Paris. Maybe not outside the hairdresser's, but this morning. He'd withdrawn into the obscurity of dusk and denial, unsure how or whether to let her know he was amongst the living. But he hadn't been able to tear himself completely away.

Not, at least, from the trail of the money. He himself must have had hardly a penny.

"How did you live?"

"I got my ownself over to England on a boat and picked up work, shoveling rock or pushing sand. Day work you didn't need a past for. When some other Nor'n Irish come along, I'd move on. Before he could start asking the questions."

He didn't give any specifics, and she didn't ask.

"I saw when you got married," he continued. "It was written up in the English papers. I saw too whose name you took. Servant of the British crown. That's when I started feeling sure you must have done it for a reason. I took myself as far away as I could with no passport and no money to have a good one made, for a long time then. I'd seen you drawing. I knew you could do my likeness."

"I didn't betray you," she said. "I'd never have done that. Not on purpose. Ed—my husband has had nothing to do with it. I never told him."

Had he followed Edward as well? His enemy, suddenly so real, so intimately linked to his own time on this earth? Had he watched Edward leave the Residence just this morning, tall and increasingly solid in his well-made suit, seen him reach out one large manicured hand with its family ring on one finger and wedding ring on another, and open the door to the car waiting for him? Her Edward, who had protected her all these years. Her Edward, in Niall's eyes. Had Niall shaken his head and asked himself, *So, that's what she chose?*

Her Edward. Clare started at the thought. She checked her watch. In two hours, Edward would be returning, bringing the P.U.S. with him, their guests following shortly.

Everyone expected so much from her. She, of all people! She was pale, beige, remote. She was cool, calm, efficient. She had molded herself into something perfect. But she wasn't perfect. She was anything but perfect. And still they would keep asking all these things of her. Now, here was Niall, wanting something from her also. Something she didn't have to give him.

"Why now?" she said, sharper than she'd meant to. She softened her voice. "If you've been following me all this time, if you decided to risk my being some sort of British informant, why did you step up to ask me about the money *now?* Why today?"

Niall cracked his knuckles and looked away. "The flowers. I stepped in here once, trying to keep out of sight, and saw right away you must come in here of your ownself, to sit. Next door to your house, and all the flowers—I told myself, this is where I'll get her alone. No one for her to run to. But the fecking rain in Paris."

"Today's the first day of sunshine," she said.

He dropped his hands and nodded.

She sighed. How could he know her so well? "Yes, but why *now?* If you were worried I'd turned on you, why not take the risk last spring, or last autumn, or last summer? Or ten years ago?"

Niall studied her, as though he was figuring out how much he wanted to reveal. Finally, he said, "Because when they closed down the Maze, they transferred Kieran Purcell to another prison facility, where he met a lad I'd once been working an oil rig with up in the North Sea. It was good pay, a good team, I'd stayed on longer than I should have. And they get to talking about tattoos and the ways the R.U.C. had for distinguishing Volunteers, 'cause there was a time some were getting new identities, and this guy tells Kieran he met a boy who was pretending to be from the south but was from Derry—he knew my accent, see—about five ten, black hair and eyes as light as the sky on a winter morning, who kept saying he'd been out of Ireland since 1982 and didn't have any family there, even though everyone has family in Ireland, who had this strange scar on his neck, looked like a sickle, and what could one do about that...Ol' Kieran, he puts it all together. So when he gets sprung this winter, he goes to my cousin and tells him he's been wondering whether it really were me in that coffin and might it not be interesting to have the old box dug out. They've got all those ways now for identifying a toenail and all that, don't they. And then ol' Kieran says if it turns out not to be me in there, where was I, and what did my cousin know about it, because he knew my cousin was like my own brother, and we queued up together to join the Struggle, and he the one who said it were O'Faolain he pulled out of the water. And that's when my cousin put the notice in the paper, like we agreed twenty-five years ago, if ever any trouble come on him."

"You mean this man Kieran wants the money? If you hand it over to him, he will leave it alone? But if not...?"

"Kieran was a good man. Dedicated to the Cause. Half the years I've been hiding, he spent in the H Block. He's not looking to go back in there for no good reason."

"I don't understand."

"I mean they're saying it's all peace and good neighbors now, but people remember. One tout tried to go back a couple years ago, had been hiding in some village in England. Did you read about him? He died an accidental death soon after. And twenty years in prison, you think ol' Kieran's going to get a job now?"

"You mean this Kieran knows about the money that went missing and if he was to get it, he wouldn't tell anyone you're still alive? That your cousin covered for you?"

"Feck, Clare, I dunno. Sure, he knows about the money. Maybe he'll keep his gob shut and disappear to Barbados. Ol' Kieran. Or maybe he just wants to know I wasn't fecking with them—he gave his best years to the Cause, spent them in prison, didn't he—and will give it all to the Church. Most likely he turns it over to whoever's still kindling a flame, and gets a pension for his woman. It's not like my cousin was asking him to spell out his plans. You don't feckin' ask questions of people like Kieran. I just know he wants the money, and if he doesn't get it, he's going to put trouble on my cousin."

She shifted on the bench. "But if you gave him the money and he handed it over to whomever... They'd know you were alive. Wouldn't they, mightn't they...?" She wasn't sure how best to put this. "You know?"

"Come looking for me?" Niall shrugged. "If they did, I'd feckin' well deserve it. But my cousin'll spin them some yarn about a tout going to the R.U.C. on me and the money, and that's why I went into hiding. He convinced everyone it was me in the coffin, didn't he? They're old men now, the ones who knew me. They get the feckin' money and that will be the end of it."

And she saw in his eyes the hesitation.

He took her hand up, looked at the palm, then laid it back

down on her knee, arranging it like a mortuary worker arranging the limbs of a corpse.

"I mean," he said, "if you still had it. If you hadn't given it over to the wrong person."

He stood up and shook his head.

"Forget it. Forget it."

But it had been there. For a moment, he'd been ready to ask her. Even though he knew she didn't have *that* money. She stood up, too, still exactly his height, still eye to eye. He knew about her comfortable lifestyle. "Where will you go?"

"Same place I've been all these years. Nowhere." He turned to leave.

"No."

He stopped and looked at her.

She reached her hand out and, gently feeling her way between his hair and collar, ran her finger down the slick silvery length of his scar, a familiarity she'd never dared when they were lovers.

He didn't flinch but took her hand slowly away with his, lowered it to her side, left it there. They stood in silence, watching each other.

"You never were like the other girls, Clare. Still aren't."

She shook her head.

"I would have come back, you know. I would have."

"Niall—"

"There's a church next to the Centre Pompidou."

He paused. When she didn't say anything further, he squeezed her hand and stepped back. "Tomorrow I'm gone. That's how you want it, you'll ne'er lay eyes on me again."

He walked away, disappearing amidst the sharp-edged trees.

She heard the lock-release click of the Residence's downstairs foyer and leaned her weight against the heavy oak front door. Before stepping in, she took one last look around the courtyard. The day was fading. The blue of the sky was thinning. Niall was somewhere out there.

"*Bonjour, Madame.*" The door swung open behind her to reveal the concierge's husband.

She caught the jamb to keep from tumbling. "*Bonjour, Monsieur.*" She regained her balance as he held the door open for her and, stepping inside, nodded. "*Merci.*"

He cradled a lightbulb in one hand. "*Il fait très beau aujourd'hui.*"

"*Oui, il fait beau.*"

"*Le Ministre va bien?*"

"*Oui, merci.*"

"*Et les enfants?*"

"*Oui, merci.*"

"*Ah, bien. Alors, tout va bien.*" He climbed up onto his step stool under the entryway light fixture.

She pressed the elevator button. When she didn't hear the cage begin its noisy descent, she pressed the button again. She could sense the concierge's husband look up at the sound. In the Residence, there was still the same dinner to put on, still the same problem with Jamie. But a different woman would be handling them. She could even go to Dublin now. A new, limitless world expanded before her.

Niall hadn't betrayed her. And together they hadn't *done* anything.

"Will you help?" he'd said, and unzipped a corner of the duffel.

\*　　\*　　\*

The euphoria she'd felt evened out. Yes, she could go to Dublin now with impunity. Yes, she hadn't provided money that was then used to buy guns or explosives. But she had still agreed to bring it over. The intention had been there. Plus, she'd rented that camper. She'd made that trip to the Eastern Shore. Niall, at least, had considered himself a soldier. And she? Just a pliable schoolgirl.

Her phone hummed to signal a text message. She extracted it from her pocket.

Where are you??? E

Edward using multiple question marks? She checked her watch: 6:10 p.m. He would be clearing off his desk, readying to head over to the cocktail reception being held at the embassy before the P.U.S.'s more intimate dinner.

Home, she typed back.

But her phone showed *three* missed calls. She quickly switched to the voice mail, skipping over Edward's to get to the other two.

Jamie had called but had left no message.

She rapid-dialed his number.

His voice-mail message pounded her ear: "'*Don't want to be an American idiot....*' This is James. Leave a message. Or don't. Like I care."

She clicked off. If she didn't find him at home now, she was going to call the house of every single friend he had in Paris until she tracked him down. Enough was enough.

She could hear the elevator clanking its way down, but it still had not descended to the foyer. She drew her sweater close. The air was getting crisper as day walked into evening, in the treacherous way a warm spring day had; a cool shock that creeps up and, before noticed, has already invaded the body. Like aging: the world seemed so warm, and then suddenly was chill.

The past twenty-five years felt like a dream. "Did you hear Niall's disappeared?" her cousin Kevin had said, stopping by her room in Cambridge a couple months after she'd returned from Dublin. "Dad thinks he went home and picked right back up with what he'd been doing. You know. With *them.* And, sure enough, something went wrong." She'd gone straight to the library after he'd left and checked every newspaper Harvard subscribed to, hoping in vain to find some additional information. Failing there, she'd been forced to get it out of her aunt and uncle. "Thank you again for last summer," she'd said, making a special trip to see them, a Sunday before Christmas. "We all had such a nice time here. Do you think Niall will be coming back next summer?" And her aunt had buried her face in her hands, and her uncle had shaken his head and explained why that was never going to happen: Niall's people had wound in a sheet what was left of his corpse after the fish and tides had got to it, and closed it up in a coffin. And so, over the years, she'd seen his face in the crowds and had thought she was seeing the memory of what she herself had been. But she *had* seen him. Just this morning, even, at Le Bon Marché, peering at her over the canned goods from Britain and the cheese from Ireland. Without doubt, also many other times. He'd been following her. She was *not* crazy. She mixed numbers up but not faces.

The Turk. He, too, was still out there.

The elevator clunked to a stop in front of her. She stepped in, rattled the door to the cage shut, pressed the button for their floor. She hoped there really had been a doctor and that he would come forward. *Punto.* She wouldn't give another thought to the Turk today.

But she couldn't ignore Niall. He would be waiting for her.

The elevator began slowly to rise. Upstairs were Amélie, Amélie's cousin, Mathilde, this evening's waiter. Maybe, if she was lucky, Jamie. They would all be expecting something from her. There was the rest of everything else waiting for her as well, the rituals—birthday celebrations, anniversaries, weddings, the baptism of grandchildren—and the attendant smaller routines, like straightening Edward's ties in the morning. All the things that kept daily life in order and outlined her existence like the penciled edges of a still life, giving constant definition to what otherwise would seem like an endless tunnel, would feel like the same vacuum that had sucked her into the vortex of the Dublin airport two decades earlier and now was pulling her at every moment one minute closer to life's inevitable conclusion. *I have measured out my life with coffee spoons.* How wise she and her classmates had felt back in college when they'd studied T. S. Eliot. They'd torn *J. Alfred Prufrock* to pieces until they'd unveiled every nuance—without having understood a thing. "Can you read aloud and then translate Eliot's epigraph from Dante's *Inferno* for us?" the professor had asked her, she that class's resident Romance language major, and she'd picked through Dante's Italian like it was something she could defeat: *"Ma perchiocce giammi de questo fondo/Non torno vivo alcun, s'I'odo il vero/Senza tema d'infamia ti rispondo."*

And then she'd repeated, in English, "But since never from this abyss has anyone returned alive, I'll answer you without fearing infamy."

She would walk through the front door of the Residence as she had a thousand times before. A marine landscape by Turner that greeted her every time she entered the apartment, hanging over the dark rosewood Regency console in which she would store her purse. The elegant silver bowl they'd received as a wedding gift from Edward's scull mate at Oxford, now a powerful barrister in London, and which—like the Turner—they carried from apartment to apartment, where she would place her keys, then remove them, knowing Edward would worry they would scratch the silver. The small inlaid box acquired during a holiday in Croatia, hidden from sight within the console, where she would deposit her keys instead.

A home, a spouse, children, a vocation if not a real career. She had all of these. Could Niall have somehow, along the way, picked up some version of these things also? A woman who was willing to know nothing about the father of her children? Maybe, a voluptuous forgiving Italian, with a long nose and laughing lips and thick, dark shiny hair, full breasts and hips. Or a young, independent-minded Scandinavian. Or both of the above, and many others?

A surge of jealousy rocked her body, followed by a rolling wave of self-loathing. How petty she was! How foolish!

*A church next to the Centre Pompidou....Tomorrow I'm gone. That's how you want it, you'll ne'er lay eyes on me again.*

He hadn't abandoned her. Could she now abandon him? Didn't she owe him if not the money, at least the succor he'd now handed her?

The elevator clinked to a stop.

She remembered her unsent text—Home—and clicked "send." She opened the front door; the foyer assailed her with its resplendence: the incandescent burst of the crystal chandelier, the gleam of the dark Regency console, a brilliant splash of yellow and green in a vase on top. She closed the door softly behind her, walked over to the console, leaned down to place her keys in the box from Croatia, not in the silver bowl.

"*There* you are."

The broad forehead, the gray eyes, looking down at her, over her shoulder. "Edward!" she cried, knocking against the console in her confusion. She dropped her purse and grabbed for the vase of lilies and bells of Ireland, a massive green-and-yellow shudder in the corner of her eye, just before it fell. Water sloshed around her, on the shining wood, onto the floor.

"I rang the landline," he said, ignoring the flowers, looking right past the water, gesturing to the BlackBerry still in her hand. "Amélie said you'd be here."

"I was delayed—" she began.

Amélie appeared from the direction of the kitchen, her thick legs moving swiftly. She blushed and stopped short. "*Excusez-moi, j'ai entendu...*"

"It's all right. Everything's all right," Edward said, stepping back, rubbing his hands together. Amélie withdrew a cloth from her apron pocket and began to wipe furiously at the spillage, careful to keep her eyes from either of theirs.

Clare slipped her phone into her purse and stuck her purse in the console. "At least the whole thing didn't fall over."

"*Oui, Madame.*"

"How clumsy of me."

Amélie said nothing, wiped.

"That's good now."

"*Oui, Madame. Excusez-moi, Madame, Monsieur.*"

"For God's sake, Edward," she said, once Amélie was gone. "You startled me. What are—"

"I had a call from Barrow," he said, cutting her off. "You *knew?*"

She shoved Niall from her thoughts. All the twisting and turning she'd done to keep Edward from getting involved in Jamie's mess before tonight's dinner. She looked around the foyer for telltale signs—a knapsack, a sweatshirt, a bottle of Orangina—abandoned on one of Amélie's well-polished surfaces. Nothing. "I spoke with them . . . ," she said.

"Bloody Hell! And you didn't tell me? Clare!" Inside his jacket, his own BlackBerry buzzed. He withdrew it, read the half-truth she'd sent before entering the front door. "Right," he said, raising his eyebrows. "Did you speak to James?"

"He's upset," she said, still trying to figure out how much to reveal about Jamie's whereabouts. "I told him to come home."

"As though we have a choice! When will he arrive?"

She turned and busied herself with resettling the flower arrangement. She could tell Edward how Jamie had arrived unexpectedly this morning, how he'd flown over without even telling her beforehand, how he'd written a request in her name without telling her either. But if Edward had no inkling of any of this, to whose benefit would be telling him? Not his own. Certainly not Jamie's.

"He'll be here on the weekend," she said, moving a stem, adding softly, "They're called bells of Ireland. Do you see? Green bells with white clappers? They're supposed to bring good luck. That's probably why so many brides carry them."

"Clare! Don't change the subject. What about that girl Barrow sent away?"

She dropped the flower back into the vase and swiveled to face him. "There aren't any girls at Barrow."

"There aren't *now*." That buzzing sound from somewhere on Edward's person. "Hell!" He withdrew his phone from his inner jacket pocket again and surveyed the text. "The P.U.S.'s car is downstairs. I have to go."

"What girl?"

Edward stopped putting his phone back into his jacket long enough to look at her. "I thought you said you'd spoken to Barrow."

*Right.* She was supposed to know this already. She was supposed to be on top of everything. She nodded and stepped back. "Yes, I meant was there another girl?"

"I'd say, in this case one was enough, wouldn't you?"

She processed all the possibilities as quickly as she could. In the overall scheme of things, getting caught with a girl was less serious than cheating, although how those two things related she didn't see. Maybe he'd gotten so caught up with the girl, he'd neglected the lab. Then cheated on it to catch up. "Yes, it certainly is...," she said.

"Did he give you any explanation? What in all hell happened? What was he thinking?"

Not thinking. Kids aren't *thinking* in those circumstances. She lifted her hands, helpless.

"I'm sorry," she said, "that I got back so late."

He opened the door. "We need to talk about this." The elevator was already there, fresh from her arrival. He unlatched the cage, stepped in, turned to face her, frowning. "I can't keep the P.U.S. waiting." He clanked the door shut.

"I'm sorry," she said again as the elevator began descending.

She closed the front door to the Residence. If Jamie had been caught breaking two rules simultaneously, he really was damn lucky he hadn't been expelled. But how did this relate to the other kid? What was his name—Ryan?

She stopped short under the chandelier. An image came to mind, and she winced. No, the other boy would have been caught *cheating* with him, not being with the girl with him.

She hurried down the hall to Jamie's room, flipped the light switch on.

"Jamie? *Ssss.* Jamie?"

There was no one in there. The pale reflection of her face stared back at her from the window. The sun had almost set now. She pressed her hands together and sank down on the bed. Jamie, hardly more than a baby himself. The hours Clare had spent walking up and down their apartment's hall in Cairo. He'd cried endlessly any time she surrendered him to the baby nurse. She'd take him back in her arms, and his sweet smile, toothless and trusting, that milky smell. Sometimes she still caught a glimpse of that smile underneath the adolescent hint of stubble and the slogan T-shirts.

She drew off her sweater in the warmth of his room, letting it fall over the length of his bed. Well, Jamie had found his first girl, and lost his head temporarily over her. Maybe he'd enlisted a fellow student to help him get the answers, which would explain why only Jamie was being held accountable. It wasn't really all that strange. Until now, Jamie had had no experience with girls. Edward had even said, only half joking, when she'd first proposed Barrow, "Maybe an all-boys school wouldn't be quite the best thing. You know. Things do happen."

"What are you trying to say, Edward? *Honestly.* Anyhow, I saw Jamie taking a good look at Amélie the other day while she was leaning over a bed, smoothing the covers."

"Amélie? You must be joking. She has legs like a piano."

"She's not even thirty. Anyway, since when have you been checking her legs out?"

"She spends a fair amount of time up on stools dusting the light fixtures," he'd said and added, laughing, "It's hard *not* to see them."

"Not nice, Edward."

"Yes," he'd said sheepishly. "You're right. That was uncalled for." But she'd sensed his abashed relief.

Amélie must be in the kitchen now, helping Mathilde, wondering what had happened in the foyer. Clare needed to go in, restore Amélie's faith, let Mathilde know she was paying attention. The guests would arrive in hardly an hour. She rose from the bed, turned out the light, closed the door on the room. Like salt, she'd let Jamie slip through her fingers. After she made sure everything was in order, she'd start the calling around. Embarrassing for him, even more embarrassing for her.

She walked back up the hall. The formal living room looked pristine, its vast space aglow with polished brass and mahogany. Just the sight of it soothed her. This was what she would think about. Her house. Her dinner. This much she could do. A fire had been set, but not lit, in the fireplace. The shiny brass heads of the andirons—"firedogs" Edward called them, using their British name—turned the rest of the room upside down inside their globes; the split logs brought candor to the ensemble. She moved a bouquet from a side table onto the fireplace's ornate mantel; placing a vase on that table blocked the view from the two chairs beside it to the rest of the room, and people liked to keep an eye on what was going on with other guests, to know with whom everyone else was speaking. She eased a few stems from the vase and reinserted them, causing the bells to face out, pausing to touch their curious domes. Jean-Benoît had done well, as usual. Not only did the combination of the white-and-green bells of Ireland with the yellow lilies convey everything she'd wanted to say about springtime and the bridge between different nations, but they also matched the room.

The flowers perfected, she swept the room with her eyes.

Would it pass muster with their illustrious guests of this evening? In their first year at the minister's residence, with permission and funds from the FCO, she had changed the drapes, the seat covers, the cushions on the settee and matching armchairs from the heavy peach silk favored by the previous inhabitant to a swirl of cool blues and pale browns. She'd bought the fabrics in England and had them sent over, spending hours combing through the samples in Harrods, Osborne & Little, and Chelsea Textiles. For the cushions she'd used woven fabric from Normandy. She had set about sleek pieces of silver from Edward's family and classic pieces of crystal from her family on the room's heavy dark furniture, inlaid with golden trim. Under the elaborate chandeliers, and amidst the heavy gilt-framed portraiture belonging to the Residence, she'd hung the large abstract painting by Farouk Hosni they'd bought during their posting in Cairo and the small Sam Gillian they'd purchased while they were first living in Washington. Shortly after the renovations had been completed, she'd straightened up from arranging a vase of simple yellow tulips before a cocktail party to find Jamie standing in the doorway, watching her. "Hey, Mom," he'd said, his young forehead pleated with puzzlement, "this room matches you now." She'd laughed, but secretly she'd wondered at his precocious perspicacity.

Yellow tulips symbolized hopeless love. Thank you, Jean-Benoît.

The door to the dining room was open. The table dazzled with fourteen settings of china, crystal, and silver. Amélie had used the pale gray jacquard as instructed, and the royal crest on the plate gleamed against it. Three small bouquets dotted the table. A fourth perched on top of the sideboard. These vases were just right. She didn't need to readjust them.

She extracted fourteen silver place-card holders from the sideboard and dropped them the length of the table, as though creating a trail. In a short while, her guests would follow them, observing what status they'd been awarded. She did not plan to put up a seating chart outside the door; a seating chart felt too stuffy. For the place cards themselves, she would have to return to the study. She couldn't hear any sound from the kitchen—usually a good sign. No explosions from Mathilde. After she put out the place cards, there was still her suit to slip into and evening makeup. She'd best check the cheese plate, too, to make sure Mathilde had used the cheddar as directed.

Then she would set herself to locating Jamie.

*"Plus doucement!"* she heard Mathilde bark as she passed through the kitchen door. The room's vibrant jumble of odors, industry, and color came as an assault after the regal serenity of the reception rooms. Copper-bottomed pots and smooth gray pans with angular rims, and mounds of green, white, red, and yellow on fat brown cutting boards. A pasty mound of dough covered by a cloth, a second darker mound beside it. A cloud of steam from a pot, a small twister of smoke from the saucepan beside it, the splatter of butter. An aroma of parsley, lemon, and garlic. The scent of chocolate. *"Vous les massacrez!"*

Amélie was seated at the long central table with her cousin, a twenty-something who wore her frosted hair on top of her head in a vertical ponytail. Stacked rows of asparagus flashed chalky white in two rectangular bowls of water, floating with ice cubes: one with the spears that had already been denuded of their thick exterior and the other for those awaiting disrobement. Clare couldn't see Mathilde's face, but she did catch a glimpse of Yann, the waiter sent over from the embassy to stand in for the butler, raising his eyebrows while lining up wineglasses on a tray.

Mathilde cut the air above Amélie's cousin's head with a thick red-stained hand. "You're useless, *donnes-moi,* I'll do it!"

"Everything all right?" Clare asked.

Mathilde favored her with a brief glance and practically spit.

*"Très bien, Madame Moorhouse,"* the waiter responded.

Amélie echoed, *"Oui, Madame."* Her cousin made a face into the asparagus and said nothing. Mathilde turned, threw her hands up in the air and retreated to the other end of the table.

"These girls haven't the faintest idea how to wield a knife," she said, returning to fashioning rosebuds out of a grasp of strawberries, with a tiny but very sharp-looking paring knife. White and dark chocolate peels curled on a plate beside them. Husked pistachios waited in yet another dish for their turn in the cakes' assemblage. The cakes would be a masterpiece, like all of Mathilde's desserts. "They're making a mess of the asparagus."

*"Et depuis quand ou la Suisse ou l'Ecosse informe le monde gastronome?"* muttered Amélie's cousin, whose grasp of docility did not match her comprehension of the English language.

Since when does either Switzerland or Scotland have the last word on haute cuisine? Clare couldn't believe her ears. Amélie's cousin had helped out many a time before. She knew Mathilde's temper. Was she *trying* to ruin dinner?

"I heard that!" Mathilde growled, dropping a strawberry. Red liquid dripped from her short, strong fingers and the paring knife. "I heard that!"

"I didn't hear anything," Clare said, quickly. She looked around at Yann. "Did you say something?"

"No, *Je n'ai rien dit. Ni entendu.*" He pointed to an ear and shook his head. He'd also served at their house tens of times.

"Good heavens, that is going to be incredible," Clare continued, stepping in between the two ends of the table, blocking

Mathilde's view of Amélie's cousin at the same time as gesturing towards the fourteen little cakes and the mounds of homemade chocolates and strawberries and pistachios waiting to join them. She suspected there was a freshly blended red-fruit *coulis* waiting in the refrigerator as well. "You've outdone yourself again, Mathilde. Honestly, you make me the envy of every hostess in Paris."

"I know," Mathilde said, sniffing. "It's a wonder, too. Without any decent help. And those pills you bought haven't done anything for my fingers. Plus, working one extra evening this week."

"Oh, Mathilde, we are so grateful. I will definitely make it up to you. And the pills, you just have to hang in there a little longer. Homeopathic medicine works a little slower. But you know that. The Swiss are masters of homeopathy. Very medically advanced people, the Swiss. Very advanced period. As well as wonderful cooks." Clare had to avoid catching the waiter's eye, or they both might burst out laughing. The cousin bent lower over her stalks. "I'll go get dressed now. Send Amélie back if you need anything."

"I don't need anything from you, Mrs. Moorhouse," Mathilde said. "You're the one who keeps needing things from me."

Clare sighed and left her staff to finish the dinner.

# THIRTEEN

S he closed the door to her bedroom and sat on the stool before the rectangular mirror on her vanity. She rubbed the crow's feet beside her eyes and the crease that separated the top and bottom halves of her high forehead.

She laid her hands on her waist, pressing in against her abdomen. Real children had nestled within her, Edward's children—not just pounds of paper, dollars destined someday possibly to have other children's blood on them. Those were the only children Niall had offered her. A British diplomat's wife with two British sons—that's what Niall had seen today, what he'd been seeing all this time that he'd shadowed her. That's what she saw now in the mirror. She turned her face one way and then another. The world she'd inhabited with Niall had seemed so alive, so physical. Yet what she'd had with Niall paled beside the reality of bearing children within one's body and into this world. She wasn't sure how it stood even against the mundane profundity of daily life. As a twenty-year-old, she wouldn't have understood such a thought, but when she'd accepted Edward's marriage proposal, she'd stepped through a passageway into a parallel universe where the consequences of her every action rolled out in front of her like a carpet. Wars were not fought and won based upon the countless phone calls and lists she made or instructions she issued. Multitudes of faceless souls were not saved or lost in response to her actions. But the very real people who spent their days beside her—her children, her husband, her staff—would be happy or unhappy, would be hungry or tired or satisfied or distraught. The tiny gestures that she repeated day after day sustained them. *That* was reality. The world Niall had shown her was a dream world that had sucked her in, in the way a nightmare does, leaving you confused in the morning as to whether you are awake now or were awake then. Niall's world possessed a hatred too big for her heart.

*You surely have beautiful hands, Clare.*

She stretched out her fingers, slipping her wedding and engagement rings off, and examined the whorl around each knuckle. Two decades had passed since she'd seen Niall. He still sat with his thighs apart, his hands clasped between them. When he leaned forward, the strange streak of shiny scar tissue that ran up the back of his neck, like a sickle cropping the edge of his hairline, still pulled tight, a scar she'd always yearned to caress. The scar that had eventually betrayed him to his countryman.

"Don't touch it," he'd told her once. "It's bad luck."

"Like stepping on a crack?" Their vehicle was stopped on a highway in Maryland alongside the shore, waiting for a drawbridge to come down, third in line. She peered into the rearview mirror. Cars unwound behind them like a string of Christmas lights.

"Stepping on a crack?"

"Break your mother's back."

"My ma's back already broke. From working double shifts at the shirt factory after my da was sent up. No, bad luck like the guy who tossed the petrol bomb what caused it." He rolled his window down farther and tapped his cigarette ash onto the street.

"He got blown up with it?" she asked, resting her hands on the steering wheel, keeping her voice level. A warm wind stirred the air between them.

Niall smiled at her. "No. I broke his front tooth when we were in school because he was kissing my sister."

She'd known he would have sisters. The Irish all had sisters. But he'd never mentioned any of them before. His words felt like a present.

He drew on his cigarette. "End of story," he said.

The drawbridge came back down. She put in gear the little Toyota camper they'd rented under her name and inched it forward. A yellow light flashed at them as they passed over the bridge, glinting off the gold-plated band he'd given her to wear on her wedding finger. She could smell the dark water of the Atlantic.

"Go right here," he said.

She spun the steering wheel and edged the camper out of the main stream of traffic onto a long straight road along the seaside. They headed out of the town into a sort of no man's land, populated by grocery stores advertising beer and fireworks, and run-down motels with neon vacancy signs in pink or yellow.

The last moments of dusk dropped down over their car. Seagulls swept around them and landed on litter by the side of the road. They passed a boarded-up vegetable stand. It looked as though years had gone by since anyone had stood there. A calcified pumpkin lay riddled with holes on the ground before it.

"Should I put on the radio?" she asked.

He shook his head. In the seaside dark, she could feel his movements more than see them. But any changes of position were rare. His body had become a repository of calm in the squall growing over the Atlantic, as still as the darkness that was deepening around them. She knew him well enough now to recognize that this was his attitude of extreme concentration. She squinted at the road and kept driving. Wind pushed against the camper.

After another twenty minutes had passed, a long ugly building came into view, the worst-looking motel of all.

"Here," he said.

"Here?" she asked.

He pointed to the motel's vacancy sign, swinging in the Atlantic wind. "We'll be sleeping the night here."

She swerved into the parking lot. There were ten doors, not including the door of the reception. Only two had cars parked before them.

He was mixed up with things back home, his home, far beyond her experience, and she felt sure his unexplained absences from her aunt and uncle's weren't to shack up with other girls. When she'd descended the bus in New Jersey to pick up the vehicle he'd reserved and seen it was a camper, she'd felt a whisper of relief—he'd rented them a mobile hotel room. They climbed onto the thin mattress in the back of the camper, shedding all their clothes, that first night, and she'd decided: it's just a vacation as he'd said, and she'd twirled the gold-plated ring he'd told her to wear around her finger. Each day, as they'd zigzagged the coastline, she'd permitted herself to fall further into this fantasy.

Now, though, when he told her to go into the reception and get them a room, she felt no surprise. She tucked her long blond hair up into the scarf he handed her, and put on the tinted glasses he pulled out of the bag at his feet. They smelled of his cigarettes.

"They won't ask for your ID," he told her.

The wind had died down. The outer door to the office was open to the warm night, but a locked inner metal guard door kept her from entering. A man with a heavy face and wearing a turban sat behind an old desk, his feet up on a crate, watching a portable TV. The only other light in the room came from a desk lamp. The turbaned man narrowed his eyes and laid one hand on a half-open drawer when she knocked on the door. His eyes squinted into the night at her.

"Yeah?"

"Do you have any rooms?" The question was ridiculous, but she felt no temptation to laugh. Laughter didn't exist here.

He showed no sign of getting up to let her in. "How many?"

"Just one."

He dropped his feet to the ground. She saw there was a second man sitting behind him in the corner. His eyes were riveted to the television.

The first man fumbled in a box on top of the desk and lumbered towards the door. He did not unlock it. "That your car?" he asked and pointed to the camper.

She nodded.

He nodded back. "I see. Number ten." He held a key up. Its silver face slipped and dangled in the fluorescent lighting over the entrance. She put her hand forward to take it, but he kept it out of reach. "Twenty-five," he said.

"Oh, yeah." She felt her face go warm. "Hang on." She fished around in her little sack for her wallet, and extracted two tens and a five-dollar bill. He accepted them through the metal bars and slipped the room key back through them to her.

"Thank you."

The man waited until she was behind the steering wheel before turning his back on her. She handed the room key over to Niall. In the obscurity of the parking lot, she could hardly make his face out, just the light of his eyes. He lit a cigarette.

"He gave me the very farthest room," she said. "I don't know why. They're not busy."

Niall didn't reply, but she felt his hand slide onto her thigh. Warmth slipped through the skirt she was wearing. He squeezed.

She turned the ignition back on and drove to the bottom of the lot. Their room was almost barren: a large bed covered with a cheap, worn orange bedspread, a bedside table with a clock on it, a linoleum chest of drawers with a television on top. The tiled floor was rugless. She didn't like to take her shoes off; she didn't want the feel of the floor on the soles of her feet. When she went to flip on the light in the bathroom, the bulb burned out in a pop and a fizz.

"I'll walk over to the office and get a new one," she said.

"Leave it," he said. He came up behind her, his body so similar in height and size that it felt like a shadow, and ran his hands under her T-shirt and over her chest. She turned to him, forgetting about the burned-out lightbulb in the bathroom.

She woke in the night to the sound of cars pulling up, farther down the parking lot. She could hear what sounded like a black man's voice and then another's, car doors opening and closing. Drug dealers, she thought, then chided herself for being racist. She crept to the window.

"Come away," he told her.

"I thought you were sleeping," she said, climbing back into bed beside him.

He didn't answer and she fell back to sleep.

She awoke again what must have been a couple hours later. A sense of emptiness had penetrated her dreams, disturbing her.

She lay quietly and listened. The men's voices were gone. Niall also was gone. The room was so dark that she could only feel his absence. She could see nothing. She sat up, waited for her eyes to adjust to the dark, and when they didn't, realized that the shutters on the room's window must have been closed from the outside. She felt her way to the door, banging one of her knees against the foot of the bed. The door was locked, and the key was missing. She couldn't leave if she'd wanted to.

She made her way back to the bed, because there was nothing else for her to do. She lay there awake, reminding herself over and over that Niall would never let anything bad happen to her, until, overwhelmed by heat and exhaustion, she fell into a sweaty stupor. Then it was morning and Niall was back in bed beside her.

"Mommy?" A voice broke in through her memory.

She almost jumped out of her skin. She swiftly slid her rings back on her fingers and turned around. Jamie was sitting on the end of her bed.

"*James.*"

"Don't get all mad. Dad didn't see me."

"You've been here this whole time?"

Jamie shrugged. "I got back around five. When I heard Dad come in, I hid."

The drapes were open, and the last moments of sunlight illuminated her son's pale face. He looked so much like her as a teenager for a second there that she was startled. There it was: the same taciturn but curious hazel eyes, same hesitant upper lip. She could almost see how others must have looked on her as a fifteen-year-old.

"You don't need to hide," she said.

Jamie shrugged. "Whatever. You're the one who said Dad had

some big dinner tonight, and I shouldn't mess it up for him. I was just trying to be helpful."

"Helpful?" Clare stared at her son, trying to figure out whether he was being sincere. "Well, Jamie, I wouldn't say that 'helpful' is the first word that came to mind regarding your recent behavior." She glanced at the clock on the bedside table. 6:48 p.m.

"You're busy," Jamie said.

"No, I'm not."

"I saw you look at the clock."

"I'll dress while we talk. You're not going anywhere," she said. "What about this girl?"

Jamie flopped backwards onto her bed. "Hmph." He had been a wakeful baby, and many were the times Clare had profited from one of Edward's work trips to bring him into their bed. He would giggle in his sleep, even before he was old enough to say "Mama," and she'd hear the sound as part of her dreams. Sometimes, she still heard it in her sleep.

She sat down on the bed beside him. "You didn't mention her."

"Whatever," Jamie said.

"'Whatever'? Are you kidding? What's going on, Jamie?" When he pulled away from her, she added, "The school called your father."

Jamie flipped up beside her, so violently his face almost hit hers. She had to restrain herself from recoiling. "It's a whole class thing! It's because she's *Irish*."

She bit her lip. A "whole class thing" could only mean a Catholic from Northern Ireland. She'd never engaged in any discussion with her sons about the Troubles or any part of Irish history. On the contrary, she'd spent two decades avoiding all discussion of Ireland, except as pertained to leprechauns, four-leaf clovers, and claddaghs. But she knew how a Catholic from Northern Ireland would be viewed at Barrow, and she knew Jamie would refer to a Catholic girl from Northern Ireland not as British but as Irish. Despite how it might gall his father. Perhaps because of how it would gall his father.

"*You're* Irish," she said.

"No, I'm not. I'm half American and half English. Superpowers! Colonizers! What could be less Irish?"

"I see." She took a deep breath. There'd been no other boy. It was the girl he felt was being mistreated. Not himself. "What was because she's Irish?"

"The way they treated her. The way they . . ." His voice trailed off and he looked away.

"Right." She took a deep breath and steeled herself. "Were you . . . ? Did they find you . . . ?"

"Mom!" Jamie protested, his cheeks flooding with red. He folded his arms over his chest.

"I need to know, Jamie. At least what Barrow knows."

He dropped back down flat on the bed, turned away, buried his face in the pillows.

"No, Mom," his muffled voice. "Nothing like that. You don't understand what happened."

"Okay, okay," she said. "You're right, I don't. Tell me."

He didn't answer.

In the silence between them, she felt as though she could hear the ticking of his heart, hidden and subdued but just waiting to go off, ready to explode his young life into a million ragged pieces. All the passions her son experienced, and yet he managed to hold them so close, so much the same as she'd been when she was younger. She stood up.

She just hoped Jamie's girl was a *nice* girl. And that being in love for the first time, if that's what they were talking about, wouldn't compel him to pull any more stunts like faking his mother's signature and hopping on planes without permission. And all the rest. Barrow strictly forbade bringing girls on campus, outside of the specific events to which they might be invited.

"Well," she said, "let's start from the beginning. I gather this was the Ryan you mentioned?"

Jamie didn't say anything.

"I guess Ryan can be a girl's name, too?"

"Mom!"

"Okay, okay." She sighed. "Do you like her?"

He rolled his eyes and pointed to the clock on the bedside table. "Hadn't you better get ready? Won't Dad's dinner be soon?"

"You're going to have to tell me everything eventually. It's not like you're just going to stay home from school a week and then go back without any discussion."

She got up and opened the door to her wardrobe. Her outfit for the evening hung inside, the top part still wrapped in paper, as the dry cleaners did it in France.

"Rian," he said softly, pronouncing it with just a hint of a lilt. "R-i-a-n."

R-i-a-n, she thought to herself. R-i-a-n.

She stopped, her hand on the suit. Edward had said Barrow had sent the girl away. Not that they'd "sent her home" or "sent her back to her own school" or even "sent her packing." If she wasn't a Barrow student, how could they have sent her away? Unless he meant *fired*.

"Jamie," she said carefully, "was Rian a student? I mean, what was she *doing* at Barrow? Was she just visiting?"

"What's the difference?" he mumbled and said nothing more.

She turned to face him, putting her hands on her hips. "Listen, James, you are going to have to talk about it whether you want to or not. You are just making things worse for yourself with the way you are behaving."

He shook his head again.

"Jamie."

Jamie rolled his eyes. "No, she isn't a student. I mean, she is, but *obviously* not at Barrow. It's all boys, Mom."

"You don't need to take that sarcastic tone with me," she said. "I'm not the one who's been acting the fool here." She heard herself and thought: If that's not the biggest lie on earth.

"Right, whatever. *Sorry.*" Jamie crossed his arms over his chest and pressed his lips shut.

*"Rian."* She swung her dry cleaning off the rack, selected a fresh package of pantyhose from a shelf within the armoire, and carried them into the bathroom. She left the door ajar, just enough so she could still hear him. "Okay. Where was she a student, then?" she said. Her sweater and pants fell away from her body. Underneath, her skin felt cool. His knee next to hers. She turned on the tap, dampened a washcloth, and turned the water back off so Jamie could hear her. "At another boarding school? At a school in London? One of the Catholic schools?"

When Jamie didn't answer, she widened the opening of the door and looked out. He was kneeling on the floor, whispering into his cell phone. She hadn't heard a ring, but maybe a call had come while the tap was on. "Whom are you talking to?"

Jamie frowned and cupped his hand over the phone. "Not *her,* if that's what you mean." He looked away, from her, from the phone. "I don't even have a number to reach her now."

She pulled her head back into the bathroom. She knew as much as she needed for the moment. If the girl was staff, there would be all hell to pay at Barrow. No wonder they weren't expelling Jamie. *They* were the ones responsible. But the main thing was, she had him here now, safe, away from any immediate trouble. Like all kids should be.

She closed the door and peeled off the rest of her clothing. She drew the washcloth across her cheekbones, and around her neck, careful not to touch her hair, then gently smoothed in cleanser. How warm the sun had felt on her and Niall's heads as they sat beside the statue of Andrieu. The sun was gone by now. She dipped the washcloth under the tap and slid it across her face. Then she dabbed at her skin with a clean dry towel.

"Don't," he said the morning after they'd stayed in that seedy motel, when she'd gone to open the back of the camper.

She felt as though the horrible night still hung to her. "I'd like to change my clothes. My bag's back there."

"We're going to the beach today. You don't need to wash." He pointed to the cab of the camper. "I've put your suit and a towel in front already."

Towel, he'd said. Singular. She climbed into the driver's seat. There was, indeed, only one towel bunched up against the dashboard.

She decided not to ask any questions about it. Niall never swam. Maybe he didn't plan to get wet at the beach.

"Can we stop for breakfast?"

He nodded. "I'll tell you."

They drove north until the motel was well behind them. After about forty minutes on the road, he indicated a diner with big glass windows.

"Leave the car right in front of the window, by the door," he said.

They sat down by the window that gave out over their rental camper. He kept his sunglasses on, and instead of slipping into the side of the booth facing her, pushed into her side after her. He threw an arm over her shoulder and drew her into him.

"Coffee, black," he told the waitress. "My wife will take hers with cream. You fancy pancakes? With a wee bit of sugar on them?"

Once, while sitting around her aunt and uncle's kitchen on a Saturday morning, her aunt cooking up breakfast for all of them, her cousin had started teasing her for eating her pancakes with sugar on them instead of maple syrup. Niall remembered how she liked her pancakes.

He'd never touched her, not even her arm, in front of another human being before. Now he was calling her "my wife" to this waitress.

"What are you having?" she asked.

If he had next announced that they were going to visit a justice of the peace, she would have said yes without hesitation. She didn't even care what had happened at the motel. She didn't want to know what he'd been doing.

Niall laughed and nodded to the waitress. "She'll have the pancakes, no syrup. I'll have the eggs and bacon super, the toast." He smiled. "Honeymooning makes you hungry."

The waitress smiled back at him and tucked a bleached lock behind one ear. She was just a girl, about the same age as Clare but with an already tired-looking face and a creamy bosom and round bottom. While Niall watched it sway back behind the counter, Clare made a boat out of her napkin. She reminded herself he didn't like heifers.

"You planning to sail away on that?" he asked her.

"Never," she told him. And she meant it.

When she came out of her bathroom fully dressed, her hair combed and lip gloss applied, Jamie was asleep on the bed, his phone clutched in his hand. She checked her watch. His flight over from London this morning would have left very early, and who knew when all this had happened? In his room, in the dark, he'd have opened his computer to write the fake e-mail from Clare granting him permission to leave, packed up some things—the novel by Philip Roth, his passport—and slipped out before his roommate was even awake. Maybe he'd even slept in the airport. She checked her watch again. Edward wasn't scheduled to be back with the P.U.S. for another twenty-four minutes. She'd give Jamie fifteen minutes to nap then shepherd him back to his own room, where Edward would be unlikely to venture during the course of the evening. Jamie could eat later, after all the guests were gone. He could go back to sleep in between times, and even if he woke before the dinner party ended, he'd know better than to wander out into his father's evening.

She racked her brain. She'd get the ring out of the safe now and put the place cards into their proper spots on the table. That was all there was left to do before Edward's dinner. All the rest would have to wait.

She knelt down before the safe, careful not to snag her stockings or wrinkle her skirt. "It's a question of fire," Edward had said about the safe when he'd brought it home, "not security." They were living in Cairo at the time, and Edward had had the safe built behind what looked like the lower two drawers of a three-drawer side table inlaid with mother-of-pearl. They'd moved it from residence to residence ever since, along with the Turner, Sam Gilliam, and Farouk Hosni paintings, the silver from his family and crystal from hers, and the handful of other personal mementos they used as homing devices as they traded residences every few years. Placing the safe in whatever was to be Peter's room had become part of their moving ritual. He stored his stamp collection in its top drawer.

Only she and Edward knew the combination, though; they kept a written record of it in their safe deposit box at Barclay's in London, along with a duplicate version of their will, in case something ever happened to both of them. She twirled the knob to the right three times, twice to the left, once again to the right, and tugged.

The safe swung open. Clare pulled out the papers: her and Edward's will, their marriage certificate, the children's birth certificates, everyone's passports, and Jamie's Consular Report of Birth Abroad. Some jointly owned stock certificates, the certificate of ownership for the Turner. Underneath them all, in the back, the box holding her maternal grandmother's ring.

*I mean, if you still had it. If you hadn't given it over to the wrong person.*

His clear eyes on her.

*I never told anyone, never will. If I had done, you'd be in the ground now yourself for what you did, wouldn't you?*

"Aren't you coming, too?" she asked, grasping the towel to her chest.

"I'll be back. You go for a swim." He climbed into the driver's seat of the camper and looked into the side mirror before putting it into reverse. And there she was, in a beach parking lot, somewhere on the middle Atlantic shoreline, like a little crumb waiting for a seagull to sweep down and devour it.

She watched the camper disappear. She picked her way through the beach grass down to the sand. All around her, families were

setting up for the day, children racing for the water and returning, squealing from the cold, mothers laying out hampers. She
found a rounded-out hollow in the base of low dunes and dug in
a space for herself.

When he returned to get her, the families were all gone. The sun
was already setting. Her skin was painfully red, and her nose and
arms were erupting in freckles. She trailed him back to the parking lot without saying a word. He opened the back of the camper
to get her a beer, and she saw that whatever had been in there had
been emptied. There were his knapsack and her tote bag. A paper
grocery bag with cokes and beer in it. And the duffel bag.

When she got behind the steering wheel, she couldn't help herself. She checked the odometer. He had driven one hundred and
fifty miles since he'd dropped her off that morning. But she had
no idea to where. She didn't ask either. She turned the key in the
ignition and put the car into gear.

"That's it," he said, sliding into the cab of the camper with the
duffel. The mixed smell of sun, sea, and cigarettes entered with
him. Sweat glued her naked skin, where her tank top didn't cover
her shoulders, to the car seat. The feeling was pleasant, even the
sunburn, like summer vacations were supposed to be. "We can return the camper to the car hire now."

She didn't ask what was inside the duffel, now tucked between
his legs half under his seat. Nor did she ask why he took it in
with him when he stepped out to use a service station restroom
north of Philadelphia on the Jersey shore.

When they dropped off the camper at the rental agency, she
looked at the odometer again. She didn't know when, but sometime before they'd returned—maybe when she'd gone into the
restroom herself—Niall had managed to alter it. Almost none of
the miles they covered, together or separately, were recorded.

\*     \*     \*

She put the certificates back into the safe and opened the ring box. Granda had been first generation in America, born on a dirty street in Brooklyn, but he grew up to be a baseball star of sorts in addition to a canny businessman. He'd kept his baseball jacket, Phineas O'Donnell printed across the back, in a glass case in his den and, until the year he died, would take Clare's brothers out into the backyard of their house in Greenwich, Connecticut, and throw a ball around with them. He met her future grandmother just off the boat from Sweden, working days as a clothier's model and nights at a nightclub as a coat-check girl. She was just taller than he was, with a twenty-two-inch waist and icy blond hair that she wore in a neat chignon at the nape of her long neck. He found out when she'd be working at the nightclub and reserved a permanent table for those evenings. He sealed the deal by offering her the grandest emerald she'd ever seen, held in place by a Celtic trinity knot in 18-carat platinum and two diamonds.

"Go Irish," he famously told her.

"Yah," she said. "I better."

Granda's cheeks turned fatter and redder with every year they were together. Mormor stayed as tall and sleek and taciturn as when she graced the pages of the Franklin Simon & Co. catalog. She outlasted him by a decade, growing paler every year, until one morning she simply didn't wake. Their descendants received two surprises at the reading of her will. The first was that Mormor had been six years older than she'd told everyone. The second was that she'd bequeathed her famous emerald engagement ring to Clare.

Clare closed the ring box and slipped Mormor's ring on her finger. She wouldn't fuss over not having time left to clean it before the dinner. The emerald, cosseted by the diamonds, sparkled on her finger, casting deep green-blue prisms of light over her thin skin and polished fingernails. Delicate coils of platinum wove around it, shooting pinpricks of silvery light, like moonlight breaking over the crests of waves. It was a ring that demanded to be looked at by everyone who came near it.

"It's a dinner ring, in truth," Mormor had once said to Clare. "Your silly Granda, always making a big show. You can't wear a ring like this daily." But she had.

The clock in Peter's old room chimed once, marking the quarter hour. Clare laid the stock certificates back into the safe, placed the empty ring box down on top, and swung the door shut, turning the knob. She needed to get the place cards out before their guests arrived. And she needed to wake Jamie, bundle him off into his room before Edward and the rest of them got there.

# FOURTEEN

Within five minutes, she had slipped the place cards into their little silver holders around the table. She peeked into the kitchen. Amélie and her cousin were finishing a quick supper. Mathilde was standing over them, ladling out potatoes like a character from Dickens. Half-readied plates of starters marched up and down the other side of the long central table, waiting for the asparagus to be added to them. Yann, the waiter-cum-butler, was out of sight—on the little kitchen balcony having a last smoke, no doubt.

Just enough time to nip back into the bedroom and wake Jamie. She strode back down the long hall, listening to the sound of her heels. The efficiency of their *clip-clip-clip* reassured her. Everything else was crazy, but she'd managed to get dinner in place.

She sat down on the bed next to her son and brushed aside the hair that had fallen over his face. The scent of his breath, warm and slightly rancid, wafted up to her, clashing with the coolness of the coming evening. "Jamie," she said, and patted his shoulder.

When he rolled away, she shook him a little harder. Then she left him to brush her teeth.

When she came back out of her bathroom, Jamie was awake but not up.

"You need to go to your own room," she told him, sitting down beside him again. "Daddy will be here any minute."

Her son stood. He rubbed his eyes.

"Are you hungry?" she asked.

"I had pizzas with Marc and some other guys. I met them after they got out of school. I had to borrow some euros from them..."

"Okay, then. Just stay in your room. You can see Daddy afterwards."

Jamie wavered before her. "Mommy?" he said.

"Yes?"

"I love you."

"Why, Jamie," she said, reaching towards him, but he was gone.

She swam her hands up and down the length of the coverlet. And if they did end up in some place like Kyrgyzstan? What then would happen to Jamie? The emerald snagged on the fabric, and she carefully disengaged it. All those Thanksgivings Clare and her brothers had seen it winking from their grandmother's hand as Mormor carried out the turkey she would never learn to make correctly, which, in fact, Clare's mother would arrive in the morning to dress and put in the oven to keep them all from being poisoned. But still her grandfather would take the heavy platter from Mormor's hands and kiss her cheek admiringly. "My bonny Swedish prize," he would announce, even as her blond hair faded and her shoulders tumbled inward. Clare had always planned to pass the ring along to Jamie; she wanted him to be able to share it with a wife who would protect him as well as she had tried, or maybe a daughter who would clutch at his heart the same way as he had at hers. Peter would have the Turner, which he'd hang on the wall of a well-appointed home, wherever around the world it might be, and feel at ease on the honorable path he would undoubtedly take. Peter had already made his choice—he belonged to England. But Jamie? England, so far, clearly wasn't working out for him. Maybe he would find his place in Ireland, if Edward got the posting there. Maybe he'd be able to feel a pride and even comfort in his Irish ancestry. From what she'd just learned, Ireland already seemed to hold its appeal for him.

The way he had said her name—*Rian,* with that lilt—as though the girl's very name held magical properties.

Clare stilled her hand and stood. She went down the hall, and surveyed the formal living room. Amélie had set out silver plates of nuts and tiny burnished crackers. She had also closed the windows, so Clare went in and reopened them. She wanted the spring air of Paris. The night's chill hadn't settled yet, and the light evening breeze carried in a remembrance of the warm scent of earth awakening and blossoms opening.

The house bell rang. That would be Edward, arriving with the first guests, undoubtedly the P.U.S. amongst them. He wouldn't open the door with his key, not when accompanied by guests. For one thing, it wasn't dignified. For another, it didn't give the household—including her—proper warning that guests were about to enter.

She could hear Yann's footsteps heading for the door, echoed by those of Amélie's cousin. The cousin would hover in the background, helping Yann hang up coats and pass out cocktails—her own hair neatly arranged now, her T-shirt and jeans traded for a white blouse and pair of black trousers—after the guests had passed through the front hall, Clare there to greet them. It was a science. They were all cogs in its machinery.

She still had a few seconds to run the guests through her mind, matching mental snapshots of their faces with some piece of information about them that would separate them from the scores of other individuals whose hands she shook or cheeks she kissed weekly, a trick she'd learned from Edward. If she did it quickly—

The P.U.S., Toby Pessingham, whom she'd met only a few times and who had been wearing a red tie each time. Perhaps he would be again this evening.

Alain LeTouquet, tennis-loving director general at the Quai D'Orsay, and his wife, Bautista, who was Florentine and took a great personal interest in art. Clare would speak Italian with her, at least initially. They would discuss Clare's latest translation for the Rodin Museum.

Those de Louriacs—Rémy, Cécile, and what were the son and fiancée's names? Clare fished around in her memory, saw her own hand inscribing their names this morning. There the names were: Frédéric de Louriac and Agathe Gouriant D'Arcy. Someday soon, especially if Edward got the Irish ambassadorship, she and Edward were likely to see their same names engraved on a creamy wedding invitation delivered to their doorstep. Recognizing them at tonight's gathering would be simple. They'd be the young ones. The de Louriac seniors she'd run into at a reception just the week before last, and she could picture them all too easily. He'd kissed her hand, with emphasis, and Madame's laugh had sounded like a tuberculin cough, low and puffy. She would ask them about the cave paintings in Dordogne, not so far from their estate. She'd read recently about a new exhibition opening.

Sylvie Picq, ministre délégué au commerce extérieur, blond, sharp, and frighteningly effective, be it at arguing a point over dinner or simply answering her cell phone, and her self-important husband, Christian Picq, from whose latest tome on sociology Clare would have to pretend to have read at least an excerpt. Or else pretend it was too above her to attempt reading. Edward had read most of it. She'd leave it to him to do the requisite flattering.

Hope Childs, the British actress now living in Paris, whose thin face and mysterious hooded eyes everyone knew from her movies.

And the bespectacled Reverend Newsome, John, and his wife, Lucy, whose latest book for young adults Clare *had* read. Lucy had been a pediatrician, specializing in adolescent health, before John had been named chaplain at St. George's in Paris. She'd leaned into Clare after church services last Easter and, eyeing the well-heeled crowd milling about the church steps in their well-tailored spring suits, whispered, "If *I* had gobs and gobs of money, I'd invest in acne cream. Adolescent complexion crises are one thing, like death and taxes, you can always be sure of." She'd said it with a straight face, but Clare had seen her brown eyes sparkling under her Easter bonnet. Clare had ordered the latest of Lucy's novels online that very evening.

Toby, Alain, Bautista, Rémy, Cécile, Frédéric, Agathe, Sylvie, Christian, Hope, John, and Lucy. She had them now in her head. The front door clicked.

The first group entered and, shortly after, the second, like a ringlet of hair uncurling in water, strands separating and fanning out, spreading over the furniture in the reception room. She ushered everyone in, became a high-stepping waterbird, showing them towards the formal dining room, asking after children, the P.U.S.'s wife, the weather. With each cluster, she exchanged words of regret and condolence about the assassinated minister, but only gently so as not to engender deeper discussion or dampen the atmosphere.

Third came the de Louriacs with their next generation, as shiny and burnished as she had expected.

"You are *Americaine!*" said Agathe Gouriant D'Arcy, the fiancée, looking confused, as she flipped a lock of long, lustrous brown hair behind one shoulder. "Not Eengleesh!"

"But, of course, *cherie,*" Frédéric, the son, chided her. "*Maman* told you in the car. Weren't you listening?"

"*Bien sûr,*" the young woman answered, her eyes shifting over the rest of the room in embarrassment, "*je lui écoute toujours,*" and Clare had to suppress a smile.

Aperitifs were passed around but not hors d'oeuvres, as these had already been served at the embassy cocktail party beforehand and they would sit down to eat shortly. Reverend Newhouse grappled nuts into his hand from one of the silver trays on a side table. His wife helped herself to a few also. Clare saw Amélie slip from behind the kitchen door into the dining room. She looked at Clare across the rooms, and Clare nodded. With dinner preparations completed and her job done, Amélie would go home now and soak her sturdy legs in the half tub her apartment probably sported, or whatever she did when she was away from the Residence. Her cousin and the waiter would stay until the end of the meal, helping Mathilde prep, serving the meal, clearing the table, and seeing that the last of the dishes were washed and restacked in boxes. Like the captain of a ship, Mathilde would not leave until the very last course had gone down and all that was left of her glorious meal was a wreckage of cake crumbs and lettuce.

The bell rang again. Unlike cocktail parties, where she and Edward would stand near the butler as he opened the door and retrieved outerwear throughout most of the evening, so as to greet guests as they filed in and thank them as they left, dinner parties required a continuous stirring of the pot, with both of them at the soiree's center. They couldn't afford to linger in the hallway in between arrivals, but they reconvened in the foyer to greet the last of the evening's dinner guests, the ministre délégué au commerce extérieur and her husband, Sylvie and Christian Picq. Pleasantries were exchanged, and kisses and handshakes. Clare noticed a strain on their faces; undoubtedly the assassination.

Still, the evening was going well. People needed to gather when they were in shock or mourning, and why shouldn't this be at the Residence? What mattered was that no one was giving off an air of wishing to be elsewhere. She moved to join them in the living room.

"Clare," Edward said in a low voice, stopping her at the living room's threshold.

She started. Edward wasn't supposed to speak to her one-on-one like this once they had guests. They were to radiate through the group, maximizing their resources. "Jamie's still not answering his phone," he whispered.

She smoothed her suit and exchanged a smile over Edward's arm with Bautista LeTouquet, wife of the directeur général at the Quai d'Orsay. *Tutto è bello!* Bautista mouthed from across the room. *Grazie mille,* she mouthed back. Bautista was gathered by the mantel with the permanent under-secretary, the directeur général, and Hope Childs. The P.U.S. *was* wearing a reddish tie; a fat petal from the calla lilies, radiant in the evening light, brushed his eyeglasses. Theirs wasn't the ambassador's breathtaking residence but, as Bautista said, everything did look beautiful.

"I've talked to him. Don't worry. He's squared away for the moment."

He shifted, blocking her view of the living room with his shoulder. "I don't see how you can be so blasé. He was caught in her room. He had the key to the lab. The school is sure he stole the chemicals."

Clare felt the air swish out of her, as though she'd been punched in the stomach. She swept the room with her regard, trying to slow things down, like dropping a sailboat keel. Madame de Louriac was standing empty-handed, and she caught the eye of the waiter and gestured. What was Edward *saying?* "Chemicals? You mean drugs?"

"Clare!" Edward caught himself. He glanced at the room over his shoulder to make sure no one had looked their way. "*Clare.* I thought you said you had spoken with him. *And* Barrow."

"Yes, but—"

"Did you?"

"Yes. But . . . not about everything. He just told me he had been caught cheating again, and hadn't been allowed to hand in his science lab. That's about all." She hesitated. "And that this girl's name is Rian."

"*Cheating?* Who said anything about cheating?"

"Jamie. I mean—"

"This had nothing to do with cheating. Did he say that?"

"I don't know," she said. "I mean, yes. I mean, I thought so. Look, you know Jamie. He didn't want to tell me anything. I couldn't get anything out of the school either—I called but the headmaster wasn't there, and I could only get the secretary. And then I didn't want to call back before I'd heard Jamie's side of the story. I did my best, Edward. It was a busy day; I was really trying to make this dinner work. And . . ." It all raced through her head: Finding Jamie lying on his bed, reading; seeing the Turk's face flash up on the television screen; Niall sitting there waiting on that bench for her. She leaned a hand against the wall. "And, things didn't go quite as planned."

Edward bowed his head towards her. He spoke very softly, barely moving his lips. "There was no cheating. The girl is part of an antiwar group. They're planning a disturbance near Ten Downing Street: Chinese party poppers with flash powder for a bang and antiwar flyers shooting out. That's what the chemicals were for. To create an extra bang."

"Chinese party poppers?"

"They call themselves the FFF. Fight Fire with Fire."

There was a buzzing in her head, a lightness. "Fight Fire with Fire?"

"*Yes.* The girl claimed they weren't planning any actual damage—but according to what I've found on them, the group's leader was arrested just before the invasion, on suspicion of attempted arson. At Whitehall. This is no ordinary grassroots student organization. And even if they were just poppers, can you imagine? In this atmosphere? The police aren't fooling around in these times, especially not around the prime minister. They're carrying loaded weapons."

Arson? Explosives? She tried to grasp what Edward was saying. *There will be gates, there will be grounds,* he had said about sending Jamie to boarding school, then reached for the newspaper. Jamie was supposed to be safer over there. That was the whole point of this miserable transfer to boarding school.

"And the girl? This Rian?" she said.

"Ireland. County Mayo. She's related to one of the teachers, studying art in London, and was granted a staff room in exchange for working as monitor at the sports center. When they found the two of them yesterday evening in her room, they dismissed her on the spot and told her to be off the grounds by nine this morning. Barrow was looking into having her deported on the basis of antigovernmental activity, but when they called me, we agreed, as there wasn't anything actually illegal in her room, just illegally procured, and not by her but by *our* son—indeed, the only person who'd already broken any laws was our son, stealing from the laboratory—it might cause more trouble than it was worth to get the police involved. I'm working on that still."

She nodded, stupefied. Thank God for Edward; thank God he acted swiftly. Barrow wouldn't want news of what had happened to get around or their name in the papers.

But. If Barrow decided to bury the whole incident, there'd be nothing to stop Jamie from continuing to be involved with this organization. Certainly not from becoming further involved with this older girl. A week would pass. He'd go back to Barrow. The girl would still be there, somewhere, in London. He would find her. Or she would find him.

"What did they catch them doing? I mean, in her room."

"Making flyers." He shook his head, looking at a complete loss, and repeated, "Making flyers."

He pulled away from her, straightened. "We have to go in there," he said, adding, "No sign of rain, for a change," in a normal, louder voice, and she saw him reassemble his face into its usual calm as he turned back towards the room. He tipped his head in the direction of the reverend, who was chatting with the Picqs. The reverend nodded back and his hand went out; he rested it on Christian Picq's forearm.

They were discussing the slain official.

She should have canceled the whole damn evening after Jamie's phone call. Or, at least, after the parliamentarian's murder. All this desperate effort, putting off Jamie's problems, trying to ignore her own, just to make *this* happen.

She watched the group take an almost imperceptible move in towards one another, then move out, like a heart beating. The reverend was speaking.

But, no. She saw the faces on their guests, turning like buttercups towards the light. She and Edward were carrying on not just for the ambassador. They were proving that life would go on, could remain decent no matter what happened, despite the fact that someone could get up in the morning, go to work, and never come home again, because someone disagreed with their opinions, or race, or religion.

She felt flush. Fight Fire with Fire? Setting off explosions by the prime minister's residence? How could things have gotten to this? How could Jamie be so *stupid?*

"We need to go in," Edward repeated.

How? There was a filament loose somewhere inside her, and she'd passed the same disorder on to her Jamie.

"An art student?"

Edward looked at her, his expression clear, unreadable. "Not now," he said.

He went to join their guests. He left her.

She wanted to go back to Jamie's bedroom and shake him awake immediately. "What were you thinking!" she wanted to shout. "How could you? Do you think it stops with Chinese party poppers? Do you think it *ever* stops?"

She wanted to call Barrow and interrupt the headmaster from whatever he might be doing—eating dinner, having cocktails, settling down to a nice book. "Why didn't anyone there *see* what was happening to Jamie?" she wanted to say. "What was Barrow doing hiring a girl like that in the first place? At the sports center of all things." Had she access to the lockers? To the showers? How could they be so stupid as to put young boys together with an unattached girl in that way in such a setting?

Edward had joined the group around the reverend. He was leaning in to listen, looking grave but composed.

*"Tout le monde est arrivé?"* Yann said, coming up from behind her, holding a tray of empty wineglasses in his hand. *"On passe à table?"*

*"En dix minutes,"* she said.

The waiter nodded and returned towards the kitchen.

Chinese firecrackers were a party popper. The Chinese set them off at their New Year: a bit of a bang and then brightly colored streamers shooting out into the sky. Tiny translucent parachutes, like aerial jellyfish floating down against the clouds. Catching the parachutes was considered good luck by the Chinese, and the party poppers were operated even by small children. A toy. That's how Jamie must have seen it, as though he were playing at superheroes, like he and Peter used to do when they were little, tying towels around their backs as they zoomed up and down the apartment, and the popper would be his magic wand.

A pretty, older Irish girl. The first he'd felt an interest in. Or, perhaps, the first that had shown an interest in him. An anti-war conviction with which he already sympathized, over which he'd even obsessed. Of course he'd agreed to help the girl. Peter wouldn't have. Edward wouldn't have. They would have been able to differentiate between what was right and what was wrong—such as stealing from a school lab, such as setting up explosions in central London less than a year after fifty-two civilians had been slaughtered on public transportation—and too sensible to participate during times as troubled as these, no matter how much they liked the girl or agreed with her politics. But not Jamie. Not her Jamie.

"We'll go for a wee holiday, you and me," Niall said. He handed her a beer. They were sitting on her aunt and uncle's patio, and the heat still hadn't abated. It would turn out to be one of the hottest, driest summers in Boston's recorded history.

Her heart jumped up. A trip together out in the open, like real couples did?

"To the shore. You'd need to hire the car for me."

"You don't have a license?"

"I'm not twenty-five yet. I wouldn't be old enough as a foreigner. But I found a company that will hire to a twenty-year-old with a license if you are a U.S. citizen."

She didn't ask anything more about it. She didn't even ask where precisely they were going. She followed his directions. She took a one-week leave from her summer job at the museum. She told the landlord of the room she'd rented in Cambridge for the upcoming school year that she'd move in immediately upon her return. She packed a bathing suit, a towel, and a change of clothing. She packed a camera. She did not pack film for it. She put the gold-filled band he gave her into her wallet.

"People pay less mind to a married couple," he said.

She arrived at the bus station in Boston on the designated day two weeks later. He was there already, lining up to board a vehicle. She shuffled in after him, settled in a separate seat without so much as glancing at him, and got off where he got off in New Jersey, still without saying a word to him. In this second bus terminal, with no one looking, she slipped the false wedding band onto her ring finger. She went to the counter of the car-rental agency without him and filled out the papers for the camper he'd reserved under her name.

"If anyone ever asks where you were," he'd told her back in Boston while he was explaining how they would travel, "if the car hire comes back to you, you just tell them you were meeting a man and you didn't want anyone else minding your business.

If you put it that way, no one will ask anything more about it, not even your ma and da. They'll assume it was someone married. And if someone does interrogate you, you just make up a first name, or use the name of someone you know at school, and say he never showed up."

She hadn't asked him how or even why anyone would ever find out about her having rented a car in New Jersey. She'd blocked that word "interrogate" right out of her thought processes, though it would come back to her over and over later, like remembering the sound of brakes squealing right before an accident.

She'd just nodded and said okay. She and Niall were going on a trip together. They would be alone, far from the eyes of her aunt and uncle. That was what mattered.

And so, she pulled out of the rental-car lot, mindful to check the side mirrors for incoming traffic—she'd never driven a camper before—and proceeded to the street corner where he'd instructed her he would be waiting. She pulled up to the sidewalk.

"Drive south," he said, slipping in beside her. Sun beat in through the front windshield; the front seat smelled of chemical solvent. He rolled down his window and flipped down both of the windshield's sun visors. "Fancy the beach?"

They spent the first night of their trip sleeping in the back of the camper in the parking lot of a public beach, opening up the back doors with slumber still in their eyes and treading down to the lips of the sea at dawn to watch the sun awaken over the Atlantic.

"My green island is on the other side of all that water," he said.

She whispered, half hoping he wouldn't hear, "I'd like to go there."

"You would, then?"

"Of course."

"Maybe you will. Maybe we will together." He threw his arm around her and drew her in close to his warmth. She realized he smelled of her. She must smell of him also. "I wonder," he said, "what it would have been like had my great-granda made the trip to America like yours did, instead of north during the famine."

"If he had——" she said. The clouds moved above her, huge masses of effervescence. She left her thoughts to billow up to them.

Niall grabbed a handful of sand. He let a few grains run through his fingers before tossing the rest of it towards the ocean. "Ah, I'd probably just turned out another freckled-nose Mick in Boston, tending a bar somewhere." He laughed and tugged on her braid.

She slipped her braid back over her shoulder. "Let's go for a swim."

He shook his head.

Their aloneness, the intimacy of their two bodies out in the world, the night they'd spent in the camper, made her feel bold. "Aw, come on. Are you afraid of the cold?"

"I don' swim. I don' know how."

It was like a precious gift, this confession. She understood why he wouldn't ever go to the Cape with her aunt and uncle and the rest of the family. What he couldn't do that she and all of the rest of them could. She also understood why he didn't know how to swim: his childhood had been nothing like theirs. She said nothing more, gathering in every millisecond of that moment to her: the Atlantic dark and deep gray-blue, the sky a softer gray-blue echo with ribbons of the palest pink and a burning white orb radiating out from its core, its rays tracing a brilliant golden path across the water almost directly to their feet on the shore, the cool

feeling of the sand under those feet, the sound of the tide shifting and the twitter of waterbirds wandering the beach disturbed.
Their shoulders, side by side, level, his arm around hers. Over
and over she would come back to this moment, to this feeling.
She understood that in giving her this piece of knowledge of a
weakness, he was giving her collateral. A pact was being signed
between them.

If only she had it to do over! For twenty-five years, she'd been im-
prisoned within an invisible vault of guilt and self-hatred. Today
had arrived like a miracle. But—why hadn't she known better
then? And now Jamie. *Fight fire with fire.*

"She's not as beautiful in person, don't you think?" Dr. Lucy
Newsome said, joining her in the doorway, keeping one eye on
her husband, the reverend, as he approached Hope Childs, the actress. "And yet, you do have to look at her."

Clare struggled to return to the Residence, the evening, the
right now. Her eyes swept around the formal dining room. There
was the reverend, standing just slightly too close to the dazzling
Hope Childs, and there was the imposing Sylvie Picq, turning
away from them. Dr. Newsome, as intelligent as she was, was
detritus on an evening such as this. "Wives" at these events had
limited choices: either they could stay by their husbands' sides
to coach them on other guests' names and remind them of the
ages of their children when asked, or they could congregate with
other wives in a corner, like pedestrians caught in a rain shower
with only one umbrella between them. But the reverend didn't
need this sort of help, and there wasn't much in the way of other
wives tonight for Dr. Newsome to huddle with. One didn't huddle with Mme de Louriac, and Christian Picq was a husband,
not a wife, and not even a trailing spouse, as he had his own

established career in Paris. That left only Bautista for huddling purposes, and Bautista was currently engaged with Agathe and de Louriac Junior, whose mutual gloriousness probably intimidated Dr. Newsome.

She gestured towards a collection of eighteenth-century British Romantic poetry perched on a side table close to the entryway, the first thing she could think of. "I've been wanting to ask you, Lucy," she said. "Do you devise your wonderful books longhand or directly on a computer?"

Dr. Newsome laughed. "Are you thinking of taking up writing, Clare?"

"Good heavens, no. What sort of story would I have to tell?" She cupped a hand behind Dr. Lucy Newsome's upper arm, guiding her back into the formal living room. "Tell me, have you met Bautista LeTouquet? May I introduce you?"

She attached Dr. Newsome to Bautista and the affianced couple and began making the circuit, stuffing her own thoughts back down, allowing her guests' conversations to weave a tapestry in the chilling spring evening air around her, the daytime smell of blossoms ceding way to the scent of candles and wine and cologne. Still, all the while, she kept one eye towards the hall. Jamie was in his room; they were in between him and the door. This time he couldn't slip out without her knowing. She exchanged glances with Edward, and then with Yann. She nodded to Amélie's cousin, who stood waiting in a corner of the dining room.

"Shall we go in to dinner?" she said, scattering the phrase amongst the guests like rose petals at a wedding.

At the table she was flanked by men, the permanent undersecretary on her right, Directeur Général LeTouquet on her left. Edward faced her, down the long, dark length of wood at the other end, the rest of their dinner companions between them. She pressed the bell attached to the table leg by her knee. Instantly, their servers appeared, bearing plates of tender white shafts of asparagus and thin pink cuts of ham, decorated with a buttery vinaigrette and clusters of round mustard seeds and rose pepper-corns.

"*Ah, les asperges!*" LeTouquet intoned as Clare's plate was set down, and Clare knew she'd made the right choice. And here were the dinner rolls Mathilde had stalwartly made herself rather than order from Poilane's or one of Paris's other excellent bakers, pounding that pasty dough into the clouds that Amélie's cousin was now carrying around the table in a silver bowl. Beside each dinner guest she stopped and proffered a selection from the bowl; only the fiancée could resist taking one. Would she be able to re-sist Mathilde's dessert?

"Yes, a moment of silence," Reverend Newsome was saying.

Clare's emerald sparkled under the candlelight, and she turned her palm upwards to quiet it. Who had brought the assassination up? Could it have been Newsome? But that's right—she and Ed-ward had agreed to ask Newsome to give a blessing when they sat down. Edward must have spoken to him about it privately, prob-ably over the phone this afternoon. Of course he had. She lowered her head.

Newsome's elegant British voice rolled over all of them, quot-ing Donne's famous words, like a tonic: "'One short sleepe past, wee wake eternally/And death shall be no more; death, thou shalt die.' Amen," he eventually said and looked up.

"Amen," Edward said and looked up also.

"Amen," she and the others but Hope Childs added.

"Amen," Hope Childs said, her voice deepened.

Clare paused before lifting her fork, to make sure everyone was ready. It was her and Edward's job now to move the conversation forward to another topic, but tactfully.

"Thank you, Reverend," Edward said. "John Donne. Lovely."

"I wonder if children still read him in school," Reverend Newsome said.

"Sometimes I wonder if children read anything in school these days," Lucy Newsome said. "I mean other than computer programs and about biogenetics and all these things that didn't even exist in our day. Certainly, I could bear to sell a few more of my books."

The table laughed, a little. It was weak, but the others appreciated her effort.

"The asparagus arrived early this season," Clare said, to keep things going, having swallowed her first bite of the starter and before taking another. "Despite all the rain."

From his seat at the center of the table, Christian Picq began a discourse in French on the Alsatian village of Hoerdt and why the very best asparagus in the world grew there. His voice was sonorous, probably from giving lectures on sociology year after year in drafty Sorbonne halls; it carried to both ends of the table. *"Donc, c'est grâce à la terre très sablonneuse—"*

"In Alsace," Madame de Louriac interjected, also in French, "they would have this as their *main* course. They wouldn't serve it as a starter."

Clare smiled at her guests and sipped from her water glass. Had she made a mistake in serving the asparagus this way? She let an asparagus tip melt into her mouth. It hovered there and evaporated. She looked around. Everyone was eating it. The problem wasn't the asparagus. Madame de Louriac had expected to be entertained at the ambassador's residence rather than the minister's. It had been a shock not just to Clare to discover she'd be entertaining such a lofty gathering in the Residence. It had been a shock to the guests themselves. They *felt* it. Madame de Louriac wielded her knife in sharp little strokes; she lifted asparagus towards her mouth's dark oval, creasing the bloodred lipstick she'd used to line it.

"It's perfect as a starter like this," Sylvie Picq announced in a clipped tone, and in English. She clinked her fork on the edge of her plate and picked up her glass of white wine. "When they serve *les asperges* as a main meal in Alsace, they do it completely differently. With thick slabs of *jambon blanc* and a choice of three sauces. Frankly, it's old-fashioned to eat it that way. People still do, but it's an exercise in nostalgia. This is the new way to enjoy it."

"They are just superb," the reverend said, wiping his lip with his napkin.

"This is a wonderful time of year," Dr. Newsome said.

Clare pressed the table-leg button again, and the plates were cleared. The table fell into small pockets of conversation. New wine was poured and the fish was brought out, its lemony sauce streaking the lightly spiced new potatoes. It mingled with the pesto, a springtime pageant of yellow and green. Mathilde had again proved herself a genius. The dinner was going all right. Everything was going all right. She could see Edward down at the other end of the table, nodding at whatever Sylvie Picq, sitting at his right hand, was saying. Clare couldn't make out the words. She turned to look at the P.U.S. on her own right hand.

"Very impressive, the French police," the permanent undersecretary was saying. "They caught the culprit in a most expedient manner."

Here was the waiter again, stepping forward from the shadows to check on their glasses.

"Convicting him is another story," Lucy Newhouse said, her brown eyes sharp. "He hasn't confessed, has he?"

The conversation was ricocheting around her. Clare lifted her glass. "Pardon?"

"There's an eyewitness," LeTouquet said. "It's as good as done."

*As good as done?*

"Do you mean the assassination? Do you mean the suspect?" she said.

LeTouquet looked at her with surprise. "Haven't you heard, Mrs. Moorhouse?"

She dropped her hand back on the table. "But *how?*" she said. The police were not supposed to find him that quickly, not this evening, not until after Edward's dinner—not, in fact, *at all.* The doctor was supposed to have come forward to bear witness, to stop the police from going after him.

But maybe there really hadn't been any doctor. Maybe that had all been one big story. Maybe the Turk had been sweating from nerves and not because he was ailing.

"Is he all right?" she said.

Eleven heads on swaying necks, peonies on thin stems, shining in the white and gold of the tableware, swiveling to look at her.

"All right?" asked Lucy Newsome gently.

"I mean, did the reports say anything? About his physical condition?"

"The assassin?" asked LeTouquet.

"This isn't America," Hope Childs said from the other end of the table, seated as she was down by Edward. "If that's what you mean. They don't practice waterboarding and the like in France."

Childs was a cofounder of an organization called Actors Against Torture. They had gobs of money and a direct conduit to any media outlet they wished, which made them powerful;

Edward had explained it to Clare last evening. "What I don't get," he'd remarked, "is if they're against torture, why don't they set their attentions on some of those films that come out? Not only do they glorify violence in their own right, most of them are torture to sit through." He'd smiled then, but he wasn't smiling now. He was staring down the table at her.

"Maybe not, but I doubt the French police will treat a Turk who's murdered a French official to champagne and a feather pillow," answered Lucy Newsome, doing her level best to make Clare's comment seem less startling.

She couldn't explain what she'd meant, not without betraying what she'd kept hidden. She couldn't think what to say. She stared back at Edward.

"Our beloved British poet John Donne," Edward said, cutting into his fish as though she hadn't said anything, "eventually became a priest in the Church of England, didn't he, Reverend? Have there been many poet clerics?"

A pause hung over the table, and then, as though in mutual agreement to leave this uncomfortable moment behind them, all heads turned towards Newsome.

"Oh, gobs," Newsome said. "Here in France, Philip the Chancellor, Hugues Salel; in the U.K., Jonathan Swift, Robert Herrick; in Africa, Desmond Tutu... These are just a few examples. And if you expand the meaning of the word 'cleric' to include all religions, you have all the mystics like Sufi or Kabir... Remember, for a long time, members of religious orders were amongst the only people who were literate."

Clare was saved. Her slip would be forgotten, or at least digested and incorporated into something different. They would probably wonder if she wasn't criticizing America, which wasn't good, but it wasn't quite as bad as suggesting the French would treat their prisoner anything but humanely, especially as there weren't any Americans present. Or maybe they wouldn't take it that way either. Even the permanent under-secretary would know she was uncontroversial, apolitical. They would take her strange question as one of those inexplicable Americanisms most likely—a sort of reality-TV response. In what state had they brought him in? Only Edward would know better. She pressed her knee against the table-leg button for the dishes to be cleared.

Conversation picked up again, and wineglasses were raised as the salad course was brought out. Sick or not, doctor or not, the man she'd met on the street wasn't an assassin. At the very least, he hadn't been the only person involved, and hadn't been the one to do the actual killing. She had seen him, she had seen the time. She wasn't mistaken about that.

"The Musée d'Art Moderne will be opened again soon," Bautista LeTouquet commented.

"How wonderful," she said. "Have you had a chance to see it?"

Breeze wafted into the room, and with it the odor of evening. In the gardens of the Rodin Museum, the marble limbs of the statues would be incandescent in the moonlight and cold to the touch, like the memory of a great passion that had faded. The daffodils would cast an eerie glow, the hyacinths be nothing more than dark shadows. The breeze stirred the table, lifting an edge of the tablecloth and setting the flames of the candles dancing. Clare pressed her hidden button again. When the waiter appeared, she beckoned to him to lean in closer.

"*Fermez les fenetres dans le salon, s'il vous plaît,*" she whispered in his ear.

Cheddar cheese and brie were passed, then cleared away, and the dessert brought out.

"*C'est impossible,*" the de Louriac fiancée said, probing the plate before her. Even she finished every last bit of cake, strawberry, and chocolate.

And then there was just the coffee to get through and the cognac. Clare watched the orangey liquid swirl in their glasses.

Dinner was over.

# FIFTEEN

The last of the dinner guests were on their way out, and even with her slip, and although it wasn't late, their early departure didn't mean the evening hadn't been a success. What counted was that the dinner had gone on despite the ambassador's indisposition, thanks to her and Edward's last-minute intervention, and his guests had left pleased and relatively satisfied. Certainly the food had been good. Everyone enjoyed a good dinner; they weren't as common in diplomatic circles as people might think. Insipid roast beef, another stuffed chicken breast in white wine sauce—meals that Mathilde would never permit to exit the doors of her kitchen. Clare patted down a chair in the living room while Edward walked the reverend and his wife to the door. She moved the flowers back from the mantel to the side table. Everyone had been accepting, ultimately, of the ambassador's sudden indisposition and their equally sudden subsequent intrusion. Clare and Edward hadn't even been on the original guest list, but hierarchy wasn't personal in the Foreign Service; the hosts of the dinner that they had had to back out of to hold this one wouldn't be insulted either. There was something wonderfully pure about the way life within the diplomatic service dispelled any ambiguity as to the link between the personal and professional. People might criticize diplomats for their glibness, but perhaps the transparency of their motives might be considered more honest than the underhanded networking that went on in most professions.

The front door shut, and Edward rejoined her in the quieted living room.

"Well," he said.

"It went well."

"Yes. Even with this business about Jamie."

He sat down in the chair Clare had so recently plumped and folded his hands over his lap. She glanced towards the dining room. "I really should check the kitchen."

He leaned back and closed his eyes. Still, he tapped his fingers against his thigh. "It's been a long day."

"Yes. I'll just be a moment." She slid away, passing through the dining room past the now-barren table, the chairs pushed in, the candles and chandeliers darkened, the silver place-card holders back in their spot in the sideboard, all that glimmer and polish retired into silence.

Light streamed from under the closed kitchen door. She swung it open.

Mathilde sat by the central table, dressed in her thick winter coat. Her oversized handbag stood on the wiped-clean table in front of her. She looked up as Clare came in, and grunted. "I'm still waiting."

When Mathilde worked dinners like this, one of the embassy drivers would take her home after. "No one's come round yet?" she said. "I'll call. I'm sorry."

Mathilde shrugged. "The *asperges* weren't bad," she said, gathering her coat in close to her. "Did the minister like the potato? I went light on the garlic. But can you get someone else in next time? That cousin of Amélie's is a numpty. *C'est un vrai idiot!*"

"What's a 'numpty'?" Clare asked.

*"Un vrai idiot."*

Clare shook her head. She was too tired to humor Mathilde. "She's a nice girl. And she and Amélie work well together." She looked around for the kitchen phone, but it wasn't in its cradle. "Let me get my phone."

She left the kitchen to collect her purse from the console. She couldn't hear any sound from the formal living room. Who knew how late Edward had had to stay up last night, prepping for today's meetings? She heard no noise from the rest of the Residence either; perhaps Jamie was also sleeping. She returned to the kitchen. When she opened her purse to retrieve her phone, she caught a glimpse of the Turk's map.

She snapped her purse shut and pressed the number for the embassy drivers on her phone.

Mathilde eyed her and said, "Thank you, Mrs. Moorhouse."

"Thank *you*. I apologize again for making you come in on your day off. Dinner was excellent."

"I'll rest here a minute, whilst I wait."

"Of course. You must be tired. Please don't worry about lunch tomorrow. And we're set for tomorrow evening as well. Perhaps you can make a Bundt cake on Saturday."

Mathilde looked at her good and hard, as though she was memorizing Clare's face. "Mrs. Moorhouse," she said.

"Yes?"

"I know there's ones that say, What can a Scottish woman know about fine cuisine?"

"No one says that, Mathilde."

Mathilde shrugged this off. "And, I know there's others that say, What can a Swiss woman know about cooking?"

Clare suppressed the desire to look at her watch. Time seemed to be crawling. The embassy driver had said ten minutes. "Mathilde, you are a wonderful cook. No one argues about that."

"My father met my mother in a hospital during the war. They started a little hotel together, right after, peaceful-like, in the countryside. I grew up in its kitchen."

"I'd guessed your childhood must have been something like that." There was nothing to do but wait. It couldn't be that much longer. And she'd waited this long—what was another few minutes? "You have such a natural sense for cooking; it's not something one could learn in a class. Did you just hear the bell?"

"I never took to school," Mathilde continued, ignoring her question. "I didn't get on with the other kids. They thought I was suspicious-like, see, because one of my parents was foreign. This was after the war. And I didn't like sitting there on a wooden chair studying maths and geography from a torn old book either. I was doing my own maths back home, measuring out herbs, figuring out how much flour and how much sugar. And my own science. Making a cake rise—that was what I'd call science. I took first when I did get myself into a cooking course, but I only took the course so I could get a certificate. To get a place somewhere."

"Yes, I saw that on your résumé," Clare said. "I'm sure you were ten times better than any of the others." She wasn't going to ask how Mathilde had figured out Edward was angling for a new posting, but she could see where this conversation must be headed. Not everyone would put up with Mathilde the way Clare had. But Clare would find someone else in Paris willing to endure

Mathilde's caprices in exchange for the splendor of her culinary skills; the French were at their most tolerant when procuring a good meal was involved. "And when it's time for the minister and me to leave the Residence, I'll make sure you'll be okay. Don't worry."

The cook continued to watch her.

"Mrs. Moorhouse?" she finally said.

"Yes?"

"If I might say something just between you and me?"

When had Mathilde ever asked permission to say anything? "Yes, Mathilde?"

"Just remember: What's for you no go by you."

Clare had seen this old Scottish saying on a needlepoint pillow-case once, when she'd brought Peter up to school at Fettes. She'd asked the teacher who kept it in his sitting room what it meant. *What's meant for you will not pass you by,* he'd told her.

"Thank you, Mathilde," she said.

The lights were off in the living room. She walked down the hall to her and Edward's bedroom. Standing at the foot of their bed, Edward was holding his BlackBerry in one large smooth hand, scrolling down through his messages. "No word from Jamie still," he said. He laid his phone down on the bureau. "I've left I don't know how many messages today. When did you speak to him?"

"This afternoon," she said. "Hang on." She stepped back out into the hall to check that Jamie's door was still closed and there was no sign of light under his door. It seemed cruel to leave Edward worrying about Jamie, but she had enough things to handle without the midnight revelation that she had Jamie hidden here in the Residence.

"Just wanted to check I'd turned the hall light out," she said, returning. She took her suit jacket off and hung it over the back of a chair.

Edward loosened his tie and lifted it over his head. He undid the knot and looped it in half, the dark violet silk slipping through his blunt fingers.

"Clare," he said, his eyes trained on her, "why did you go out to check the light was off and then come back in with it still on?"

"I—it was just...I'm tired."

Edward removed his own suit jacket and hung it up. He unbuttoned his white shirt.

"I forgot," she said.

"Yes," he said, unfastening the buckle on his belt.

"Okay, then," she said.

"All right," he said. He slipped the belt out of his pants' belt straps. "Clare?"

"Yes."

"At dinner. You made an unusual comment."

Her fingers fluttered up before her. How they beat at the air, grasping for something to hold on to. "I know. I'm sorry! I don't know what came over me."

"You surprised me."

She shook her head. "I know, I know. I don't usually make mistakes like that." But I do make mistakes, she thought. If only you knew.

Edward pulled his pants off and laid them over the shelf of his suit rack. He walked across the room to her, his bare legs long and white in his boxers, his chest under his unbuttoned shirt also white, softer than it used to be. "*Everyone* makes mistakes," he said. "It's only human. 'To err is human,' right? Alexander Pope?" He smiled. "A Pope, but not a cleric poet."

She didn't smile back. She shook her head. "Not everyone does. You don't."

"Of course, I do. It was probably a mistake sending Jamie to Barrow. That was my idea."

"No, you wanted to send him up to Fettes. At Fettes, Peter would have taken care of him. He would have made sure nothing like this ever happened. Barrow was my bad idea."

The heat of the bills wrapped around her stomach as she'd walked through Dublin customs. The heavy weight in the back of that camper, driving it up along the Atlantic shore, and the sound of wooden boxes shifting as she went around a corner. She and Niall had never discussed it, but she was sure now that there had been guns back there. Maybe Niall had traded them for the money she later carried, or maybe they also were being gathered to be sent to Ireland and she'd help transport them. All she knew was that she had gone ahead and married Edward and given birth to Jamie and Peter—and her life with them had been built on lies, the biggest lie of all being that she was perfect. She wasn't perfect. Far from it. She couldn't continue pretending.

"Edward, I did something bad once. Very bad."

Edward held a hand up. "Stop," he said. "Wait. Before you say anything, think whether you need to."

She shook her head and seized his hand. "I led you to believe I'd never been to Ireland. It's not true."

"Oh, *that*. Clare," Edward said. An expression of vague relief flitted across his face. "Is that what all this is about? All this strangeness from you? I know that."

She withdrew from him, releasing his hand so forcibly that her own fingers clattered up and almost hit her face. "You *knew?*"

"Clare, I'm career Foreign Office. I'm working for the British Embassy in Washington with Irish Affairs as part of my portfolio. I meet a lovely Irish-American girl, already in her twenties, who says she's never been to Ireland and shows no interest in going. Doesn't even want to talk about it. *No Irish-American girl doesn't want to go to Ireland.* Half the Irish-American girls have even managed to get themselves Irish passports. Did you think I wouldn't notice?" He shrugged. "Never mind that last statement. I didn't mean that how it sounded. I'm not angry about it. Whatever you did, your personal life before you knew me, is your own business. You seem to want forgiveness from me, but I don't need to forgive you for anything, Clare. I'm not Divine. But of course I noticed."

"And...?"

He stopped to close the door before continuing. "And when I decided to ask you to marry me, I had it checked out. I had to make sure something wouldn't come up later. For you as much as for me; in this world, we're both under scrutiny. And I saw you'd been there. Passport records are easy to come by. But the trail ended there. We checked Northern Ireland, too. I'm sorry. It was the times. I had to. Your name didn't come up there either.

"So, I don't know whom you went there to see or what you did while you were there or why you wanted to keep it secret from me. I just know you went, and I can surmise the visit didn't go as you wanted. End of story. I tried to suggest we visit Ireland a couple times, thinking maybe you'd gotten over whatever it was, and when you brushed me off, I dropped it. I hope nothing very bad happened to you there, that someone didn't hurt you, and that it won't affect how you feel about moving there now. I mean, *should* I get the embassy in Dublin. If it would, then, yes, maybe we need to talk further. But you didn't say anything last night when I mentioned the possibility; instead, you worked hard to make this dinner happen. And you are still wearing your claddagh. So if this is just about having pretended not to have been there, and if there is something you'd still prefer to keep to yourself about it, I can live with it. I didn't know you when you went to Ireland. The person you were when I met you, the person you've been every day of our married life together, *that's* whom I am married to."

Clare felt dizzy; she felt breathless. She saw the calm gray-eyed face she woke next to in bed all these years. Then she saw the slightly doughy, creased face of a stranger with a British accent and receding hairline. Was this what life came down to? A succession of shadows, each darker than the last, masking the consummate isolation of human existence. Puff, you dissipated like the sprung seeds on a dandelion weed, one last shadow obscuring the garden furniture.

"You checked up on me? You checked up on me behind my back? And you never told me?"

"That's a bit like the pot calling the kettle black, isn't it?"

He was right. He had married her in good faith and she had lied to him, and lied to him again and again. She'd been far more deceptive than he'd ever been, and than he realized. And in addition to all the rest, she'd pretended she was unattached when she'd still been as attached to Niall as the rusty unbending clasps on an attic trunk. Every waking hour, every night, she'd thought about him. And so she'd stretched her fingers out to Edward before a linen-draped altar and let him slip his family's rings on her fingers and swore before God and their families and a church full of witnesses that she would love and cherish him till death parted them without letting him know that she'd already done the same in an imaginary world over guns and blood money with someone else. As though, with Niall's disappearance, she could make that whole summer evaporate into nothingness by pretending to the rest of the world it had never happened.

"Edward, I—"

"Wait, Clare. Think. You can tell me whatever it is you are about to say. I will listen. But, for the more than two decades of our life together, you have not wanted to and once you've told me, you can never *not* have told me. I do not want you to wake in the morning regretting anything, and I do not need you to explain to me. I *trust* you."

There was Niall, sand in his wavy hair, the freckles popping out of his fair skin, the sound of the Atlantic at their feet, the way their same-size bodies had curved into each other. There he was, disappearing into the crowd at the airport in Dublin, like the last drops of water plunging into a funnel, her trying to cling on to them.

His scent, the heat of him sitting on the bench next to her today.

There was Edward, undressed but for his socks and underpants and unbuttoned dress shirt, with a fat golden band on his ring finger. He thought she was going to tell him about something personal, something intimate; he had no idea the enormity of her betrayal. If she told him now what she'd done all those years ago in Dublin for Niall, he would be worse than betrayed. He would be forced to become an accomplice.

She shook her head. "How can you be so accepting?"

Edward sat down on the bed and pulled off a sock. "It's simple, really. Look, I don't know why suddenly, at almost midnight, after two decades, you have decided to admit to me you have been to Dublin any more than I understood why you felt obliged in the middle of dinner to ask after the well-being of an accused assassin of an important government official. But I do know—whatever it is you are trying to sort out in your heart and head at this moment—in the end, you will do the right thing." He pulled off the other sock and held them in his hand. "Actions mean something. You're a good person."

She felt like crying out. There he was, Edward. The face she saw each morning, the hand that rested on her shoulder came back into focus. She sat down on the bed beside him and slid her arms around his broad chest, laid her head against his neck. He wrapped his arms around her and held her. She looked up into his face and kissed him.

"Jamie's here," she said. "He's in his bedroom. I hid him."

Edward sighed and released her. "Well, at least he's safe. You better go make sure he's sleeping and not waiting up for us. It's too late to talk sensibly with him."

She hesitated before Jamie's door. If she knocked, she might wake him up. But she didn't want to step in on him unbidden, possibly embarrass him, a teenager. She laid a hand on the door as though by doing so she might be able to feel whether or not he was awake. She hoped he wasn't. Edward was right—talking with him would have to wait until morning.

Edward was right about so many things. He was wiser even than she'd given him credit for. She'd done everything in her power to make herself as unnoticeable as possible, swathing herself in beige cloth and neutral opinions. She'd buried the pivotal choice of her life, like the city of Troy, under layers and layers of sediment, even as she carried the remembrance of it with her every minute. And still she hadn't managed to fool him. He had watched her lie, year after year of their marriage, and had never said a thing to her about it.

Was he right also in thinking he could trust her?

*Actions mean something.* Sitting beside Niall on the bench at the Rodin Museum this afternoon, she'd felt as though they knew each other better than anyone because they'd shared this one thing that no one else on earth knew about and that had defined her every waking moment since it had happened. But she didn't even know where he'd slept the night before. And people weren't just their pasts, or their dreams for the future. They were the drugstore where they went to purchase shampoo, and the shampoo that they purchased. They were the jobs they got up and went to in the morning or didn't get up and go to, the movies they chose to watch, the magazines they read. The way they dealt with the people they employed or the people who employed them, whether or not they enjoyed the scent of calla lilies. Whether they brushed their teeth before or after breakfast, or both. When you are young, you can believe you still are your dreams. Then you *become.*

She pushed open the door to Jamie's room. The desk lamp cast a dim halo over the edge of Jamie's bed, its neck stooped down and forward like a swan's. Jamie lay just out of its reach, asleep. He'd pulled her sweater, which she'd shed on his bed and forgotten earlier in the evening, over his shoulders, so that one arm flung out around him in an empty embrace. She lifted it from over his neck and chest and drew the afghan on the foot of the bed over him. His long, thin limbs shuddered; he groaned and sleepily pulled the blanket in around him.

No one planned to grow up and become a bad person. As a young girl, she'd cried over a neighbor's three-legged cat and tried to stanch the bleeding of an injured chipmunk. She'd been horrified by the televised images from Vietnam. Then, one day, she'd found herself combing the dunes of the Atlantic for seashells while her Irish lover was probably delivering guns, and smuggling dollars in a bandage around her midriff.

She understood the source of Jamie's confusion. He had picked up her ambiguity. But she was not going to be ambiguous anymore. She wasn't going to allow the sum of her life to be based on one sole defining moment that had happened when she was too young to know better. Maybe there was no going back, but there still could be going forward. People had to be able to change. A better world had to be possible.

Jamie's face looked flushed, but when she laid the back of her hand against his cheek, his skin felt cool. A wisp of night flew in, and she rose and shut the windows, carrying her sweater over her arm. She returned to the bedside and tucked the afghan in still closer around him. She stood looking at him a few minutes longer, twisting the emerald ring on her finger. Then she kissed him softly, so softly he'd be sure not to awaken.

Edward had drawn a bathrobe on over his pajamas, making him look strangely formal for being in his nightclothes.

"He's fast asleep," she said, "and so should you be. You look exhausted." She slipped her sweater over her shoulders.

He sat down on the bed, swung his long legs onto it. "Aren't you coming to bed?"

She came to the edge of the mattress and smoothed the hair back from his brow. "I have some things I need to do. Don't wait for me." In the silence of the night, the sound of heavy, even breathing from Jamie's bedroom grew like a heart between them.

Edward propped himself up on his elbows.

She withdrew her hand. "Just a couple of chores. Cleaning up. You should take off your bathrobe before you fall asleep in it. You'll be too hot otherwise." She leaned down to kiss him also, and he pulled her down to him.

"Thank you, Clare, for this evening."

"It was a good dinner."

"Yes, it was."

She turned off the overhead light, closed the door to their bedroom, and continued down the hall. She stopped in the formal living room to turn off a lamp that had been left on. In the dining room, she closed a door of the buffet that had opened. She checked that the china plate, with the queen's crest printed around the rim, stood neatly washed and all in its crates, ready to be picked up as soon as the sun rose. She slipped into the kitchen and made sure the back door was double-locked.

Returning to the front hall, she opened the heavy door as gently as she could.

Outside, the courtyard was slippery with darkness. So bustling in the day, the Rue de Varenne yawned before her, a stretch of crooked teeth in the moonlight. She wrapped her sweater closer and wished she'd put on a coat. The early hours of the morning would come before her so-called chores were finished.

# SIXTEEN

The taxi couldn't fit into the narrow streets behind Beaubourg, the futuristic modern art museum plopped down amidst the ancient houses of the fourth arrondissement, so she had to get out and complete the last two blocks on foot. Young couples, bound in skintight black or purple jeans, cropped leather jackets, sneakers or boots, pushed by her, the girls swinging their purses, the boys throttling the necks of wine bottles. A busker wearing a bowler hat and ripped jeans played his guitar to the night, with a dog draped over one thigh, a mostly empty paper plate in front of the other. Two girls, their young faces studded with silver knobs, shared a cigarette. All the activity was disorienting after the desolation of the seventh arrondissement at night; she was flotsam, slapping back and forth against the sand, tossed by tiny but continuous breaking waves, splashed around with pieces of bark and shell and seaweed. Decades had passed since she had had a place in the chaotic nocturnal world other than in taxis or limousines. After she'd returned from Dublin, the pubs of Cambridge might as well have taken flight. That last year at Harvard, she'd hunkered down in the little room she'd hoped to share with Niall, night after night, alone, reading French and Spanish and Italian for hours. Her youth had ended when he'd asked her.

"Turn off the light," he said.

They were sitting on her mattress, on the floor of the little room she'd newly rented. It was far from the campus, in a part of Cambridge where she normally would never have ventured, but she'd signed the lease thinking it was a place where Niall could come without being seen by any of her classmates. If she wanted him, this was the requirement.

"We're cousins," she'd said, the first and only time they'd ever discussed being seen around Boston in public together, "aren't we? Not blood related, but still. We could go to a bar just like that. You know, like family. We could at least act like friends."

"And watch some other feck looking at you like a piece of skirt?"

She turned off the light and settled back next to him. She waited for him to ease her down on the bed where she would feel his taut contained energy against her. But he didn't. He looked at her for a long time, holding her gaze in his sharp blue eyes.

"Clare," he finally said.

"Yes."

"You've heard of Bobby Sands."

"Yes."

"They said he and the others were nothing but common criminals, and the screws treated them worse than that. Even after Bobby was voted MP of Fermanagh and South Tyrone. Even after he starved to death."

She watched his face, waiting for him to continue. He seemed to be deciding something.

He got up and extracted the duffel bag from her closet. He'd stashed it there the day after they returned. *Don't you be opening it,* he'd told her. She hadn't.

He grasped the zipper hook between his thumb and forefinger and pulled. The hook slid along the tracks of the zipper, allowing the lips of the bag to part. When he'd opened it about two inches he stopped and looked at her.

White paper printed with green. The corner of a bill. A "1" followed by two "0"s.

"Ordinary, decent people. That's all it comes down to. They stole our country from us, Clare."

He clasped the bag in his two hands and placed it between them.

"It's up to yourself," he said. "You can say yea or nae."

She saw the way his Adam's apple rose and fell as he said it. She had laid her cheek against it, smelling the salt air on his skin, while seagulls picked around them.

She nodded.


She'd made the choice. No one had forced her. He'd said it was to help regular people, but, as a linguist, she knew better than most how any given phrase could have numerous interpretations. She'd believed what she wanted to believe, when in her heart of hearts, if she'd asked herself any hard questions, she'd have understood that that money wasn't intended to be distributed through any church's coffers. Just as she'd known that whatever she wasn't supposed to look at in the back of that camper had been contraband. Ignoring wasn't the equivalent of ignorance.

But that was long ago.

Clare gathered her sweater around her and quickened her pace. After twenty-five years, there had to be some hope for clemency.

A guardian stopped her at the door to the church, gesturing over his shoulder into its darkened cavity. Billows of clear music echoed out from behind him. Just visible under the dim light cast by a wall sconce, a sign read *IIIème Festival de Musique Ancienne, 22.00.* Clare checked her watch. It was nearly midnight; they must be playing an encore.

*"J'ai oublié quelque chose dedans,"* she told the guard, to gain entry. She *had* forgotten something inside or, if not forgotten, mislaid it. She took a twenty-euro bill from her wallet and placed it in the contribution basket.

The guardian looked her up and down. She knew what he was seeing. She was foreign but not touristic. She was well kept, dressed expensively. She was tall and naturally blond.

He shrugged and waved her in.

Cold rushed her as she entered the church's ancient interior. Centuries of unheated winters seemed to have settled into its stones, a chill that no amount of summers would ever dissipate. She waited for her eyes to adjust to the dimness, then let them sweep the pews, raking the audience. Only a smattering of people were there, tossed amongst the front half of the pews like droplets of rain. A few were gray-haired, but most seemed of that indeterminate age around twenty when teenagers discover they've somehow become adults. Music students, probably; friends of the performers.

She sorted through them until her eyes located an older, sparer figure.

He was on the far left, in one of the last pews, several rows back from anyone else. He didn't look up when she tiptoed in beside him. He moved over to accommodate her, as though she were returning from having stepped out briefly to make a call or use the lavatory. Chanting echoed around them, and she felt she knew this song; it was the story of her years of waiting. The sound filled her body with a supreme sadness. Defying the skeptical look of the peaked arches above them, he took her hand in his, cradling it as though it were a fragile, curious object left tossed up on the banks after the tide receded.

The music stopped and people clapped, but still he held on to her hand. People rose, some to depart, others in order to view the bowing musicians over the heads of the people already leaving. Niall stayed seated, and so did she.

People began streaming back towards the doors. He lowered his face from any hint of light.

"What kept you?" he said with a bit of a smile. He was dressed in the same clothes as earlier in the day but wearing a worn leather jacket. It looked soft against the sharp lines of his body, as though it would melt against her cheeks if she were to bury her face in it. Looking down, she could see the edges of his knees pressing through denim. He was still so handsome. That would have been another one of the reasons they'd sent him to the States to collect the money.

"I never knew you liked music," she said. There was so much they had never talked about. They'd shared so little except for that most intimate act, a crime.

"All Irish like music." He laughed. "I saw you were having people coming round for dinner, and there was a notice for this concert at the museum. I didn't know it would be so bloody cold. I could have just as well waited on a park bench."

She shook her head. "The Luxembourg Gardens would be closed. The Rodin also."

Up against the nearest wall stretched a heavy stone tomb, its contours rubbed away from centuries of frigid obscurity. This was Niall's life, shadows and austerity. The first time she saw him, he was standing on top of a stone wall in a comfortable suburb outside Boston, the sun playing on his hair, and ever after, she'd had the feeling he was taller than he really was. He hadn't bothered to hide his disgust for her and her cousin's ignorance, and she'd taken that to mean he himself knew everything. Sitting beside him in her aunt and uncle's kitchen, she'd been surprised to look into his face and realize he was barely older than she was. He'd been so young and full of life and promise, not much older than Jamie was now. She'd gained much in the years since— Edward, her children, a world so much bigger than the cloistered one she'd begun with in Connecticut. A world she understood so differently. If only he had.

*This is a war,* he'd said. He still believed it.

"I need to tell you something," she said. "I'm glad I lost the money. I'm not saying you were on the wrong side of the argument. I'm just saying I'm glad I don't have that at least on my conscience."

Niall let go of her hand. He nodded. "Right. You married a Brit. And not just any Brit either, but a feckin' servant of the Crown. Diplomatic service."

"That has nothing to do with it. Edwa—my husband's a good person."

"They all..." Niall stopped. "Well. I hope so."

The church was nearly empty now. Up by the altar, the musicians had returned from the vestry to fold chairs and gather their music stands. The guardian was with them, helping. The church's bell rang out: midnight.

"Do you know that's the oldest church bell in Paris?" she said.

Niall studied her. "You always were a clever one," he said softly for the second time that day. He rose and she followed him out of the pew, out of the church, into the street. The inky night air felt gentle and smooth now, after the cloying damp of the church interior. They walked silently through a narrow alley, absent of street lamps, away from the random sounds of motorcycle and car engines and nightclub music, falling back into a long-buried habit of not speaking until they were no longer within view of others. A stray cat ran in front of them.

*I never knew you liked music.*

*All Irish like music. I saw you were having people coming round for dinner.*

She stopped. "What did you mean you saw I was having people round for dinner?"

"I figured you weren't buying all that cheese and asparagus just for you and your husband. He's a Prods. You can't have too many children."

He had never seen her sons. He didn't know anything about them. She brushed the air with her hand. "Did you see me buying flowers before that?"

"I saw you come out of a flower shop."

And so had her Turk. Niall must have seen the Turk also, there, with her, at 10:29 a.m.

"Did you see me talk to someone?"

"A man. And then you were in the shop with a woman. But I'd seen how you go about the city. I thought of the flowers and how they'd come out with the sun shining. I knew this was the day I'd find you in the garden, alone by the statue."

Niall had seen the Turk, too, yet another horrible quirk of fate. There couldn't be a worse witness on earth to corroborate her word. Niall. A *dead* man.

"Never mind him right now," she said. "Look, I want to help

you, and your cousin. But if I gave you money, how could I know it wouldn't end up in the war coffers now? I mean, if things started up again." How could she explain to him? The weight that had been lifted from her shoulders this afternoon, all those years of thinking about what she'd help do. What they'd help do. "We're so lucky. God, Niall, we are *so lucky.*"

"Lucky? Are you taking the piss out of me?"

"Yes, lucky."

Niall stopped. He stepped in towards her, letting a bit of the streetlights glance off his profile. He seized her hands and held them to him. In the moonlight, the emerald on her finger sparkled, dark and green as the Atlantic under a troubled sky. "I'm not lucky, Clare. I'm not even *alive.*"

The feel of his skin against hers, so rough against her smoothness, the energy within them. Twenty years of his life, wasted.

*My green island is on the other side of all that water,* he'd said. Then another voice, a smooth, calm one: *I trust you.*

She withdrew her hands.

There was a flurry of dark wings in the street, only roosting pigeons awakened by their passage, but Niall shied away, receding into a doorway. He was hiding, forever hiding. A younger Niall, with the summer sun bouncing off his dark hair, his white skin; his every movement an expression of committed, concentrated energy. A Niall who, already as a teenager, was prepared to risk his life for what he believed in. She and her youthful crowd had learned to play tennis competitively and read the important tomes by the important Johns: John Maynard Keynes, John Milton, John Quincy Adams. They'd worn the right clothes, seen the right movies, and supported the right political causes. But if something went wrong, it had always been someone else's mess to clean up.

She stretched her right hand back out.

They both looked at it.

"Take it," she said.

"Are you trying to buy me off?"

"No. I want to give you something of mine. Because..." She looked away. "I want some part of me to go with you. Look, I know nothing I can give you will equal twenty years of your life. But this is what I have that is mine and mine alone to give. For the first time in decades, I feel hopeful, and I want you to have some hope, too."

She held her hand out for what seemed like ages, one long hot summer rising between them, twenty-five long cold years pressing back down beside it.

He held her wrist fast as he slid the ring off her finger. He turned it over in his hand, as though he were reading it. One arm looping around in platinum, two posed hands holding a huge heart-shaped emerald betwixt them, secured further by diamonds; how that ring had sparkled on her grandmother's graceful, slowly aging hand. *Go Irish,* Granda had said and *Yah, I better,* Mormor had answered, the start of a love that had seemed to stretch beyond the grave. Every time Clare slid the ring over her finger, she felt the pride her grandfather had had for his motherland in having it made, as well as his pride in the woman who would wear it. All that love. All that certainty. In Niall's hands now.

"It's a claddagh," he said softly.

She nodded. "Yes."

"That can't have come from your man."

"No."

He examined its deep green edges, felt the smooth of its facets with his thumb. "I'm not fighting anymore, Clare. If you were ever to read about some bastard down Derry way lifted for blowing up a police station, it wouldn't be me. That much I can tell you."

She hesitated. "You're going home."

He shrugged, held the ring under the light of the street lamp, causing it to sparkle. "If I tried to sell it, they'd think I stole it. Or worse, for both of us, that I blackmailed it out of you. Either way, it could come back to you."

He didn't say anything further for a while, and she had no idea what was going through his mind. She wasn't sure what was going through her own. He looked up, gazing at her face with the same air of appraisal he'd given the emerald. "The British government didn't give us any other choice, Clare."

"I'm not saying you were bad men. I'm not saying I even understand any of it. But innocent people got hurt, on both sides, and that can never be right. There has to be a better way."

"Not all wars can be fought around a conference table. You think we were risking our lives for a bit of craic?"

"Of course, I'm not saying that. But while very few things in the world are black and white," she said, "maybe one or two things are. It can't be right to kill innocent people. It can't be right to go blowing up cars in the middle of the street on a Friday afternoon."

He sighed. "Think what you want. I'm glad if it's over. I'm not glad the British are still there, but I'm glad if there's peace in the streets and bread on the tables. But remember this. You don't get peace unless first you fight a war. And for the one man to be a peacemaker, the other has to have made the war. I don't like those stories either. But we had our own stories." He handed her the ring back. "Not enough, Clare. You keep your ring. You keep your guilt also. And I'll keep mine."

"Niall—"

"I deserve what I got, but not for what I tried to do. For the amateur way I went about doing it. And for involving an innocent American girl. I'm sorry for that, Clare. I am. Honest."

"You aren't hearing me, Niall. I *am* keeping my guilt. I know neither of us can change the past. But we can use it to do better tomorrow."

The night air stirred, caressing her neck. A piece of paper glanced off her calf, vanished. Niall leaned against the door behind him and shook his head.

"I made a fecking hash of it, didn't I?" he said. "But I paid the price, too, didn't I? That's the big laugh—I might as well have just gone straight to the R.U.C. myself, said I'd dropped the money in the Liffey, then after I got out of prison, told the lads the Brits took it off me. No one would have known about you, I would have done ten, fifteen years, been out in time to enjoy the benefits of the Good Friday Agreement. Not stuck in this hell of my own makin'.'"

"So, you're going home."

He shrugged. "There's my cousin."

"Even without the money."

"Feck the money. Feck it *all*," he said, stepping out of the gloom. He drew her to him, kissing her as though he were kissing right through her. There was nothing but that feeling, that feeling of *him*, spreading through her gut, her limbs, into her fingers, obliterating all the time that had passed between.

He released her, and she felt him drain from her body slowly; a shock, that iridescent glow that came at dusk as the light leveled and faded until all that was left was a glimmer, a silhouette. It spilled away, another life's blood, into the night, into the Parisian gutter.

His eyes searched hers, and she remembered the first time she'd seen them. How startled she'd been by their color. So bright, so clear, like a winter day.

She shook her head.

He held her in his gaze. Finally, he nodded. "You always were a clever one," he said, for the third time, the last time.

She put her ring back into his palm. She folded his fingers around it. "Have it taken apart. It will be worth a lot. It'll give you a head start."

He lifted the ring in his hand, not so differently than he'd lifted her hand so many years ago in her aunt's steamy kitchen, as though it were not just an object or a small piece of a whole he'd just come upon but something that, thanks to the greatness of its fragile beauty, possessed an existence of its own. After so many years, his history, her history, their history, had all been rewritten. She would no longer try to forget Niall, but he would no longer haunt her.

They looked at each other one last time.

"You go that way," he said. He pointed down the unlit street towards a beacon of light, a busier thoroughfare. "I'll watch till you're out of the darkness before I go the other way.

"Good-bye, Clare," he said.

She forced herself to say it. "Good-bye, Niall."

# SEVENTEEN

S he would not look back.

They'd said good-bye now; the good-bye they hadn't said in Dublin. She placed one foot ahead of the other until her steps took on an existence of their own. She listened to the rhythm of her heels on the pavement and allowed it to lead her through the narrow cobbled streets of the fourth arrondissement. They twisted and turned, and slowly they felt firmer and surer, and she knew she was going in the right direction. Now she was on the Rue de Rivoli, and the street widened and flattened out. The Ile de la Cité was a short way; she would walk there. How far she had come from yesterday morning, when she'd woken up to the feel of Edward's reassuring hand on her shoulder and the alarming thought of moving to Dublin. How much had happened! But this was life: random. What she would do next might make moving to Dublin impossible again, but that was hardly her purpose. The thought of moving to Ireland no longer scared her. The only thing that scared her now was the possibility of repeating her mistakes—and then watching her child repeat them also.

La Tour St.-Jacques jutted up into the blackened sky before her, its jagged heights looking like the peaks of an ornate sand castle after being hit by a wave. She turned left onto the Rue St. Martin. Again, awakened pigeons fluttered up, blackened silhouettes less a shape than a movement. They cooed overhead and bobbed from one sill to another. They were the carrion birds of the inner city, hovering over the decay and discard of urban life. A window was drawn shut, and they flew up then relanded, settling back down to sleep.

She reached the Avenue Victoria. A sprawl of couples spilled out of a restaurant across the street from her. The restaurant front read The Green Linnet, written in spindly white lettering against a green background. Of course she would now come upon an Irish pub, on probably the only street in Paris named for an English monarch. Could this day become stranger? But it was no longer the same day, or day at all. It was past midnight, in those odd hours where night flirts with morning. The women teetered on spiked heels, reaching for cigarettes and their companions' arms to support them. The men bantered loudly amongst themselves. One pulled out a lighter. How happy they looked. How vulnerable! A violent burst of nails in a London tube stop during the morning rush hour, an airplane shoved through an office wall. Who was to say that a bomb wouldn't go off right here, right now? La Conciergerie's majestic spires rose up in front of her. People had died here already; Marie Antoinette spent her last hours here before being carted off to La Concorde for beheading. The tiny gilt tube of lipstick, smooth black-leather wallet, shoe heels, forearms, calves, and ankles, hours spent loving, dreaming, arguing, plotting, fussing . . . exploded into millions of pieces splashing through the air. It took one moment: the wrong place at the wrong time and someone with a wrongheaded notion of justice. How insane. She'd secretly lived a lifetime in the shadow of this world, well before 9/11 occurred and checking under waiting-room seats for unclaimed luggage became a global habit. But all those years of thinking about what might have happened, what she might have helped make happen, had taught her something. Fear could be converted into a kind of terrorism of its own. She had to live in the world, for good or for bad. She had to be part of it.

The sight of the Seine interrupted her thoughts. There was a song to the way the water moved. It swayed like a woman's body, nudging the banks of the Ile de la Cité, the lights of the Pont Notre-Dame burnishing her liquid flesh in gold. Reaching the Ile de la Cité, the small island at the center of Paris in whose soil a raggle-taggle group of Celtics known as the Parisii first jabbed their spears and unfurled their animal skins amongst the willows, thus founding what was arguably the most lovely city in the entire world, Clare had to stop a minute to take it in, to make a final assessment of herself and her surroundings, before surrendering herself to someone else's description. She was Clare Siobhan Fennelly Moorhouse, forty-five years old, married with two teenage sons. She was born in Hartford, Connecticut, and grew up in a suburb of false colonials with clapboard finishes. She was standing all alone on a bridge in the middle of the night in the middle of Paris, something she hadn't done since she first visited the city as a college freshman. And the world before her eyes was beautiful.

A drunk passed by, his body bent in her direction by an invisible wind. She returned to walking. She crossed the bridge, reached the streets of the Ile de la Cité. A young couple, a careless amalgam of loosely draped scarves and shaggy hair, leaned into each other against a tree on the Quai de la Corse. She resisted the urge to stop and stare. She was walking through a coffee-table book of Paris. But she had her final errand of the day to carry out. She kept walking.

A few more moments of moving through the silence and she reached her destination. On her left loomed the monumental Hôtel-Dieu. On her right the massive stone walls of the Préfecture de Police. She'd been here before to process papers. Locals came to the Préfecture to obtain driver's licenses, and foreigners to become legal. But criminal investigations were also launched within its warren of dim, dusty rooms, as well as projects for municipal public safety. She'd heard as much at a cocktail party. And an office was kept open twenty-four hours to receive criminal complaints.

First she needed to find it. Nothing was ever streamlined in France, least of all bureaucracy. She hesitated in the Préfecture's shadows, wandering the length of the street until she reached the other bank and Notre-Dame Cathedral. She felt eyes on her, not those of late-night carousers or ambling tourists. Were there guards watching? Normally, she would have sought one out to ask directions, but these guards wouldn't bob their caps toward her like those she passed every day and had come to know by sight along the Rue de Varenne. She waited until she saw movement around one corner. She followed in its direction. A lone policeman, obscured by the light of night.

"Officer," she said in the politest French she could muster, "I'm looking for the police station."

He screwed up his face. *"La Préfecture?"*

The Préfecture loomed over their shoulders, a huge lacy monument to French bureaucracy. She shook her head. He must think her an idiot.

"No, I mean I wish to speak with someone. About a crime?"

"You have been a victim of crime?"

"No. Not exactly. I want to speak to someone about someone else's crime."

"You must go to your central police station if you wish to make a report. In your district."

"No, but it's not that kind of a crime. I mean it's not related to my district."

He continued to stare patiently at her. "Are you all right, Madame?"

"Yes, yes, I'm fine. It has nothing to do with me." There wasn't any point in arguing. Instead, she asked, "Could you tell me please where the closest central police station is?"

After he'd finished explaining, she turned back towards the right bank. The kissing couple was still there; the drunk had moved on. She crossed back over the bridge. A lone taxi waited at the stand by the nightclub. He must have just let someone out. She peered in and saw the driver speaking on his cell phone. She tapped on the window, and he jumped, then scowled with embarrassment. She climbed in.

"*Bonsoir, Monsieur. Dix-huit, Rue du Croissant.*"

When he drew up by the modern glass-fronted police precinct, the driver betrayed no interest. He put out his hand and accepted her money.

She showed her *carte speciale* to the policeman at the entry. He lifted the diplomatic identification card between two fingers to examine it, raised an eyebrow.

"Are you here alone, Madame?" he asked in French. And when she nodded, added "Why?"

"Because."

He looked at her as though to check whether she was insulting him. When he seemed to have decided she wasn't, he handed her

ID card back and pointed to the waiting room. She tried not to look at the others who were waiting also—a young man with an old woman, two middle-aged men—willing herself to become invisible by virtue of not seeing.

Hours seemed to pass rather than minutes. Years, even. The time was late now; the very air felt tired. Finally, the policeman filing complaints motioned to her. To her surprise, when she approached the counter, he smiled.

*"Bonjour, Madame."*

"I am here about the murder this afternoon at Versailles," she said in French. "I have information about the suspect."

Something almost imperceptible shifted behind the face of the police officer. His smile slackened, and he looked more closely at her. He requested her identification and studied it, glancing back and forth from the photo to her face. "Please take a seat right there," he responded in French finally, pointing to a nearby chair. "It will be just a few minutes."

She sat down to wait, his eyes keeping track of her. She felt as though there were eyes in the wall watching her, too, as though she might bolt for a door or evaporate or somehow disintegrate and the building itself wanted to be able to grab hold of her sweater before she might do that. About fifteen minutes later, a plainclothes detective appeared, with as many rings around his eyes as the cross section of a tree.

"Madame Moorhouse?" he said.

*"Oui."*

*"Suivez-moi, s'il vous plaît."*

He led her down a long, narrow corridor into a tiny linoleum box of an office.

"You are American," he said in English after she was seated.

"Yes."

He fingered the forms she'd filled out and the identity card she'd handed over. "But married to the second at the British Embassy here in Paris."

"Yes."

"Does your husband know that you are here?"

She shook away his question as though it were a fly buzzing around her. *"Monsieur—"*

"There is no one here with you?" He looked around as though someone might have suddenly appeared. Finding no one, he looked back at her.

"The man you arrested—I saw him on the street yesterday. The reason I believe it's the same man is I saw a photograph of him on a television broadcast. It looked just like him, even the clothing was the same as he was wearing."

The detective nodded, curious but now impatient. She screwed up her courage.

"But I saw him in the center of Paris, miles away from Versailles, about two minutes before the assassination took place. I *spoke* with him."

The detective laid his pen down. "You spoke with him."

"He gave me a piece of paper that has his handwriting on it."

"Where?"

"On the paper. It was a map."

"No, I mean where were you when he gave you this paper?"

"On the Rue Chomel in the *septième arrondissement.* Outside a flower shop. I had been ordering flowers."

He sucked the spaces between his teeth. He examined her face, seemed to be considering every last line and angle to it. His jacket was a worn gray herringbone weave; he wore no tie. Finally he asked, "What are you doing out alone at this hour, Madame Moorhouse?"

"Lieutenant, *s'il vous plaît.*"

"You understand that there is enormous interest in this case, yes? It is very high profile?"

She nodded.

"You are sure?"

"Yes."

The detective said nothing, made no motion.

She repeated herself. "Yes."

He waved a hand in the air. "*Alors.* You are ready to identify him? If it is the same man, you will sign an affidavit?"

She nodded.

"Very well." He picked up the desk phone and began punching in numbers. "This is not the average crime, Madame Moorhouse, you understand. You understand this, Madame Moorhouse?" He addressed his attention to the phone. "*Oui, c'est tard.*" He continued in a low rumble for a few minutes. After he'd hung up again, he stood.

"Very well," he said again. "We need to go to the *Direction centrale de la police judiciaire* at Rue des Saussaies."

She followed him out of his office. She stopped to search the street before climbing into the backseat of his car. Was there someone walking towards them? Was there anyone there, a guard, to bear witness to her departure? She was used to climbing into backseats of cars, used to being driven, but this man was a stranger, and no one, not even Edward, knew she was with him. All around them night glistened; the dark lapped at the old stone buildings across the street from them and at the detective's and her faces. No one at the French Ministry of the Interior would be happy if she discredited the arrest, no one in the French police force. No one at the British Embassy. The news would be on every television station in every city around the world. It would be in every newspaper. The wife of a prominent British diplomat frees a known terrorist and discredits the French police.

But the guy I spoke to on the street is innocent, she thought to herself. He didn't do it. Not this crime, anyhow. Not if he is the same man they have in custody.

Another detective joined them from within the police station. He mumbled his name, nodded at her rather than offered his hand to shake. She ducked her head and clambered into the car. The front passenger seat was pushed back too far; there wasn't room for her long legs. She turned them sideways.

The first detective drove. They raced along the Rue de Rivoli, and for the second time in twenty-four hours she felt herself drawn towards the centrifuge of the Place de la Concorde. He turned his car up the Champs Elysées. The two men sat up front while she sat in the back, like a criminal. Their heads from the back looked worn, as though they'd rubbed and rubbed against car headrests. The car smelled of stale cigarettes and fear. There was junk in the backseat: mail, newspapers, empty Vittel water bottles.

She looked at her watch. 2:00 a.m. She was tired, but she had no desire to sleep. On the streets, there were still people walking. She pulled herself to the edge of the car seat and stared out the window. Normal people going home from a night of revelry.

She sat in darkness on the edge of the hotel bed and waited for morning to come to Dublin. With the first light, she stood and went to the window. She tugged on a strand of her hair, pulling it out of the disheveled braid that crossed her shoulder. There was a man weaving his way down the street, a woman sweeping a doorway. The air felt damp, cold, in the hotel room. She drew her arms around herself. She couldn't imagine that anyone could do what she had just done. She didn't know how people like Niall, and now her, existed. He'd said bringing the money over would help people, but what had he meant? Help people do what? Was this money really going to help someone buy a First Communion dress for his daughter? Or was it to stain someone else's dress with blood? She wished Niall had never shown her the contents of that duffel. She wished she had never seen the bills piled up so tightly within it. She wished they were back still combing the sands of the Atlantic while she pretended they were on their honeymoon. And still she wanted Niall with her. Her longing for him was so visceral that she had to sit back down on the bed. She wrapped her arms around herself.

The first time she saw him he was standing on a stone wall. Forever after, she would have the impression he was taller. He was wearing corduroy pants so threadbare she could see the white knobs of his kneecaps through them. He...

Clare's head knocked against the car window. She sat back and tightened her seat belt as the detective swerved around a double-parked car. They were approaching the Arc de Triomphe. Clare tried to return to her memory, but the image of Niall's face slipped from her, there but out of reach, like a fish in lake water.

Instead, she saw Jamie's flushed cheeks, his lips swollen with sleep, her sweater wrapped close around him. She saw his face earlier in the evening as he sat on her bed while she dressed for dinner.

"Madame. Why didn't you wait to come in the morning?" the detective behind the steering wheel asked her. He was viewing her through the rearview mirror.

In the morning, after the sun had risen, she would be en route to London with Jamie, to speak with the headmaster of Barrow before the weekend was upon them, if the police allowed her to leave Paris. Jamie was within his rights to dissent, but the method had been all wrong, and, just as he'd said, it wasn't right one person take all the blame. Evasion wasn't the same thing as absolution. She'd needed twenty-five years of silence and a fifteen-year-old son to make her see this, and she wasn't going to allow Jamie to make the same mistakes. She would not let this episode become a dark package shoved to the back of his dresser. And she wasn't going to leave him to return right back to it. If he believed what he had done was justified in some way, he needed to argue his side before facing his punishment. And then he needed to move on.

But she couldn't leave Paris until she had finished with the police. Not without being sure the man they'd detained was guilty. What if she had not only refused to help Niall but had set herself to stopping him? She couldn't let another man's life be wasted because of her cowardice.

She shook her head. "Morning would be too late."

The detective looked at her again through the rearview mirror. He raised an eyebrow. "Why did you not come earlier?"

She shrugged. She didn't need to explain to him.

The two men conferred. The one in the passenger seat craned his head around to look at her. He wrinkled his brow and scratched his head. *"Vous ne voulez pas téléphoner à quelqu'un à l'Ambassade?"*

She shook her head. No, she did not wish to call anyone at the embassy. They'd know all about this soon enough.

The men exchanged glances.

They wove through barren side streets, empty of life or sound, warrens of shadow. They stopped for traffic lights, or didn't. They pulled up by a stolid fortresslike stone building with none of the glamour or grandeur of the central police station on the Ile de la Cité, though at least as many French flags flew before it. A no-nonsense, double-jointed metal door guarded the entrance. What the gates to Hell would really look like, she thought to herself. No Thinker, no Adam and Eve. No embellishment. She knew of this place. During the German occupation of Paris, it was used by the Gestapo for questioning prisoners. The Ministry of the Interior now had offices on this block.

The second detective slunk out of the car and opened the gate. She and the detective behind the steering wheel drove over cobblestones and through a shadowy archway. He pulled up in front of a group of buildings, got out, and stood there in the night, waiting.

She slid from the backseat.

The second detective joined them on the cobblestones. *"Par ici,"* he said, gesturing towards a door. There was a strange moment while they hesitated in the night, all unsure of the protocol. She was a female, a well-dressed and blond one at that, and a diplomat's wife. A person of a certain importance. But she was a troublemaker. She stepped forward, leading them, leading herself. Now they followed her. The first detective reached out and opened the door for her. She passed through. They registered her with a clerk, who nodded his head to her but then took her cell phone, led her into an empty room, and asked her to wait. They left her alone with a long solid-wood desk, several folding chairs, not much else. Dustlets floated through the air around her like a clock with no sense of time. She didn't bother to check her watch again. Eventually the detectives returned, led by a third man, more erect in bearing than the first two but with the air of having recently been awoken.

*"Madame,"* he said. He stretched out a hand to shake hers.

"*Commandant,*" she said, accepting it.

"*Merci d'être venue.*"

He spread a rack of photographs of different men in front of her. She felt a wave of exhaustion buffet her body. This day had been too long. She hesitated, one image swimming before her. Her Turk no longer wore the cheap leather jacket, and his face appeared bruised, or maybe it was just the photo's lighting. Gone was that gentle expression when he told her about his wife's homemade yogurt. Still, the photo seemed to be him. She brushed it lightly. The *commandant* asked her to consider again.

"*C'est difficile avec une photo,*" she said.

"*Il faut être sûr.*"

She nodded and thought for a moment. The newscaster had said the suspect had been photo-identified by the witness to the assassination. "*Je veux le voir. Le prisonnier. En personne.*"

The commandant considered her. He turned and spoke sharply to one of the detectives. "*Reveillez-le.*"

They would rouse the prisoner. He was in a holding cell within the bowels of the building, awaiting the morning for further interrogation. Which they would want to avoid if they had the wrong man. Again—what a terrible embarrassment this would be for the French police services if the material proof she'd promised proved this to be the case. Even worse if in the meantime they'd mistreated the man they'd picked up. They'd been proud of the speed and efficacy of their forces; this man, the commandant, would have to step forth and admit to their error. His face, like hers, would be all over the newspapers.

She considered the moons on her fingernails, the shine of her engagement diamond, the blank space on the stretch of her hand where the emerald had sparkled and shone such a short while ago. They'd both walked away bearing their own responsibilities—

no, she couldn't go backwards. She couldn't make what she'd done disappear. That would always be with her. But she could go forward. She no longer blamed Niall for anything.

"*S'il vous plaît,*" the commandant said.

A part of her hoped against hope that their Turk would be another Turk that looked just like hers. Perhaps the news stations had mixed up her Turk and the police's Turk's photos? The man in this photo looked so faded, so crumpled, it was impossible to focus on him. Or maybe it was her exhaustion. She would peek at the real living body and shake her head. She would go home and slide into bed beside Edward and close her eyes against this whole day. She would not sign an affidavit; they would not file her report. No one would be the wiser for it. The British Embassy, the permanent under-secretary would never hear of it.

She shook her head. She and Edward would move to Dublin or not; it made no difference. And whether Niall was *alive,* whether he would return to the island he loved so much that he was willing to risk all for it, whether he would be forgiven his debt or not and, if he was lucky, meld back into the crowd, another fair-skinned freckled man nearing fifty, scraping by with whatever he could pull together—all of this made no difference to right now. She'd made her decision. And she was sure it was the correct one.

The room spun in front of her. She was so tired.

The second of the detectives returned. She rose and followed him and the commandant along yet another hall and down a set of stairs.

Reaching the bottom, the commandant slowed his step. "*C'était courageuse d'être venue,*" he said.

The numerous headlines and photographs and, after, the years of Internet traces. Every time anyone Googled her name: her photo, the Turk's photo, little head shots side by side. Words underneath morphed into whatever shape the public wished to make it. What this might mean for Edward's career. The boys' friends, their classmates, their teachers staring at them, whispering as they passed: *His mother was the one that stepped forward for that terrorist.*

Her, the detective's, and the commandant's footsteps slapped rather than echoed through the next hallway. She felt they must be underground, with nothing but earth beneath them, but she'd lost all bearing.

They reached a doorway, and the commandant stopped. *"Mais pourquoi vous n'êtes pas venues plus tôt? Pourquoi vous avez attendu pour minuit?"* He laid his hand on the doorknob and waited for her to explain. What was she to tell him? That she hadn't come earlier because she was preoccupied with organizing a dinner party? That she'd waited to bid Niall good-bye, to make sure he could leave Paris without being followed, in case she would now be watched? That she might not have come at all had she not learned that her own son seemed close to repeating her own errors?

*"Je suis venue,"* she said. That she had come had to be enough.

"Madame Moorhouse," he said, suddenly in English. "You understand that this is a bad man. Even if he is not the one to do this murder today, this is still a bad man."

"Because he belongs to a nationalist organization?"

"It has been associated with terrorist acts."

"Is there any proof that *he* has?"

"Does that matter?"

"Maybe. Does he still?"

"Still?"

"Belong to this organization? Is he still active in it? And if not, was it involved in terrorist acts when he belonged to it?"

The detective shrugged. "Does this matter either?"

He opened a small window in the door.

She looked at the prisoner lying slumped over a cot. He looked yellower, but his breathing was slightly less heavy.

"He is ill?" she said to the detective. "He is on medication?"

"Yes," he said, shrugging. "He had *une ordonnance* in his jacket pocket."

*"C'est lui."*

She withdrew the Turk's crumpled map from her sweater pocket, with the name of the doctor scrawled on it. She pointed to it

"He was on his way to see this doctor. Here is the name and number," she said. "It should correspond to the prescription, and if so, you will have a corroborating witness. That will make two witnesses in his defense to one against him. Contact him." She paused, seeing the commandant's hesitation. "This is the writing of the man I encountered in the street; you can easily check it against your prisoner's. I got the map from him. It probably has his DNA on it as well. He was sweating so heavily, he probably sweated right onto the paper. You can check that against your prisoner as well."

The commandant frowned. He took the paper from her. "Are you sure?" he said, giving her one last chance to turn away from her responsibility.

So little, in the end, was black and white. Perhaps the only thing was humaneness—the innate human response, the thing that made prison guards light a cigarette for a condemned murderer. *"Monsieur le Commandant,"* she said as he closed the door to the cell, "don't you see? If you keep the wrong man, no matter what he may have once done, all you achieve is that someone is punished for what he didn't do and the one who shouldn't goes free."

# EIGHTEEN

The commandant brought her back to the room in which she had waited. He handed her a pen. She accepted it. He laid an affidavit on the desk. She signed it. He nodded. He led her out to the foyer. A policeman handed her her cell phone, and she cradled it in her hand. It felt strangely warm, and she thought of how just pressing a few buttons would connect her directly to Edward and Jamie. The original detective, the one with so many rings around his tired eyes, reappeared, the lines in his face looking even deeper. The commandant explained Clare's testimony.

"I shall drive you," the detective said.

"No, that's all right, thank you. Perhaps you could call me a taxi."

He and the commandant nodded. There would be enough excitement surrounding her in the upcoming days without her now emerging from an unmarked car in the wee hours of the morning in front of the Residence. The concierges would have something to gossip about after all.

*"Merci, Madame Moorhouse,"* the commandant said, extending a hand to be shaken.

*"Merci, Monsieur le Commandant,"* she replied, accepting his hand.

The detective led her out. They trod across the cobblestones, the weakening moon still bright enough to show their way towards the entrance. He dragged open the heavy metal doors to the street with a creak and followed her out onto the sidewalk to wait for the taxi.

"What will happen to him now?" she asked.

"The prisoner?" he said.

She nodded.

He shrugged. "We will hold him until we speak with this doctor. You understand this is not that we do not believe you, Madame. It is how things are done. If the doctor can also identify him and we determine that this is entirely a case of mistaken identity, as he has no *carte de séjour* and does have a significant history, we will turn him over to the Turkish government. France will have no more interest in him. Maybe *les Turcs* will, maybe not. That's a question for them. It will have nothing to do with this case and nothing more to do with *la France.*"

She nodded again. The Turk would be deported. His own government would scour his life for signs of unsavory connections and activity. Probably he hasn't been active in this organization for years, maybe decades. But they would try to find something. Meanwhile, he would be photographed and interviewed, would possibly bring forth a complaint against the French police for their treatment. If the Turkish government did manage to find something they could hold against him, he'd go to prison there. If they found nothing against him, or maybe even if they did, outrage would be stirred up at the French government's rash response to the crisis, their speed to mistake one Turk for another. Either way, a photo of her, dug up from some cocktail party or charity event or official gathering or another, would be produced beside his. Guilt by association, even with the nonguilty—the Internet was especially brilliant for innuendo.

"Excuse me," she said to the officer.

She had one last thing to do before the sun rose.

She turned from him to press the familiar button on her phone.

"Edward," she said when his sleepy voice answered. "I'm outside the Ministry of the Interior."

She could feel his immediate transition to wakefulness. She'd witnessed his ability to do this before, from the depths of her own milky haze, in the middle of the night when he'd received sudden word of some crisis.

Now *she* was the tinny bearer of bad news on the other side of the receiver.

"You're where? Are you all right?" he said.

"Yes," she said. "I am all right. I am fine. Wait."

She cupped her hand over the speaker and turned back to the detective. "I am free to come and go from France?" she said. "You won't need me on hand to bear further witness?"

"You plan to leave when?"

She considered. "This morning. Midmorning. I can be back by evening, or tomorrow."

"Of course, Madame," he said, his eyes with their multiple folds of tired skin blinking slowly at her. "We will need you only if we cannot find this doctor."

She nodded and turned back to her phone again. "Yes, I'm fine. I will explain everything. But first I want to tell you: I'm going to go back to Barrow with Jamie as soon as he wakes up. To settle with the headmaster. And make plans for next year."

"Clare—"

"I'll try to set things up so he can finish out the school year without additional trouble. Maybe I'll have to stay in London myself. But we can't leave Jamie behind, alone, without support. Even if I hadn't just spoken up about the assassination. This isn't mollycoddling—trust me, Edward, I know something about this. He needs help. He needs us around him."

Moonlight played on the paving stones, splashed across the metal gates, the car, her feet, her hands. The sun would be rising soon. She could imagine Edward sitting up on their bed, the room lit only by his phone's screen. He would sit there like that for an hour if necessary, waiting for her to be ready to explain. He had been doing this already, after all, for the twenty years they'd been together.

"I've been in to give a statement to the French police," she said. "I saw the man they picked up for murdering the parliamentarian today. I was with him at the time of the shooting. Just on the street; we crossed paths. I've borne witness to his innocence."

"You were with him at the time of the shooting?"

"Yes," she said. "I'm sure of it. I happened to check my watch. I have the flower-shop receipt. I didn't tell you right away because of the dinner."

She could hear Edward breathe on the other end of the phone line. He was seeing it all in his head, all she'd seen herself: the photos of her with the captions, the phone calls both from the media and the embassy, the hate mail and threats that would arrive from people convinced she was part of a conspiracy against France, a defender of terrorists, of terrorism. He was seeing the permanent under-secretary considering whether or not her actions, and subsequent infamy, would make them unsuitable for the ambassador's post in Dublin, or anywhere.

"Well, then," Edward said, "you did a very good thing. You can't let an innocent man go to prison."

She reentered the courtyard of the Residence as the first hint of dawn lightened the facade of the building. She didn't bother to press the hated elevator button but headed directly for the stairs. She opened the front door to the Residence, stopped to view the marine landscape by Turner, and stowed her purse inside the Regency console, mindful to settle her keys within the inlaid box from Croatia. She took a moment to breathe in the scent of the lilies and bells of Ireland.

She withdrew her feet from her shoes, leaving them by the door, and reached out to switch off the light. But she caught sight of her right hand and stopped. It was unadorned now, no emerald ring, nothing but the whorls of time to decorate it. But it was still graceful and tapering, her nails still smooth and rose-hued. Was that a new freckle by the wrist? She rubbed it gingerly. The spot did not budge.

She turned around to face the Turner. The painting was an early work, a minor watercolor, which Edward had bought from a great-aunt's estate on the occasion of his and Clare's first wedding anniversary, because Clare said she found it so beautiful. A funnel of yellow broke open over a mystery of pinks, then, below it, grays and violets and blues. White crests skipped across the bottom, where waves broke against a shore. Dawn.

These were the colors she had seen the morning that she and Niall had stood side by side along the Atlantic seaboard, the sand running over their toes and through Niall's fingers, and dreamt that somehow they might have met in a different way or that somehow they might end up in some other way than they were destined. Nothing would stop this rising sun's radiance, so delicate but determined. What joy the painting gave her every day as she entered and left the Residence, whatever residence she and Edward might be calling home. A quick feeling in her heart, a recollection of anticipation. And yet she never stopped, like she was right now, to really look at it. She traced the paint with a finger, allowing herself to touch its surface. She examined how strokes of white infused the yellow, giving it dimension. The blues and grays melted into each other, a smoky haze under the dazzle of the yellow.

She flipped off the light switch. She was lucky to have known so much love in her life. To think that she'd always considered it a burden.

She trod the length of the hallway and stopped at Jamie's room. He was asleep still, cradled in the afghan she'd wrapped around him. Tomorrow, on their way to Barrow, she would begin to tell him about the mistakes people made, and the prices that had to be paid for them. She knew she wouldn't be able to keep him from making his own. But at least she could try to keep him from the one he was in the middle of making and give him some thoughts to hold close for the future.

Edward was stretched out across their bed, awake, his eyes points of intelligence in the dark. He would go to England in the morning to face Barrow with Jamie if she asked, but she would not. There would be time enough for him to talk to Jamie, for him and her to talk together. Everyone was a compilation of right and wrong steps, like the steps that had brought her and Edward to the same stretch of road together. The point was that they kept on walking.

"I'm back," she said.

She dropped her sweater on her vanity, next to the scarf she'd laid there so many hours earlier, and draped her skirt and stockings over it. She slipped into bed and felt against her bare arms the coolness of the sheets where her husband hadn't been lying. He shifted his weight, making room for her.

"Clare," he said, reaching out for her.

Yes, she said to herself. It's Clare here.

# ACKNOWLEDGMENTS

Thank you to my mother, MaryAnn, and my late father, William, and to my sisters, Alice and Caroline.

Thank you to the peerless Gail Hochman, and everyone at Brandt & Hochman.

Thank you to Judy Clain, Michael Pietsch, Nathan Rostron, and the whole wonderful team at Little, Brown.

Thank you to Alice Mattison and C. Michael Curtis.

Thank you to Mina Samuels, Eva Mekler, Laurel Zuckerman, Anita Chaudhuri, Ronna Wineberg, Louise Farmer Smith, Susan Malus, and Melanie McDonald.

Thank you to the many others who also offered valued pieces of advice, assistance, and information, including but not limited to Ian Whitehead, Jocelyn Ferguson, Sandee Roston, Tom Kennedy, Julie Metz, Nancy Woodhouse, Niamh Casey, Stef Pixner, Corinne McGeorge, and Christina Haag. Thank you, Jörg Brockmann.

I am indebted to Drue Heinz and the International Retreat for Writers at Hawthornden Castle, within whose ancient stone walls in Scotland I was fortunate enough to undertake a last revision.

Last but never least, thank you to Antti, Susanna, and Laura.

# ABOUT THE AUTHOR

Anne Korkeakivi was born in New York City and currently lives in Geneva, Switzerland, where her husband, a human-rights lawyer, is with the United Nations. They have two daughters. Her short stories have been published by *The Yale Review, The Atlantic, The Bellevue Literary Review,* and other magazines, and she is a Hawthornden Fellow. Her nonfiction has run in numerous periodicals in the United States and Britain, including the *New York Times,* the *Wall Street Journal,* the *Times* (London), *Gourmet, Ms.,* and *Travel & Leisure.* She has also lived, among other places, in France and Finland.